A blood hot, historical tale from the Scottish Highlands, where the 19th Century Industrial Revolution is ravaging the clans. Village after village is gutted by the greed of capitalists who evict the local populations, divesting them of homes, land and honor. Until they advance on Greenyards...

There the home grabbers face a fiery, flashing-eyed widow, Catherine Ross, who rallies the villagers to fight for their rights, land and heritage. Into the ferment comes Ian Macgregor, a tall and strapping RossShire advocate of law and order. But as battle is joined one misty morning in a field by the River Carron, with Catherine leading against drunken and belligerent lawmen, Ian must choose sides. And as a truncheon comes down aimed at Catherine's skull, he makes his choice.

BLOOD ON THE TARTAN is the powerful tale of a little known ugly time in Scotland, where raw, fighting Scottish spirit gathers itself to challenge injustice. In Catherine Ross and Ian Macgregor the reader is treated to a rare romance and love triumphant as they fight for Scottish honor.

~ Robert Middlemiss, *A Common Glory*

~~~

Against overwhelming odds, Catherine Ross fights for the land and heritage of common villagers in Chris Holmes' page turning historical romance, *BLOOD ON THE TARTAN*. When Catherine refuses to stand aside as a large, drunken posse challenges her, Ian Macgregor must choose between enforcing the law or defending the love of his life. An incredible read from the first to last page.

~ John Hamilton Lewis, *Lost River, Cry Havoc, Samsara*

HIGHLAND WISHES by Leanne Burroughs. This reviewer was easily captivated by the story and was enthralled by it until the end. The reader will laugh and cry as you read this wonderful story. The reader feels all the pain, torment and disillusionment felt by both main characters, but also the joy and love they felt. Ms. Burroughs has crafted a well-researched story that gives a glimpse into Scotland during a time when there was upheaval and war for independence. This reviewer is anxiously awaiting her next novel in this series and commends her for a wonderful job done.
~ *Dawn Roberto, Love Romances*

* * *

REBEL HEART by Jannine Corti-Petska - Ms. Petska does an excellent job of all aspects of sharing this book with us. Ms. Petska used a myriad of emotions to tell this story and the reader (me) quickly becomes entranced in the ways Courtney's stubborn attitude works to her advantage in surviving this disastrous beginning to her new life. Ms. Petska's writings demand attention; she draws the reader to quickly become involved in this passionate story. This is a wonderful rendition of a different type which is a welcome addition to the historical romance genre. I believe that you will enjoy this story; I know I did!
~ *Brenda Talley, The Romance Studio*

* * *

IN SUNSHINE OR IN SHADOW by Cynthia Owens - If you adore the stormy heroes of 'Wuthering Heights' and 'Jane Eyre' (and who doesn't?) you'll be entranced by Owens' passionate story of Ireland after the Great Famine, and David Burke - a man from America with a hidden past and a secret name. Only one woman, the fiery, luscious Siobhan, can unlock the bonds that imprison him. Highly recommended for those who love classic romance and an action-packed story.

* * *

INTO THE WOODS by R.R. Smythe - This Young Adult Fantasy will send chills down your spine. I, as the reader, followed Callum and witnessed everything he and his friends went through as they attempted to decipher the messages. At the same time, I watched Callum's mother, Ellsbeth, as she walked through the Netherwood. Each time Callum deciphered one of the four messages, some villagers awakened. Through the eyes of Ellsbeth, I saw the other sleepers wander, make mistakes, and be released from the Netherwood, leaving Ellsbeth alone. There is one thread left dangling, but do not fret. This IS a stand alone book. But that thread gives me hope that another book about the Netherwoods may someday come to pass. Excellent reading for any age of fantasy fans!
~ *Detra Fitch, Huntress Reviews*

* * *

ALMOST TAKEN by Isabel Mere is a very passionate historical romance that takes the reader on an exciting adventure. The compelling characters of Deran Morissey, the Earl of Atherton, and Ava Fychon, a young woman from Wales, find themselves drawn together as they search for her missing siblings.

Readers will watch in interest as they fall in love and overcome obstacles. They will thrill in the passion and hope that they find happiness together. This is a very sensual romance that wins the heart of the readers. This is a creative and fast moving storyline that will enthrall readers. The character's personalities will fascinate readers and win their concern. Ava, who is highly spirited and stubborn, will win the respect of the readers for her courage and determination. Deran, who is rumored in the beginning to be an ice king, not caring about anyone, will prove how wrong people's perceptions can be. ***Almost Taken*** by Isabel Mere is an emotionally moving historical romance that I highly recommend to the readers.

~ Anita, The Romance Studio

* * *

PRETEND I'M YOURS by Phyllis Campbell is an exceptional masterpiece. This lovely story is so rich in detail and personalities that it just leaps out and grabs hold of the reader. From the moment I started reading about Mercedes and Katherine, I was spellbound. Ms. Campbell carries the reader into a mirage of mystery with deceit, betrayal of the worst kind, and a passionate love revolving around the sisters, that makes this a whirlwind page-turner. Mercedes and William are astonishing characters that ignite the pages and allows the reader to experience all their deepening sensations.

There were moments I could share in with their breathtaking romance, almost feeling the butterflies of love they emitted. This extraordinary read had me mesmerized with its ambiance, its characters and its remarkable twists and turns, making it one recommended read in my book.

~ Linda L., Fallen Angel Reviews

* * *

HER HIGHLAND ROGUE by Leanne Burroughs. In a stunning sequel to Burroughs' HIGHLAND WISHES, the reader will find a powerfully emotional and passionate love story that focuses on Duncan MacThomas, who was introduced in that novel.

Against the sweeping backdrop of Scotland's war of independence, this author continues an epic of a heart wrenching and positively beautiful love story. Duncan and Catherine were painstakingly developed with such realism that you'll be sharing their emotional journey.

At its very heart you'll share the love, the joy, the anguish, and the tears. Along the way, you'll revisit old friends, gain new ones, and thoroughly wish the story would never end. Burroughs gifts you with a terrific story, straight from her heart to yours! A most excellent novel that I whole-heartedly recommend!

~ *Marilyn Rondeau, The Best Reviews*

* * *

CAT O'NINE TALES by Deborah MacGillivray. Enchanting tales from the most wicked, award-winning author today. Spellbinding! A treat for all.

~ *Detra Fitch, The Huntress Reviews*

* * *

RECIPE FOR LOVE - I don't think the reader will find a better compilation of mouth watering short romantic love stories than in RECIPE FOR LOVE! This is a highly recommended volume –
perfect for beaches, doctor's offices, or anywhere you've a few minutes to read.

~ *Marilyn Rondeau, Reviewers*
International Organization

* * *

Christmas is a magical time and twelve talented authors answer the question of what happens when **CHRISTMAS WISHES** come true in this incredible anthology.

CHRISTMAS WISHES shows just how phenomenal a themed anthology can be. Each of these highly skilled authors brings a slightly different perspective to the Christmas theme to create a book that is sure to leave readers satisfied. What a joy to read such splendid stories! This reviewer looks forward to more anthologies by Highland Press as the quality
is simply astonishing.

~ *Debbie, CK2S Kwips and Kritiques*

***(*One story in this anthology was
nominated for the
Gayle Wilson Award of Excellence*)***

* * * *

HOLIDAY IN THE HEART - Twelve stories that would put even Scrooge into the Christmas spirit. It does not matter what *type* of romance genre you prefer. This book has a little bit of everything. The stories are set in the U.S.A. and Europe. Some take place in the past, some in the present, and one story takes place in both! I strongly suggest that you put on something comfortable, brew up something hot (tea, coffee or cocoa will do), light up a fire, settle down somewhere quiet and begin reading this anthology.
~ *Detra Fitch, Huntress Reviews*

* * *

BLUE MOON MAGIC is an enchanting collection of short stories. Each author wrote with the same theme in mind but each story has its own uniqueness. You should have no problem finding a tale to suit your mood. *BLUE MOON MAGIC* offers historicals, contemporaries, time travel, paranormal, and futuristic narratives to tempt your heart.

Legend says that if you wish with all your heart upon the rare blue moon, your wishes were sure to come true. Each of the heroines discovers this magical fact. True love is out there if you just believe in it. In some of the stories, love happens in the most unusual ways. Angels may help, ancient spells may be broken, anything can happen. Even vampires will find their perfect mate with the power of the blue moon. Not every heroine believes they are wishing for love, some are just looking for answers to their problems or nagging questions. Fate seems to think the solution is finding the one who makes their heart sing.

BLUE MOON MAGIC is a perfect read for late at night or even during your commute to work. The short yet sweet stories are a wonderful way to spend a few minutes. If you do not have the time to finish a full-length novel, but hate stopping in the middle of a loving tale, I highly recommend grabbing this book.
~ *Kim Swiderski, Writers Unlimited Reviewer*
* * *

Legend has it that a blue moon is enchanted. What happens when fifteen talented authors utilize this theme to create enthralling stories of love?

BLUE MOON ENCHANTMENT is a wonderful, themed anthology filled with phenomenal stories by fifteen extraordinarily talented authors. Readers will find a wide variety of time periods and styles showcased in this superb anthology. *BLUE MOON ENCHANTMENT* is sure to offer a little bit of something for everyone!
~ *Debbie, CK²S Kwips and Kritiques*

* * *

NO LAW AGAINST LOVE - If you have ever found yourself rolling your eyes at some of the more stupid laws, then you are going to adore this novel. Over twenty-five stories fill up this anthology, each one dealing with at least one stupid or outdated law. Let me give you an example: In Florida, USA, there is a law that states "If an elephant is left tied to a parking meter, the parking fee has to be paid just as it would for a vehicle."
In Great Britain, "A license is required to keep a lunatic." Yes, you read those correctly. No matter how many times you go back and reread them, the words will remain the same. Those two laws are still legal. The tales vary in time and place. Some take place in the present, in the past, in the USA, in England... in other words, there is something for everyone! Best yet, profits from the sales of this novel go to breast cancer prevention.

A stellar anthology that had me laughing, sighing in pleasure, believing in magic, and left me begging for more! Will there be a second anthology someday? I sure hope so! This is one novel that will go directly to my 'Keeper' shelf, to be read over and over again. Very highly recommended!

~ *Detra Fitch, Huntress Reviews*

For Helen
Best wishes *Chris H*

Blood on the Tartan

Chris Holmes

Highland Press
High Springs, Florida 32655

Blood on the Tartan

ISBN: 978-0-9787139-8-0

PUBLISHED BY HIGHLAND PRESS PUBLISHING

An Excalibur Book

For my mother, Catherine Holmes,
a Highlander from her toes up.

Patty Howell, Senior Editor

Prologue

Saint Valentine's Day, 1845
The Scottish Highlands

Ten constables drove their mounts through swirling snow, determined to arrive at their destination before morning. Blue jackets buttoned high against the wind, silver badges layered with hoarfrost, they held down their hats with one hand. The other hand gripped black truncheons bearing the Queen's monogram—'VR' for Victoria Regina burnt into the hard ash wood.

The first glint of dawn emerged as an anemic yellow sun rising over the Cromarty Firth, the middle of three crooked fingers of water clawing into northern Scotland's eastern coastline. The men headed for Glencalvie, a small Highland settlement three miles up Strath Carron. And they meant no goodwill to the clansmen residing there.

James Gillanders, the estate manager or 'factor' for many Highland lords, and a landowner in his own right, led the posse. "Damn this foul weather!" he uttered through clenched teeth, then viciously spurred his reluctant horse.

Men in blue followed, some on horseback others in carriages, all grumbling and swearing, their woolen cloaks flapping like flags in the wind.

In one of the crofters' cottages, Anne Ross, gaunt from malnutrition and bent over from unending labor, huddled around the fire with her three children. The firepit had no proper chimney, only a hole in the roof with a barrel open at both ends stuck through it for the smoke to escape. The peats, not completely dry, burned wet and choking, and the children coughed and hacked. Their dinner of thin oatmeal porridge and soggy bannocks had failed to quiet their growling stomachs. Anne's husband, Jock, was away, traipsing from town to town at the head of the strath in a futile attempt to find work and forestall his family's impending eviction.

The posse continued on, passing chambered cairns marking burial vaults of an ancient race long gone, like the glaciers, from ancient Scotia.

Halfway up the glen, Gillanders halted, "Here, me," he said, handing out flasks of porter, ale and whisky to the men. They drank deeply. When the procession resumed, they could just make out the village of Glencalvie ahead and the cottages of the families quietly living there as their ancestors had done for generations before them.

But the new landlord had other plans for this land. 'Clearances' was the name given them by the clansmen. 'Improvements' was what the landlords called them. Whatever the name, the plans had no room for any of these families. They'd all have to go, all have to be evicted.

Gillanders spurred his horse and patted the official Writs of Eviction in his breast pocket. A wicked smile parted his lips.

With two thundering raps, Anne Ross' door burst open. Two constables, their speech thick from drink, reeled in truncheons drawn. The two younger children screamed and ran to their mother. The oldest, a firm-jawed, dark-eyed lassie, glared at the lawmen.

"Catherine!" her mother cried. "See to the children. I will gather what food and clothes I can."

The girl reluctantly obeyed.

Anne and her children soon joined other families outside and watched in silence as the constables piled their scant possessions by the roadside. When the men had finished, they looked at Gillanders. He nodded and within minutes, the first cottage was burning.

"'Tis a right bonny blaze!" one constable said with a grin, warming his hands in front of the leaping flames.

The factor looked down on the ragged crowd gathered about him.

"Please, sir, where will we go?" one of the women pleaded.

"What about the children?" cried another. She pointed to her babe-in-arms.

"How will we eat?" a third asked, her voice rising in a forlorn wail.

Gillanders extinguished his lantern. The shadows falling on the skeletal faces of the villagers startled him at first. But he'd hardened his heart years ago, had played out scenes like this many times in many other villages.

"Writs were delivered to all of you a fortnight ago," he said sternly. "You've had time to find other shelter. You've left me no choice but this..." He swept his hand around the group of constables, busily setting fire to other cottages between pulls on flasks of liquor.

Anne Ross, her plaid shawl pulled tight over her head, approached the factor and touched his leg respectfully. "Sir, could you nae wait just a few days more? Many of our men are gone with the Regiment. My own husband is away. The bad weather has prevented us from finding other accommodations." She put her hands together. "Please, sir, just a few days more."

Catherine tugged at her mother's arm, trying to pull her away. "Do not beg, Mother. Not to the likes o' him." She looked the factor in the eye and spit into the snow.

But her mother sobbed and made one last plea. "Please, sir, for the babies." She swept her arm around the children. "For all the babies!"

Gillanders answered in a voice as cold as the snow. "This land has already been leased to others. They will be here within weeks and expect it to be cleared for their use." He touched his breast pocket, bulging with the profitable leases he'd already signed with the sheep farmers.

Planting the butt of his riding crop firmly in Anne Ross' bony chest, he pushed her away, then turned to the men and yelled, "Clear them away, lads. Clear them all away!"

Chapter One

Manitoba, Canada, 1859

Catherine Ross leaned back in the old wooden rocker. Neither its comfort nor its squeak matched the one she'd had in Scotland. But it was the best she could find in the trading post at nearby Fort Garry.

She read and re-read the words she'd written in the leather-bound journal, penned from the deck of a ship on the day she'd set sail for the New World. Branded an outlaw, a fugitive from Her Majesty Queen Victoria's cruel justice, she'd watched her homeland recede from view. When she could bear it no longer, she'd written what was in her heart.

"I am a Scot, a Highland-born woman from the ancient land of the Celts. I am distant kin to Sir William Wallace and Robert the Bruce. My swaddling clothes were tartan plaid, my first spoken words Gaelic. The earliest music I can remember was the skirl of bagpipes, and the first song I learned—from my mother's own lips—was a melody by Robert Burns.

"Though evicted now from my ancestral land, cast out onto the sea and destined for foreign soil, I will remain, whilst I live and breathe, a Scot. A Scot, so help me God!"

Catherine ran her hand over the words on the yellowing page and closed her eyes. Even after all these years, she could still feel the torment in those words. Powerful words. Like animated spirits, they flowed up her fingers into her body, giving her a lump in her throat and eyes wet with tears.

The old rocker creaked and groaned against the worn carpet in time with her heartbeat. Outside, the wind howled, searching for a way in—an uncaulked crevice in the siding, a crack in a roof tile, a hole in the foundation. Finding none, it tried the chimney. There it was restrained by the stout metal flue. Defeated, it gave up, and with a banshee wail headed back to the Manitoba prairies which had spawned it.

She read the next sentences in the old journal:

"I once had a home in Scotland. In a Highland river valley known as Strath Carron. In a Ross Shire village named Greenyards. All gone now, the village destroyed, the houses pulled down and burned, the clansmen scattered to the winds. The land emptied of people. All replaced with sheep."

She looked around at her new home in the Red River Valley, close by the confluence of the Assiniboine and Red rivers. It was a sturdily built dwelling, well-crafted by experienced hands, strong muscles. She sighed. Sturdy though the house may be, its windows would never catch the morning sun's glint the way her house in the glen had. Its walls would never feel the warmth of peats burning in the fireplace, never echo the piper's trilling of the pibroch, nor the fiddler's bowing of an eightsome reel.

She pulled her red plaid shawl tighter around her shoulders, the ancient tartan of Clan Ross hand woven into its warp and woof. Another color was there as well. Blood. Her blood and the blood of her clansmen from that awful day by the river when so much of it had been spilt, so many killed, so many more injured. She'd never been able to wash the stain away, neither the one in the fabric nor the more painful one in her heart.

She listened to the wind howl, shook her head and smiled grimly. It was not a Highland wind that was for sure. That other familiar breeze would come creeping cool and misty over the hills and down the glens, lofting the smoke away from her house along the river and out to sea.

She reached for her tea. Sipping its hot broth, she washed down the still-warm freshly-baked bread she'd eaten. Its flour made from kemels sifted and ground from the hard Canadian wheat grown in fields beyond her back door.

The memories swirled back, trying like the persistent wind to wedge themselves into the crevices of her mind and stir the embers of her emotions.

That past life was gone, the memories dulled with the passage of time. Yet its ghosts lingered, sometimes illuminated like flashes of lightning momentarily dazzling a dark horizon. Her friends and family—the entire strath where she was born and thought would die—had been violently cleared out, its people dispersed, blown away by an ill wind to unfamiliar shores.

She sipped and continued to rock, the reverie washing over her like a Highland stream in full spate.

How she longed to see the heather-covered hills of Scotland again! To celebrate clan lore and tradition at *ceildh*—celebration—evenings, and dance a lively reel to the sound of the 'pipes. To listen to the old bard spin out tales of clan history to wide-eyed children. To speak the Gaelic, the language spoken in Eden it was said, and hear it in the songs and lullabies of her childhood. To sleep on a mattress made soft by heather stuffing instead of bristling hay.

Memories rolled past, the images growing darker. The pain and suffering, beatings and deaths—all of it could have been avoided if only she'd not been so iron-jawed stubborn, if she'd bowed to the authorities, had given in to the landlord's demands.

The gnawing worms of self-doubt squirmed in her mind's innards, tormenting her in spite of the passage of these many years.

Still, those tribulations had also brought her love again. That awful day of bloodshed had also been a day of spiritual rebirth. Love, like a new babe, had come struggling and screaming into her world in pain and blood and gore. That time of great sadness had become a memory of great joy. Love had triumphed, transcended all the Queen's constables who'd come to lay her low.

She wiggled her toes in front of the crackling fire and surrendered to the memories once more. She could recall the exact day—the very hour, in fact—when she and Ian first met, the exact moment love had come back into her life. It was the same bittersweet day the other struggle had begun, the one to keep her home and land. Neither struggle had started well. Not well at all...

Chapter Two

The Highlands of Scotland, 1854

Catherine had been lost in thought when it happened, leaning against the cow's flank and rhythmically pulling its teats in time to some Gaelic melody she hummed. The village bard said every Highland cow had a favorite song and wouldn't give up its milk without hearing it. This particular one, she'd learned from experience, was her cow Mary's favorite.

When she looked up, she could make out a layer of clouds in the distance along the eastern horizon, looming over the Dornoch Firth. But over her village of Greenyards the risen sun had already chased away the early morning mist. The ground, until recently frozen, was thawing, peat bogs steaming. Here and there a brave crocus boldly pushed its colorful way through the wet, black earth.

She paused her humming to take in the other sights and sounds of the village's morning routine: a hammer working on a nail, a shovel scraping through a peat bog, a lonely piper practicing a song—a familiar melody, one of the tunes of glory. Adapted from Robert Burns' poem, 'Scots wha' ha'e,' it was instantly recognizable as that stirring anthem of Scottish pride, 'Scotland the Brave.' And finally, the River Carron, in full spate from the spring thaw, playing its own song, slapping and sloshing against the rocks on its way to the sea.

A flutter of wings and a flash of color momentarily drew her gaze. She smiled—only a robin hustling for its breakfast.

Her eyes left the bird's flight and drifted with pride

around her farm, a stout cottage, its stone walls caulked with mud and heather, its roof closed over with wood beams and thatch. A thin spire of smoke streamed from the rock chimney. Nearby, but separate from the house, stood the small stone-and-thatch shed she used as shelter for her cow and chickens during the winter, for storing the harvest of her vegetable garden, and as a drying place for the peats she burned in the fireplace. Also cached there were the unsold oats and barley she'd grown, but kept for her own use. It would soon be time to plant the onions.

She turned her head at other sounds: a group of women heading for the river, loads of laundry in creels on their backs. Fragmented bits of Gaelic chatter trailed behind them like smoke from the chimney. When they stooped at the river's edge, she caught sight of a young lad walking his family's acreage in the field beyond, sizing up the job awaiting him. And beyond him on the hillsides—the *braes*—she saw framed against the sky a few cattle which had begun their day-long search for any meager pasturage growing there.

She resumed her song, drowsiness weighing on her as the sun climbed higher, drenching her in its warmth. Life was as good as it could be in these parts. She had her own home, her own land, her own cow...

A sudden shadow, cold and black, blotted out the sun. She caught her breath, looked up, and turned. A stranger had come up behind her. She could only make out his silhouette, dark and menacing.

She jumped up, both to protect herself and to get a better look.

He was tall, this stranger, and lean, about her own age she guessed, but with the rangy look of a seasoned traveler. His hair, peeking out beneath a cap, was blond, as bleached by the sun as his skin was tanned by it. A clean shaven face with high cheekbones projected inward strength, friendly hazel gray eyes, and a sharp jawline which met at a dimple in the middle of his chin, promising steadfastness.

She stepped back, placing the cow between herself and the stranger.

He snatched the cap off his head and gave a quick nod. "I'm so sorry. I did not mean to startle you," he said softly. He held out his hand and took a step toward her.

She backed up further, looked around for a weapon or an escape route.

Clearly seeing her distress, he stopped, holding out his hands in a gesture of peace.

"I'm Ian MacGregor, the new constable. I heard such sweet singing I had to stop and see for myself where it came from." He smiled. White teeth glistened.

Catherine scolded herself. *This is no way to treat a visitor. I have been taught better than this. Hospitality to a stranger comes as naturally to a Highlander as July sunshine and October snow.*

Her muscles relaxed. She managed a wispy smile and reached for his outstretched hand.

Then she noticed the uniform—dark blue and sharply creased, with a shiny silver badge over the left breast.

She stiffened again. That uniform, a black truncheon thrust through the belt, held too many memories, too many nightmares, for her clan, her village, and herself.

She stopped, withdrew her hand, and eyed him warily.

Like boxers in the ring, they stood motionless and stared at one another, each waiting for the other to make a move or say something.

Tension clotted the air.

Then, like a face full of cold water, a sharp, shrill whistle rent the stillness.

They both jumped.

Catherine looked toward the sound, threw her head back, and laughed in relief. "Finn! Ye'll be the death o' me yet."

Her six-year-old son grinned a toothless smile from

his perch in a corner of the shed atop a sack of oats. He held up his new homemade whistle. His face a mess of freckles, his hair a red mop top, he was her first and only child and the linchpin of her life.

"I see ye've found the way of it," she said. "Let's hear another."

He obliged with a series of toots.

She covered her ears with her hands and turned back to the constable.

He laughed, head back and full-mouthed. His blue eyes glinted, and his deeply dimpled cheeks flushed crimson.

She relented and permitted herself a chuckle. "Welcome to Greenyards, Mr. MacGregor. I am Catherine Ross."

"Is your husband about?" he asked politely. "I should like to make his acquaintance also."

She frowned, looked briefly at the ground, then straightened and said with a hint of defiance, "I am a widow and the mistress of this house."

He nodded silently, touched two fingers to the side of his forehead in salute, put his cap back on, and turned to go. His eyes locked momentarily with hers. "It's Ian," he said. "My name is Ian. And I thank you."

Her heart skipped a beat. Gooseflesh crawled up her skin. A small sound escaped her mouth, something between a sigh and a gasp. *Had he heard?*

He smiled again, recognition in his eyes that he'd heard, but said nothing and continued down the path to where he'd tethered his horse.

She watched him until he was out of sight.

Another toot from her son's whistle broke her concentration.

"That's enough for now," she said.

She picked up the pail of steaming milk and limped markedly toward the house. The pain in her foot was always greatest in the morning. She rarely thought about the original illness that had caused it, and the pain itself was more an irritation than a disability.

"Be comin' in and I'll fix yer breakfast," she told her son.

As she entered the front door and headed down the hallway, she passed the larger of the house's two bedrooms. Something caused her to stop and look in, some tug at her emotions. But everything seemed in its proper place—everything as it should be—clothes washed and folded in the dresser or hanging from two antler-horn hooks embedded into the walls; a big wooden bed with a heather-stuffed mattress on top, a chair next to it; a small writing desk and plain wooden chair next to the window. It looked neat. Ordered. And empty. Especially the bed.

"Oh, David," she whispered to herself. "Why did ye have to go off and leave me like this? Alone to raise Finn?"

She set the pail of milk down heavily on the kitchen table and remembered with a sigh the care she and her husband David had put into this house, building it stone by loving stone from the ground up. Her gaze swept the large main room—the fireplace and chimney against the wall; the old rocker, motionless but inviting on the rug before it. Countless times she'd sipped tea and rocked before that fire while David puttered about the house on some project. She'd nursed Finn in that rocking chair, softly singing an old lullaby as he suckled.

"I miss ye so. Finn misses ye." She wiped away the welling in her eyes.

Every object in the room had an aura, wisps of memories clinging to it, memories of her and David's short, sweet life together. She lightly stroked the wall and remembered how they'd gathered the heather for the insulation. Other memories flashed by—David, bare-armed and sweating as he worked in a nearby birch copse, cutting and dressing timbers for the roof. The two of them laboring together to finish the house with coats of whitewash—it was still the handsomest one in the village—then celebrating its completion by making love in that bed, giggling and frolicking like newlyweds.

She leaned on her broom, exhaled softly, and surrendered to the memories...

It's said that whom God would punish, He first makes happy. And she'd been very happy with David, her life filled with joy. The initial harvests had been good. They were very much in love. And Finn, short for Findlay, was a never-ending source of wonder and delight to them.

Then times turned hard. One of their cows died, and the potato crop failed two years in a row. They had to borrow money just to pay the rent. She remembered the lines of strain on David's face.

"Can we not borrow more money?" she asked. They'd been seated at the kitchen table, sipping illegal whisky from Angus Macleod's still.

"Our credit is at its limit. We've borrowed as much as we can against the farm."

"What about the bootleggers? Can we nae sell them more barley for their stills?"

He shook his head. "I fear not. The government has removed the excise tax from the legal brands, so prices have plunged. Their higher quality products can now be had for about the same cost as the illegal ones. Bootleggers like Angus canna compete."

"What will we do?"

"If we want to keep the farm, there's only one thing left..."

She waited in silence.

"I must join the Army."

She recoiled. "David, no! I dinna want ye to go asoldiering."

He put his arm around her, drew her close. "'Twill be all right," he said. "My Army pay will cover the loans, with some left over. When my enlistment is up, things will be better for us."

He gripped her shoulders and looked reassuringly into her eyes. "Without the farm, we have no future."

Two days later she'd stood in the doorway, little Finn in her arms, and watched her husband—dressed in his new uniform with shiny brass buttons and a Glengarry hat—disappear down the path.

Less than a year later, he'd been killed fighting in India, at some place she'd never heard of.

That was three years ago.

Since then, she'd resolved to keep her home and raise her son, determined that her husband's sacrifice shouldn't have been in vain. Her widow's pension from the Crown, plus the small income she received from her potato patch and barley rigs, saw her through. She was now completely caught up in her rents. She owed no one anything.

Her heart was her own as well...

She brushed the hair off her face with the back of her hand—at the same time brushing away the memories of her life with David—and put the broom to work again.

A familiar 'hello' came from outside.

She gave the visitor the traditional Gaelic greeting, "*failte duibh*—welcome to ye."

The door burst open with a flood of sunshine. Margaret Ross, Catherine's young cousin, entered with a smile as wide as the strath.

"*Sith gun rob so*—peace be here," the lassie replied.

Catherine looked at her kinswoman. What a sight! A Highland lass through and through, Margaret had a riot of long, unruly, flaming red hair, usually worn cascading down to her shoulders in thick tresses. Now it was tied back with a heather braid. A blush of red highlighted her cheekbones. Sparkling blue eyes set off a petite nose and complemented a full mouth, almost always open in a smile or song, though it also could turn up in a pout when she didn't get her way. Aye, she was a bonny one!

A young lass of sixteen years, Margaret was a hard worker, whether at home cooking supper, milking cows, or stacking the peats her father cut at the bog. But she loved her fun as well. Many times Catherine had watched her turn and whirl and dance in delight to the scottish reels on *ceildh* evenings, times of entertainment when the whole village gathered to sing, dance, drink whisky, and hear stories by Old Pete, the clan bard and historian. Not a few of the village lads had eyes for the young girl.

"Have you met the new constable?" Margaret asked breathlessly. "Isn't he handsome!" Her eyes twinkled with mischief.

Catherine had watched her cousin's adolescent urges come to full bloom, always wanting to talk about love and romance. And about other things more intimate, things she couldn't discuss with her own mother. Like a little sister, the girl had an unrestrained curiosity about her older cousin's romantic life. Or lack of it.

"Come in Margaret." Catherine invited the girl to a chair at the table and offered her bannocks—flat oatmeal cakes—and milk. Then she sat across from her young friend, took a long comb from her apron and looked at it wistfully. A gift from her mother, an heirloom, it was one of the few keepsakes she had of her family. She carried it with her always.

She combed her hair in long strokes and answered slowly. "It has been more than three years since David was killed. I have been too busy rearin' Finn and makin' a home for us to worry about romance."

"Come, come, cousin!" the girl persisted. "I know he was here. I saw his horse tied up at the end of your path."

"Aye, he was here. And if ye knew that why did ye ask?" Catherine said casually, as if it were a matter of small importance. She rose and busied herself over the kitchen stove.

Margaret munched the bannock and sipped the milk, her eyes dreamy. "Weren't you moved by him? Even a wee bit?"

"Lassie, I have a house to run and a son to raise. I have no time for such girlish things." *Nor the inclination for it.*

Margaret persisted. "But he is sooo handsome! And

polite. He even bowed to me. Did nothing stir in ye at all?"

Catherine wiped her hands on her apron and leaned against the wall. "Aye, he is a looker, I will give ye that. But I'm not ready to open my heart again. Especially to a lawman, one of the Queen's own. Besides"—she turned back to stir a pot of boiling oats on the stove—"I dinna even know if he is already married."

"He's not."

Catherine chuckled. *Never underestimate a Scot's love of gossip, nor the speed of the village grapevine.*

The lass patted the last of the milk from her lips with a cloth napkin. "What is it about that uniform that riles you so?"

Catherine collected her thoughts. "I've always been suspicious of the authorities. One look at their badges and I stiffen like a dead cat. I canna help it."

"Because of Glencalvie?"

Catherine grew quiet. "Aye," she answered sadly. "My father's village, the one that used to be at the end of our own strath but is no more. It was there my parents met, where my two brothers and I were born."

She paused to watch a wren, a blur of browns and grays, flit past the kitchen window.

"We lived happy and warm in that glen for many years," she said pensively.

"Until the evictions?"

Catherine nodded. "Until the Clearances." She'd suppressed the feelings for years. But they percolated up again. Memories of pain, rage, humiliation...

"I'll never forget that wretched day. How cold those constables were. Colder than the ice and snow that crusted the ground. My mother and I gathered what we could—barely a few personal items—and threw them onto horse carts or into the creels on our backs. The men in blue uniforms stood waiting, their black truncheons out."

"What were they waiting for?"

"For us to resist, I suppose."

31

"Did anyone consider doing that?"

"I was ready for it!" The warmth of a flush crept up her neck, and she smacked her fist into her palm. "If I had had my way, they would have had to drag me off kickin' and screamin' all the way down the glen."

"But you were only a lass."

"Aye. Even so, I was ready to fight."

"And the others?"

Catherine lowered her head and dabbed at her eyes with the corner of her tartan. "They were too beaten down, cousin. All my life I had heard stories of Highland courage. But there we were, driven whimpering from our homes like...sheep. To hear my mother begging... I was so ashamed."

The girl waited silently, then asked, "What happened next?"

"We had no place to go. Finally, we pitched camp in a nearby kirkyard with eighteen other Glencalvie families. There were about eighty of us in all. For shelter, we stretched a tarpaulin over poles and closed in the sides with blankets, clothes, plaids—whatever we could find."

"Why didn't you take refuge in the kirk itself?"

"Many thought it would nae be proper. The kirk was God's house, they said. For worshipin', not for livin' in. Some of us disagreed. God would have understood our needs. But we were out-voted."

"How did you survive?"

Catherine leaned her elbows on the table and cupped her chin in one hand as memories of swirling snow, smoky campfires, and crying babies washed over her.

"We divided the tent into compartments to give each family some bit of privacy. Then we built a communal fire in the middle of the kirkyard. The children cried and huddled around it to keep warm. There were two new babes. We put their cradles near the fire, but one died anyway. Each week one or two families left. It broke my heart to watch them trudge off through the snow, their

heads hung low, the children clutching at their mothers'
skirts. Finally, we went too, the last to leave."

Catherine wiped her eyes, rose from the table, and
cleared away the dishes. She smiled thinly, her voice
thick. "And now ye know why I am so leery of men in
blue uniforms. Even if they are as handsome as Ian
Macgregor."

Margaret nodded solemnly and rose. "I must be
getting back to my chores." She kissed her cousin, retied
her heather hair bow, and started for the door. She
turned back suddenly for a parting word. "Look behind
the badge, cousin," she urged. "Look at the man *behind*
the badge."

Catherine stared at the girl open-mouthed as she
departed. Such wise words from one so young!

Chapter Three

The next morning dawned gloomy and chill. It followed a night of brooding and ill-defined nightmares for Catherine. Mist, hanging like a shroud over the braes of Carn Bhain—the escarpment rising from the south side of the river—added to her unease. Perhaps the unexpected meeting with the new constable had stirred up the anxiety again. But about what? What was it? Like an out-of-reach itch begging to be scratched, she couldn't quite get at it, couldn't reel into her conscious thoughts the image of the feelings in her heart.

But life had to go on. The simple business of daily living was demanding in the Highlands. Couldn't be put aside. Not even for a wee touch of the melancholy.

She borrowed her uncle's horse and cart for a trip to the marketplace at Ardgay, the small town at the eastern entrance to the strath. Finn chattered and tooted his whistle next to her. She glanced up at a golden plover flying overhead, its plaintive cry seemingly directed at her.

Later in the morning, with fresh vegetables and a loaf of baked bread in her creel—luxuries in the Highlands—she was on the return trip to the village, still lost in thought and only dimly aware of the rapidly improving weather. Blue holes had appeared in the cloud cover, and the sun's perfectly aligned light rays poked through, sparkling off the black waters of the Carron.

"Look!" Finn cried, pointing to a family cutting peats in a nearby bog.

She reined in to watch. It reminded her that her own supply needed replenishing.

After a moment, she turned to Finn. "How long do ye figure this old bog has been here?"

"My teacher said some have been around for five or six thousand years."

"That old, huh?"

The lad nodded seriously. "Do you know how they came to be? Our teacher told us that too."

"Tell me."

"They started long ago," he began, his voice hushed like all good story tellers, "when leaves, twigs and branches from the ancient forest"—he swept his arm around and gave a toot on his whistle—"all this land was forested then—fell to the ground and got mixed in with dirt and rain water. Then it got squeezed by the layer above it, and so on down through many layers that built up."

Catherine nodded. "Until it finally became peat."

Finn's answer was another toot.

She laughed. "Good lad."

They watched the peat cutters for a few minutes longer.

"They have got it down right," Catherine said with admiration. "Teamwork. They all know their jobs."

The woman first used a hoe to scrape away the top layer of peat moss. Then her husband, following behind, sliced through the peat itself with a square, flat shovel, bringing up a slab of it. He put it down carefully and went on to the next cut along the trench. Two children, about nine and twelve years old, took the boggy slabs and carefully stacked them with others in a house-of-cards shape for even drying. After a week or two, they would be restacked nearer the house. Further drying would make them light and springy. When finally fed to the fire, they would burn hot, leaving a fine, gray ash.

Watching the family work together on their communal task rekindled Catherine's melancholy. She and David had labored just like that on another day in another peat bog near their home. The family working in front of her could have been her own—a hard-working wife, a strong man for a husband, another child, maybe a brother or sister for Finn.

That dread affliction, the 'might-have-beens,' crept through her. She felt them like a weakness in the body, or the start of a fever or flu. Once they had you, they had to run their course. It had been years since she was last affected. Why now? What had triggered them?

She shook her head and flicked the reins to encourage the old mare up a rise in the road. Finn turned and waved to the peat cutters, then gave them a whistle. They all laughed and waved back.

At the top of the hill, she caught sight of a man walking ahead leading a horse. Her stomach dropped away and she stopped breathing for a moment. It was Ian Macgregor, the new constable.

Finn saw him too and blasted out on his whistle.

She hushed her son. Too late! The man turned, grinned, and started back toward them.

Her muscles tensed. She sat straighter.

When he reached the cart, Ian tussled Finn's hair, then said, "Good morning, lassie. A right bonny day, eh?"

"Where are ye heading, constable?" she asked curtly.

"I'm bound for your own village, for Greenyards. The doctor in Tain asked me to deliver some medicine to the widow Margaret Macgregor. Mind if I accompany you?"

She turned the simple request over in her mind, felt a thin crack appear in the ice around her heart.

"If ye like," she said, "ye can ride along with us."

He hitched his garron to the back of the cart, slid in beside her, and automatically reached for the reins.

But she held on, unwilling to relinquish control.

"Give yourself a rest," he said softly.

An electric instance of remembrance startled her—of David and his strength, and of the many kind things he did for her. Just like this.

She finally relented and they continued on toward

home.

The watery sunshine—now pouring through the broken clouds like a pitcher of lemonade—raised Catherine's spirits. She cast a fleeting glance at Ian. He looked a few years older than she, though she wasn't exactly sure how many. Taller than average, and rangy rather than broad, he looked strong. His bright blue eyes and coppery blond hair, worn closely cropped, suggested a mixture of native Gael and Viking bloodlines, two races which had brawled in Scotland for centuries until finally making peace with one another by interbreeding.

Catherine had heard from neighbors and friends that Ian was quiet spoken and thoughtful, not quick to passion. She'd also heard he was fluent in Gaelic, with a solid foundation of English. Easy going and friendly, she'd heard rumored, with a cheery greeting for everyone. He'd ridden into the village and immediately introduced himself all around, winning everyone's acceptance.

When he glanced at her and smiled, she turned away, not wanting him to see the blush she felt spreading up her neck and across her cheeks.

When they reached her house, Ian didn't leave right away. He seemed to be searching for some excuse to linger.

"I noticed your stack of peats was low," he finally said. "Why don't Finn and I replace them?"

She answered quickly, perhaps too quickly. "That is not necessary. We can manage ourselves."

"I know you can," he said quietly. "But I would like to help."

She considered the offer, then nodded. "Yes, thank ye. That is a very kind offer."

"Fine. The lad and I will get started right away."

She watched as they set to work hauling peats from the shed and restacking them near the fireplace. While they worked, she busied herself about the house, her old heather broom quickly clearing away the dirt. She occasionally glanced out the window. Finn adored Ian, that was plain to see. And Ian seemed to return the affection. He was patient when instructing the lad, but firm when Finn wanted to go his own way and do his own thing.

Catherine returned to her housework, fluffing up the pillows and mattresses. They were getting flat and would soon need more heather stuffing.

"Heather is the housewife's friend," her Aunt Christy had told her when she'd first married and had set up her own home.

She'd never forgotten the advice and had discovered the many uses for the native plant—for insulating the house; tied together to make stiff but effective brooms and brushes; and though individual strands were wiry and tough, in clumps it was springy enough to pad mattresses, pillows and chairs.

In the summer, starting about July and reaching a peak in September, the heather bloomed and covered the braes in a carpet of lilac hues. In addition to the household uses, Catherine braided strands of it into rings, bracelets, necklaces, and ties for her hair. She remembered the first thing she'd ever made from the highland bounty. As a young lass, she'd sat at the table and watched Aunt Christy weave the purple-headed flower stems into useful objects. She'd taken Catherine's small hands and guided her through creating her own necklace. It had been around her neck every day until it had started to fall apart, then she'd gently wrapped it in a small cloth and tucked it away to save. But it had been lost, or burned, when her family was driven from Glencalvie.

Catherine warded off the sad memory.

When Ian and Finn finished stacking the peats, Ian nodded wordlessly to Catherine and ambled toward his horse.

She called out to him. "Will ye not stay for a wee bite to eat?"

He turned back and removed his hat. "That would be right bonny."

She ladled out a bowl of steaming oatmeal porridge. Two scones smeared with butter, served with fresh milk, completed his meal.

When he finished, he leaned back and looked at his new lady friend while she cleared away the dishes. The sun was up full now. It streamed bright and yellow through the kitchen window and highlighted her figure when she'd stood. Narrow-waisted and full-breasted, her neck curved swan-like, long and sensuous. His eyes were drawn to a small birthmark at her throat. An urge to kiss the rose-colored imprint, to suck on that particular spot of beauty, overwhelmed him and he shook it off with difficulty.

Her jet black hair was gathered together at the back of her head and tied with a heather braid, falling loosely from the bound part to her shoulders. It reminded him of a pony's tail. Drawn back, it framed the oval of her face—calm, direct and honest like her eyes. He'd also seen her wear it straight down to her shoulders in the no-nonsense style of most Ross women. He'd overheard some of the neighbors tease her about her generally darker complexion, a contrast to most of the fair-skinned Rosses. Some poor Spaniard, they joked—maybe a survivor of the Great Armada of 1588—had washed ashore and somehow gotten into her bloodlines.

Then there was that firm jaw, almost as strongly chiseled as his own, an ancestral trait inherited from *Gilleon na ha-airde*, father of the Celtic Earls of Ross. It complemented her aquiline nose and dark green eyes, as dark as an Irish sea, which revealed intelligence, determination, and depth of character.

When she looked up, glanced at him and smiled, her face seemed to say, 'Here I am. Take a good look... See anything you like?'

Ian had learned from her neighbors that Catherine was usually friendly and forthcoming and not prone to moodiness. But when her temper was lit, so it was said around the village, she could become as hard as the Stone of Scone. And if she straightened her back and clenched her teeth as well, woe to the man or woman who crossed her, as a pushy peddler had done one day, to his great discomfort.

Ian noticed she limped as she carried a bucket of water. He got up quickly to help her and received a smile of thanks in return.

"I almost forgot," he said suddenly, digging into his pouch. He pulled out a crumpled letter. "It's in English. From Canada."

Catherine explained she could read and speak English. She'd learned as a girl in the little schoolhouse at Glencalvie, she added. "I pestered the poor teacher for the loan of his books. I kept the Gaelic, too, since it is the language of most of the villagers. Many of my neighbors only have a middling ability in English, so they bring their important papers for me to read. Excuse me a moment while I read this." At his nod, she opened the letter and began to read to herself.

"They've made it through another winter, thank God," she whispered.

Ian waited patiently.

"My family," she explained, sitting at the table, "emigrated to Canada when we were evicted from Glencalvie."

She turned back to the letter and read in silence for a time, then announced, "The wheat harvest was good last fall, and they will be plantin' the spring crop soon enough. My father says the boys"—she looked up—"my brothers—are both well and have been a great help on the farm." She paused, read more, then folded the paper.

He was deeply moved she'd shared something so personal with him and he didn't know what to say. He shifted his weight from foot to foot. "Why didn't you go with them, lass?" he whispered. "When your family was evicted, why didn't you go with them to Canada? I hear there is good land there for farming. Readily available and cheap."

She stood and faced him, tucked the letter into her apron. "Aye, so I hear. Those were my father's very words when he announced the family would strike out for North America."

Her eyes flashed like lightning and she stomped her foot. "But I'm a Scot, by God! And I will ne'er leave my native soil. At least not willingly."

He took a step back. He was no farmer, but Green-yards looked to be poor land. Very poor. No self-respecting Englishman or Lowland Scot would have paid more than a few shillings an acre for it. But he knew the Rosses had been living in this strath continuously for over 500 years. The clansmen considered the worth of the land out of all proportion to its true economic value. It was their ancestral home, the source of their customs, traditions, songs, stories and moral values. To leave it meant death. At least that's what they believed.

He sighed, shook his head slightly, and said, "Thank you for the food. I must be goin'."

"Stop by again," she yelled, as she watched him lead his garron back down the glen.

He turned, waved, and was gone.

She pulled the letter from her apron and began where she'd left off, when she'd folded it because tears had threatened. She hadn't wanted him to know her mother was ill.

She was still thinking of him an hour later.

Chapter Four

Spring began to show herself in Strath Carron. The drying earth steamed in the sunshine. The *urlars*—grassy meadows by the river—grew thicker and greener, dandelions dotted the grass, and lilies-of-the valley sprouted up in clumpy bouquets. Scattered amid the heather, purple foxgloves pushed up through the soggy ground.

Catherine Ross felt just like those spring flowers. In bloom. Her gait was light and breezy, and she frequently —and for no apparent reason—broke into a song. She paid more attention to her makeup and washed her hair more frequently. It was bouncy and shiny. Her skin glowed, radiating warmth everywhere she went.

Ian's visits to Greenyards increased in frequency and lengthened in duration. Rarely a day went by that his horse wasn't seen tied to the post at the end of the path from Catherine's house. The three of them—Finn, Catherine and Ian—frequently strolled together along the roads and braes, Finn leading the way, a cupid with a crude wooden whistle in place of a bow and arrow.

On one especially fine day, Ian took them on a trip to the Dingwall Fair, the nearest country marketplace where farmers and merchants displayed and sold their wares. Finn's eyes opened as wide as saucers as he took in the tables piled high with food, drink, and cloth of all hues. And the animals, dozens of cows, sheep, and horses for sale or trade, not to mention the jesters, acrobats, musicians, and play actors entertaining the crowd.

The sun shone bright that day, and the food, drink and entertainment went to their heads. They wandered around hand-in-hand for hours, then spent the night at an inn.

Ian told Finn stories in front of the fire.

It took all Catherine's strength to find her way to bed alone. Even then, she tossed and turned half the night from memories of lovemaking with David, and invariably her thoughts wandered and she allowed herself to wonder—just a little—what it would be like with Ian. To have his arms around her, caress her as David had. Kiss her. Deeply and intimately.

She finally hushed the unwelcome, unsettling longings and fell asleep.

On one visit to Catherine's house, Ian pulled a large package from his saddlebag and handed it to her. It was wrapped in cheesecloth.

"For our supper tonight," he said with a wide grin. "That is, if you'll have me."

Once in the house, she placed it on the table, unwrapped it and gasped. It contained a ten pound smoked ham, a Highland gammon, a sweet and tender delicacy.

"Oh, Ian! I've not seen one like this in months. It is magnificent. But ye shouldn't have...it must have cost ye a week's wages."

He shushed her. "Don't worry about the cost. Will you prepare some for our supper?"

"Yes, of course. Then we can have soups and stews with what is left over. It will last us for weeks."

Flinging her arms around his neck, she hugged him.

Caught by surprise, Ian reached for her, wanting more, his passions stoked. But she danced away and began preparing the food. She brushed back a wisp of hair with the back of her hand, a gesture he'd seen several times. Completely innocent, it charmed Ian and only made him want her more.

When she glanced back at him smiling, he winked at her.

She looked at him quizzically, her incredible green eyes darkening like a hazy sea. He had to look away, lest he reveal his passion so soon.

One lazy morning, Catherine invited Ian to join her and Finn for a hike into the nearby hills.

"Where are we going?" Ian asked. He was officially off duty and dressed in traveling clothes, his uniform hanging on a hook in his apartment in Ardgay.

"Ye shall see." She smiled mysteriously. "I like ye better in these clothes."

They filled their backpacking creels with surplus barley and set off to find Angus the bootlegger's hidden still. Catherine's cousin Margaret Ross accompanied them, along with Davey Macdonald, a village lad with a not-very-secret crush on Margaret. The latter led the way.

The trail began on the braes past the Kirk at Croick. Up they climbed, up into the mist. A knot of concern formed in Catherine's stomach, but Davey assured her he knew the way. And sure enough, after a hard morning's hike, they emerged into a small glen. A lochan—a small loch, or lake—surrounded by heather and thistle, rested at the foot of a large cave.

Angus emerged to greet them, cocking a wary eye at Ian.

Catherine introduced the two men.

"He's the new constable," Finn said innocently.

Angus immediately backed up, tensed his muscles, and balled his fists. "A lawman?"

"I'm a constable, not a government tax collector," Ian said quickly. "What you do here is of no concern to me."

The old moonshiner still looked doubtful.

When Catherine nodded reassuringly, Angus' muscles visibly unknotted, and he reached for Ian's offered hand. "Then ye're welcome here."

Like mist in the sunshine, the tension in the air dissipated.

Catherine stole a glance at Ian. He'd passed another test, had shown where his loyalties lay. At least on this day. At least on this matter.

After the travelers unloaded their creels, Angus invited them to stay and watch the distilling process.

"Freedom and whisky go together," Angus said, quoting Robert Burns. "And I make it here," he added proudly, "Exactly the same way it is done at the large distilleries at Speyside and along the whisky trail..."—he winked—"the ones that pay the whisky tax."

Davey Macdonald checked some of the vats, stoked the fires, and read the temperature gauges. Clearly, he'd been here before. Equally clear, the old bootlegger had developed a special affection for the lad.

"I need a protégé," he remarked privately to Catherine.

"An apprentice?"

"Aye. Someone I can teach the secrets o' whisky makin' to. Someone to carry on the old ways after I am gone."

Angus had lived in Greenyards all his life. A cotter and widower, all his children were grown and scattered. He lived alone at the edge of the village and eked out a meager existence on his few acres of land, the principal crop of which was barley—none of which went into soup! White haired, with a full round belly and twinkling eyes, his main pleasure came from his still, from the joy his whisky gave his fellow clansmen, and from his new apprentice, Davey Macdonald.

Davey appeared to return the old man's affection just as strongly.

"What is it that draws ye here?" Catherine asked the lad when they were alone.

"Angus, himself. I love the old man."

"Like a father?"

Davey seemed thoughtful for a moment. "No. More like a kindly teacher."

"But there's something more, isn't there," Catherine guessed.

"Aye. The process itself. I'm fascinated by it. It's like some kind of..."

"Alchemy?"

He grinned. "Aye. Alchemy. You start with grain and water...and presto!...out comes whisky. It's magic!"

Catherine left unsaid her suspicion that Angus' tweaking of the establishment's nose through his moonshine activities was also satisfying to the lad.

She listened as Angus explained his process. "First, I soak the grain in clear, cold Highland water from a nearby stream. After forty-eight hours, when the barley has germinated, I dry it, then roast it over an open peat fire. Then I crush it with rocks, filter it through a sieve to remove the husks and twigs, and re-dissolve the powder—now pure malt sugar—in more water in a large vat."

She noticed Davey's rapt attention.

"To start the fermentation," Angus continued, "I throw in some of the yeast I get from a bakery in Ardgay." He smirked and playfully jabbed Davey in the ribs. "They must think I do a lot of bakin'."

Ian lifted Finn up for a better look. The lad watched, clearly fascinated, as a batch started the day before bubbled and frothed from gasses rising to the surface.

"It looks like a witch's cauldron," Finn said.

Angus chuckled. "Aye, lad. 'Tis is a magic potion in there. After twenty-four hours," he continued, "it will be ready to be distilled."

Davey handed him his prized possession, a big still with a copper 'worm.' Angus began to distill off the clear, potent liquor into bottles and flasks.

"The only dif' between my process and the legal distilleries," he explained, "is they use sherry casks to age their whisky. That gives it a brown color and a smoother taste. But from experience"—he winked again —"and frequent tastin', I have learned the exact proportions of grain, barley, and fermentation time needed to make any strength of final product my customers want."

"What would happen if you re-distilled that first run," Davey asked matter-of-factly, pointing to the clear, dripping liquor. "You know, suppose you ran it through your still a second time? Or even a third?"

Angus scratched his head. "Why, I dunno, lad," he said. "It would be pure alcohol, take yer head right off if ye drank it. And it would be so volatile it would damn near burst into flames from just lookin' at it!"

Catherine arched an eyebrow at the boy. What a strange question!

Davey just smiled mysteriously.

After Angus paid her for the barley—a few shillings and a small flask of moonshine thrown in for good measure—Catherine and the others said goodbye and headed for home through brilliant sunshine and a bright blue sky.

That night after supper, Catherine poured Ian a wee drop of the moonshine.

He drank, then wheezed and coughed as it went down. "Good Lord!" he gasped. But he held out his glass for another.

When Finn was tucked into bed, the two of them sat on the rug and cuddled in front of the fire. They talked in hushed tones and caressed one another.

Entranced by the birthmark on her neck, Ian nuzzled then kissed it. When he began to suck on it, she giggled and turned her head to offer him a better target. He could see the nipples of her taut breasts tenting the fabric of her blouse, and crept his hand up to cup one of them. But she stopped him with quiet words. He relaxed, put his arm around her shoulder, and drew her closer.

Catherine stared dreamily into the fire. She was almost ready to believe Ian was the one. That he was right for her. That she'd found love again.

Mesmerized by the fire's heat, they'd fallen asleep and hadn't awakened until nearly daybreak. Before he departed, she gave him a full-mouthed kiss and watched him lead his garron back down the glen.

She stoked the fire and was still musing about him when her Aunt Christy and Uncle John knocked on the door. They looked grim. Extremely grave.

John Ross was a wiry little man, with hands as thick as gloves from years of hard work. Balding, his eyebrows nearly met in the middle. Finn thought he looked like a gnome. A merry-eyed gnome.

Uncle John liked to whistle and had found a way to give the sound a throaty quality. Listeners swore it resembled the skirl of bagpipes. As one of the four principal tenants in Greenyards, he was the head of a large extended family totalling about 100 people.

It always startled Catherine how much her aunt resembled her mother. Round and friendly-faced, with pert noses between blue eyes, the two sisters even had the same habit of brushing back their long hair with the backs of their hands.

"Good morning, Uncle John," Catherine said. "Aunt Christy, how are ye?" She looked from one to the other. "Why the dour looks?"

Both offered tight-lipped greetings in return, worry etched on their faces.

"Have you seen this?" her uncle asked. He placed a recent copy of the *Inverness Courier* newspaper on the table, opened it up, and stabbed a large, bony finger at an item. "Look at that."

"FARMS TO BE LET ON THE ESTATES OF GREENYARDS"
In the Parish of Kincardine
The sheep walk of Greenyards presently owned by Mr. Alex Munro.

The above farm will be let on leases of such duration as may be agreed upon, with entry at the term of Whitsunday 1854. William Ross, Ground Officer at Bonar Bridge, will show the land. Further particulars will be communicated by James F. Gillanders, Esq., Highfield by Beauly, to whom offers are to be addressed."

Catherine silently read and reread the notice. A knot formed in her stomach. Gillanders and Munro again. Those devils!

"Oh Lord, our homes," she said under her breath.

"I have been expecting this," Christy said grimly, brushing back a wisp of hair. "Ever since Glencalvie was cleared almost ten years ago."

Uncle John's voice was heavy with bitterness. "Almost the whole shire has been emptied. We are the last of it. It was just a matter of time before our turn came 'round."

Christy put her arm around Catherine's shoulders. "We should have a village meeting, find out what everyone wants to do."

"Whatever we decide," her uncle added, "we had better all be in it together."

Catherine looked into her aunt's deep blue eyes. "It is going to happen all over again, isn't it, Aunt Christy? They will not leave us in peace." She lowered her head. "It will be Glencalvie all over again, won't it?"

No one spoke. Gloom as heavy as a funeral dirge spread through the house and blotted out the sun.

Finally, Catherine straightened, her face flushed with determination. "I will not go so easily this time. Of that ye can be certain." She smacked her fist into her palm. "This time they will have a fight on their hands!"

Finn, who'd been awakened by the loud talking and sat by the fire, innocently let out a loud squeak on his whistle.

"Stop it!" she yelled, her fists clenched.

The lad's eyes welled with tears.

Chapter Five

Alexander Munro didn't want to make this trip, didn't want to make it at all. He gripped the horse's reins and leaned into the weather.

He'd left his estate at Braelangwell shortly after this morning's clouded sunrise and now plodded eastward along the north bank of the Carron. Old Man Winter hadn't completely given up his hold on the land and had chased garland-draped Spring southward again. Snow threatened, and a steady headwind blew up the strath from the Kyle of Sutherland, the narrow strait of water which flowed into the Dornoch Firth and then into the sea. A cold, gray, depressing day, it perfectly matched Munro's mood.

The lord's factor and lawyer expected him for dinner in Tain, a small town a half-day's ride east along the Dornoch Firth. Munro pulled his threadbare coat around him, clamped his bonnet tight on his head, and plodded on, cursing the weather with every hoof beat.

His mount was a Highland garron, an uncomfortable ride in any climate. Unlike the larger European horses the more affluent gentry could afford—chestnuts and bays, roans and grays—a garron was little bigger than a pony, though much sturdier; a horse more for working than riding. Munro's legs almost touched the ground, forcing him to bend forward in the saddle, increasing the pain in his already aching back.

Like his father before him, and his father before that, Alex Munro was the holder of the leases for all of Strath Carron. That made him the legal landlord for the village of Greenyards. But Munro was only a middleman. He didn't own the land outright, but leased it in turn from the lord, the true landowner. This arrangement had always been satisfactory to all concerned.

Generally content with this lot, Munro was considered a 'gentleman' in the social order of things. He collected enough money in rents from his tenants to pay his own lease with the lord, and had enough left over to live on comfortably, if not grandly.

And it wasn't like there was much work involved. He chuckled at the thought. In his grandfather's days, the tacksman had been the lord's principal assistant, his executive officer. He collected rents, settled disputes among the tenants and crofters, and managed the lands. But that wasn't the way of it now, not since the lords had begun to hire factors—professional managers—to run their estates. Munro never saw his lord anymore. All his dealings now were with the factor, James Gillanders.

Munro glanced impatiently to his left, then up the slopes of the peak known as Meall Dhergidh. Its rocky top shrouded in clouds, he could still make out patches of snow clinging to the rocks along the upper braes. And the burns—rivulets and rills—now full of snowmelt, danced down the slopes to the river, which plunged foaming away on his right. He plodded onward, passing the big elbow bend of the Carron where it curved northeast to southeast before spilling into the Kyle.

Munro could make out the little settlement of Greenyards across the black, peat-stained river. It wasn't a town in any proper sense, not even a township. Just houses and crofters' cottages dribbling away down the strath in here-a-group, there-a-group clumps. The smoke from their peat fires streamed westward on the sea breeze. The village women were already up and moving about. Even from a distance, Munro could make out their distinctive red plaid shawls and dark, heavy woolen skirts. He watched a herd boy gather the small, shaggy-faced native black cattle for the short drive to the wet pastures down the glen.

Munro had a pretty good idea of why he'd been summoned by Gillanders. And he wasn't happy about it. Why couldn't they leave well enough alone? He knew the lord, Major Charles Robertson, had other plans in mind for this little patch of Highland turf. And Munro smelled trouble for himself because of it. He kicked his pony, lowered his head, and kept going.

Finally arriving in Tain, Munro admired the horses tethered outside. Fine horses. Proper horses. Not like his little garron.

As he entered the room, James Gillanders and Donald Stewart, the lord's factor and lawyer respectively, were sitting, warming themselves before the fireplace in their suite of rooms at the old tudor-style inn.

"How goes it, Alex?" Gillanders asked. Over six feet tall, the factor helped him off with his coat.

Munro shrugged. "It is a good day to be home with one's wife and children." His eyes darted around the room, taking in the paintings, bric-a-brac, and other expensive furnishings he couldn't afford.

The three men sat in stuffed, comfortable chairs, their footgear drying before the fire. Stewart passed around tumblers full of whisky. Munro noted with envy the other men's high-topped leather boots and cloaks—great woolen cloaks—hanging from hooks behind the door. *Must have cost them a pretty penny.* His own was a poor contrast.

Gillanders stretched his long, lean body into a chair, unmistakably a man used to the mantle of authority. His confident posture matched the assurance in his voice. He had—what was Shakespeare's line—'a lean and hungry look': cold, slate-grey eyes, a trim moustache, tight lips that never smiled, and a pugnacious jaw framing a hard, square face. With a full head of black hair, he was almost handsome. Except for the eyes. Pitiless eyes, which could pin a listener more sharply than a Highland dirk. He had one particularly annoying habit. When considering a problem, he'd pace the room, slapping his riding crop non-stop into his hand.

"Alex," Gillanders began, "the lord wants to complete the improvements he started in Strath Carron ten years ago. It's time to finish the matter. He wants to turn all of Greenyards into a sheep walk."

Munro measured his response. "I thought as much when I received yer...yer *invitation*...to meet here." It had in fact been a summons, and they both knew it. "It is going to be like Strath Oykel," he muttered bitterly, involuntarily rubbing his left arm. The broken bone from a fall in the clearance riots ten years ago had never properly healed. It still ached when the weather turned cold.

"There need not be any trouble," Gillanders said. "I have a plan. With your help, and the sheriff's, we can carry it off without another riot." His voice was almost gentle and he paused for a moment, as if debating something with himself, then continued. "In any case, it's the lord's property. He has made his wishes clear."

He nodded to Stewart, the lord's attorney. A pinch-faced man, always daubing at a wet nose, the lawyer unfolded a newspaper and laid it in front of Munro. He pointed to the advertisement offering leases in Greenyards to sheep farmers.

"The terms for these leases will start this Whitsunday. We must have the strath cleared by then," Stewart said with a sniffle.

Whitsunday, Munro thought. May 15. One of the four 'quarter' days of the Scottish calendar, when confirmations and baptisms typically took place. And when leases became due or were renewed. A little over a month from now.

Gillanders refilled Munro's tumbler. "Alex, our lord believes great profits can be made from these leases. We've had enquiries from a number of sheep farmers already. They'll pay handsomely for use of this land." He patted Munro's shoulder. "Profits the lord is prepared to share with those who help him."

Munro sat up straighter at the mention of money. He could use the extra income, could use it very well. He'd slid into greater and greater debt to card sharks in the nearby town of Culrain. They were starting to get nasty in their demands to be paid. His youngest son had ambitions of becoming a lawyer, and a professional education didn't come cheap. And he still had one unmarried daughter at home. A fat dowry would bring the right sort of suitors. None of the family had bought any clothes in a long while. A new greatcoat for himself and some woolens for the wife would also be nice. Gillanders' offer sounded tempting. Very tempting.

"Exactly how pleased would the lord be?" Munro asked coyly.

The factor winked at the lawyer then smiled at Alex. "He's prepared to offer you fifteen percent."

Munro had an idea of what the sheep farmers were willing to pay. Fifteen percent would be a handsome income indeed! Almost double what he collected from the villagers now. And it would cost him nothing. Or would it? His brow furrowed.

"Where is Major Robertson?" he asked, swirling his whisky around in the glass. "Here in the Highlands?"

"No, he's still in London. But I have spoken with him recently. I assure you, what I'm telling you came right from his mouth."

Munro accepted that as the truth. He knew the small rents the lord got from his Highland farmers barely covered his expenses. And rumor had it the major wanted to be a bigger player in the world of British politics. Munro had it figured out—if the lord was willing to part with fifteen percent of this new income, he must want his help badly. Must need his help badly.

Gillanders persisted. "What say you, Alex? Are you in?"

"I like the money," Munro grumbled. "I care not for the trouble I am likely to get." He held up his tumbler for more. He could rarely afford such good liquor himself. Smooth single malt whisky from the nearby distillery of Glen Morangie. Golden in color, with just a whisper of peat. He smacked his lips in approval.

Gillanders stood, moved to the window, and listened to the bells of the Old Tain Kirk tolling out Evensong.

He turned back to the tacksman. "Alex, I have a plan. Trust me; there'll be no trouble this time. It will all be over and done with before the villagers even realize what's happened—"

The lawyer interrupted. "Mr. Munro, what is the current population of Greenyards now? As near as possible?"

"About 400 souls. Ninety families. But only four are on my rent rolls, the heads of the four principal households. They collect rents from their own sub-tenants, then pay me annually. Their leases are due this Whitsunday. There are also a few cottars who work the tenants' acreage and receive a small parcel of land to farm in return."

Gillanders nodded. "I'm not worried about the little fry. When the heads of the four households are evicted, the rest will go quietly."

"Are any of your tenants in arrears on their rents?" the lawyer asked hopefully.

"None," Munro replied. "They're all paid up."

The lawyer shook his head. "Pity. That would have made it easier."

The two men then explained to Alex their plan for clearing Greenyards. For turning that thriving, ancient community of men, women and children into empty sheep walks.

"It might work," Munro said when he'd heard the scheme. "But I am not completely sold on it. Highlanders can be stubborn when their backs are up. And they have long memories. Some of those clansmen ye tossed out of Glencalvie ten years ago settled in Greenyards. And many of them still remember yer evictions in other straths."

Clearly, it wasn't what Gillanders wanted to hear. His voice turned hard. "Alex, these improvements are going to happen. That land can no longer support the population living there now, and it's increasing every year. The clansmen grow poorer every year and the lord is not prepared to pay a Poor Tax for a bunch of illiterate villagers who want to continue living in the old ways."

His voice rose a few octaves, and he practically shouted. "My God, man, there's a worldwide revolution going on, an Industrial Revolution! The textile mills of Manchester, Leeds, London and Glasgow are desperate for our wool, Scottish wool. Its price has more than quadrupled. And Lowland sheep farmers have the expertise and capital to make the project succeed. They are offering enormous amounts of cash for leases to our Highland straths." Red-faced, he glared at Munro, then turned to stare out the window again.

Munro had kept his own temper. He took small satisfaction in knowing he'd bested the factor, at least in that. He'd seen Gillanders' temper flare on many occasions.

"Mr. Munro," the lawyer said, his tone conciliatory, "we can't stop the march of progress. The Highland economy cannot continue as it has always done. Our plan will improve the standard of living for the whole region. If a few poor crofters have to be displaced to achieve that goal, it's worth it, isn't it?"

Gillanders came back from the window. "Who knows, Alex, this might be an opportunity in disguise for some of those clansmen. Many have already emigrated to North America, New Zealand, and Australia, where they've made new and better lives for themselves. I've heard others have learned new trades in the factories and shops of Glasgow and Edinburgh. They've all improved themselves. That's our purpose. To improve not only Highland land, but Highland lives as well."

Munro could have cared less for the fate of the villagers—his own future his only concern. True, the money looked good—the fifteen percent. But something gnawed at him. This didn't seem like just another business deal. Like wind before a storm, this smelled like something more, like a sea-change in his relationship with the lord on the one hand, and with his own tenants on the other. He couldn't see over that horizon, couldn't foretell what it would mean in the long run. But worry crawled through him like a tapeworm.

Gillanders nodded—firmly, this time—to Stewart. They had tried the carrot. It was now time for the stick.

"Mr. Munro," the lawyer said. "If you won't cooperate, the lord will not renew your own leases when they expire in a few years. Without your help, it may take us a little longer, but we will clear the village eventually. Yet without any profit for you either. It would be so much faster for us—and so much more in your own interests—if you cooperated."

Munro thought about it in silence, sipping his whisky. What choice did he have, really? If he refused, they'd just wait him out and cancel his leases. Then he'd end up with nothing. And the land would be cleared anyhow.

He shrugged. "What do ye want me to do?"

"That's a good lad!" Gillanders slapped him on the back, filled all their tumblers again, then raised his own. "Dry bargaining bodes ill. Let's drink on it."

He tossed back his shot and held out his hand for Munro to shake.

Chapter Six

The rain thrummed on the roof as steadily as a heartbeat. When it turned to hail, it beat down like a water hammer. Inside the house, however, the peats burned brightly, the fireplace drawing air from a cracked open window. Heat cozily permeated the room.

David did a good job on the house, Catherine thought. *It was built for foul weather and had proved itself up to the challenge time and time again.*

Ian's eyes upon her caused her to look up, and a thrilling shiver skittered over her.

He smiled and pointed at the ceiling. "Winter's a long time goin' here in the Highlands."

She nodded and returned to her knitting, stealing an occasional glance at him when he wasn't looking. He was busy helping Finn with some school project. She could see he was fond of the boy, and from the look of adoration on Finn's face, the affection was returned as strongly as it was received. She was touched by the close father-son relationship developing between them.

She blinked to pinch back a tear at the realization she too ached for more affection. Yearned to let herself go, take the plunge and give full vent to the passion and intimacy she craved, share the hardships and joy, the partnering that was the reward of mature love. Was Ian the one? Dared she hope? Dared she give her heart away, only to have it broken again?

She put down her needle and thread and took a deep breath. There was one big hurdle to get over first: the matter of the evictions.

"Ian, please sit down." She indicated a chair across from her. "I have something to show ye."

As he lit his pipe, an old briar, she poured tea. The

Virginia Burley tobacco filled the room with a rich aroma, reminding her of her father.

She laid out the newspaper advertisement announcing the new sheep leases in Greenyards.

He read it slowly, moving his finger along the line of print. His brow furrowed. "What does it mean?"

"Ye have not seen it before?"

"No."

"Ian, I know you travel to Tain and Dingwall sometimes. Have ye not heard talk of plans to clear Greenyards, to evict us from our homes?"

"No, not a word," he said shaking his head. "Is that what you think, that the lord's going to clear you out?"

"What else could it mean?"

He leaned back heavily, releasing a long sigh. "What does your landlord Mr. Munro say about it? Has he said he plans to evict you?"

"No. We've heard nothing from him."

Ian puffed on his pipe and blew out a cloud of smoke. "Well, the law is very clear on this," he said bringing to remembrance how it read. "Only he can evict you. Since he's your legal landlord, only he can apply for any Writs of Eviction. The four principal tenants of the village have a contract with him, not with the lord. Any such action must begin with him."

Catherine hadn't thought of this. Her eyes snapped open. She saw a ray of light, a spark of hope.

"Before you do anything," Ian continued, "you should meet with Mr. Munro. Find out his intentions. Better yet, get them in writing. A written statement from him will carry weight with the court if the lord does try anything." He smiled. "Do not buy trouble before you have to."

"I will bring this up at the village meeting." She jotted a note to herself on a piece of wrapping paper, tore it off, and stuffed it into her pocket. "Ye are right. Someone should go see Munro."

Ian puffed away, looking content.

Catherine suddenly slapped the table. "Still, I do not

trust Munro. Nor the lords. They always get their way, twisting the law to suit their own purposes. Even the kirk is on their side. What chance do we poor farmers and crofters have?"

He didn't answer, for he had no answer.

"Have ye had any personal experience with the clearances?" she asked, rubbing her hands together.

"Me? Why, no. All of my family is from Culrain. We're merchants, not farmers."

"What do ye think of them?"

He took his time answering. "I can see both sides of it. The land belongs to the lords. Legally, it's theirs to do with as they see fit. And you cannot criticize them for trying to make a profit from it." A movement from Finn distracted him momentarily. "But I am saddened by the suffering they have caused."

"Ye do not think our bein' on this land for generations gives us some right to it?" Her face flushed, her voice rising in volume. "Working it, building our homes on it, raising our families on it—does that all count for naught?"

He sighed. "What can I tell you, Catherine? I know it is not what you want to hear, but in the eyes of the law, you have no legal right to remain if the lord chooses to evict you." He stabbed a finger in the air for emphasis. *"Provided* your leaseholder, Mr. Munro, goes along with it."

She stamped her foot and folded her arms defiantly. "I will not be evicted again."

"Does the whole village feel the same way?"

"I do not know. I will find out later, at the meeting. But I have made my own decision. I aim to stay and defend my home."

Another question she had to have answered, one which could no longer be left unasked, though she feared the reply almost as much as she feared the evictions themselves.

She placed her hand on his. "What will ye do, Ian, if there is trouble? Where will ye stand if the clearances do come to Greenyards? Will ye stand with us—with me and the village—or with the lord?"

He swallowed hard. "Och, Catherine, don't do this to me. You know I'm a peace officer, sworn to uphold the law. I've taken an oath. As long as no law's broken, there's naught I can do."

She pulled her hand away and stood. He reached for her, but she moved away.

"What do you want from me?" he asked quietly.

"More than ye are givin'."

He straightened. "I'll stick by the village and defend it until someone breaks the law. Then I'll be forced to do my duty."

"Even for an unjust law?"

His voice rose a notch. His neck veins bulged when he stood to face her. "I've sworn an OATH. On my HONOR. I cannot overlook disobedience, if it comes to that. But I pray it will not."

She relented, took a step towards him, reached her arms around his neck. His male musk ignited her senses. She closed her eyes, a barely audible moan crossing her lips. "Och, Ian. I see how bothered ye are. But ye canna have it both ways. I hope ye never have to choose. But ye might." She pushed back, held his face between her hands and gave him a kiss. "I only hope ye make the right choice."

A whistle tooted. She smiled. "And so does Finn."

Ian put on his coat and hat. It was time to leave; he'd been asked to stay for dinner, but not to remain for breakfast.

"Can I touch it," she asked.

"What?"

"Your badge."

He laughed. "Of course." He turned his chest towards her.

Timidly, she reached out her hand and touched the cold metal.

He took her hand between his own, rubbed it, then put it inside his shirt against his heart. "*This* is me," he whispered, "not that other thing."

Finn stood to say goodbye.

"Fetch Ian's boots, son," his mother ordered.

The boy went to the hearth and returned with the boots a minute later.

Ian pulled on the right one without incident. But when he slipped his foot into the left, he let out a yelp and quickly pulled it back.

Finn roared with laughter and blew his whistle.

Ian turned the boot upside down. A big bullfrog flopped onto the floor and hopped madly away towards the door.

Catherine laughed.

Ian grinned and pointed at Finn. "You rascal! I will get you another time." He gave Catherine a final nod, pulled his collar high, and opened the door.

She tried to smile but couldn't hide the fear. The thorny matter of the evictions had already come between them. And they hadn't even started yet. Would she not only lose her home and land to them, but her new love as well?

Into the wee hours of the morning, she sat at the table pondering her course. No clear answer showed itself, only dilemmas, piled one on top of the other—a stack of unpleasant choices.

She finally went to bed. For the first time in many months, she prayed for guidance.

Chapter Seven

James Gillanders awoke feeling pleased with himself. He was on schedule to have Greenyards cleared by
Whitsunday, just as the lord had instructed. Major
Robertson would doubtless reward him handsomely for
his diligence and efficiency.

He celebrated his successful meeting with Alex
Munro by ordering a hearty breakfast—spicy bangers
fried with onions and creamy butter, a brook trout
fresh-caught from an ice cold stream and pan fried in
the banger's juices, and golden brown scones slathered
with butter and drizzled with honey. All of it washed
down with cups of strong Turkish coffee. He leaned
back, patted his stomach, and belched loudly. Now, if he
could just persuade the Ross Shire sheriff to go along
with his scheme...

It was already late in the day when Sheriff Robert T.
Mackenzie—'Rob' to his friends—greeted Gillanders in
his office at the Tain courthouse and jail. Once known as
the 'Old Tolbooth,' the courthouse was a historic
building, visible from all around by its tall duncecap-
shaped roof. The Highlanders called it the 'sharp-
pointed house,' and said about prisoners, 'he's a guest at
the sharp-pointed house.'

As Mackenzie talked with the factor, pale sunshine
peeped through a hole in the cloud cover and streamed
in through windows covered with layers of grime from
candles and whale oil lamps.

Gillanders handed him a packet of papers. "These
are applications for Writs of Eviction in Greenyards."

Mackenzie looked first at the endorsement line at
the bottom of the pages. "Signed by Alex Munro the

tacksman, eh?"

Gillanders nodded. "We completed the arrangements last night."

The sheriff studied the papers in more detail while Gillanders paced restlessly about the office, absentmindedly playing with his riding crop, toying with it and slapping it into his hand.

Mackenzie looked up. "They appear to be in order. I'll have the warrants prepared straight away." The sheriff then leaned back in his chair and studied the other man. *Here's an ambitious one. He's come a long way already and means to go further. A lot further.*

He finally asked, "Will you join me for some dinner, James? I've ordered from the tavern next door."

Gillanders studied Rob Mackenzie as he read the documents. The man enjoyed life, especially the eating and drinking parts—as evidenced by a belly bulging over the beltline of his stout, squat body. He also loved his pipe. Not just the smoking of it, but when not lit, he chewed on it non-stop or turned it over and over in his hands. Or used it as a pointer and stabbed the air with it for emphasis while talking. He was seldom without it.

The sheriff had one physical defect, a lazy right eye. It occasionally drifted outward. Gillanders found it creepy and unnerving.

Gillanders stopped pacing when invited to eat. "Thank you, Sheriff, I will join you for a bite and a wee drop of drink." He took a seat, and unfolded his napkin.

Mackenzie handed him a mug of ale. "How many estates do you manage now, James?"

"Four."

"And your own land? How goes it?"

"I have a small estate at Rosskeen, not far from my home. It's modest in size. Nothing like the lord's."

"But you've already turned it into a sheep walk?"

"Aye, just recently."

"At a good profit?"

Gillanders threw back his head and laughed. "Good! Why it has been a right boon, a wonderful source of income. And with little bother for it. The sheep farmers pay their rents on time, never give me a problem."

The sheriff chuckled. "Better than trying to collect from a bunch of tenant farmers and crofters, eh?"

"Aye. No trouble and four times the profit." He leaned across the table. "Land, Sheriff. That's the key to success here in the Highlands. Land and sheep. They go together like lassies and heather."

"If your good fortune keeps up, Jamie, we'll soon be calling you 'Sir James,' or 'Lord Gillanders!'"

The factor beamed at the compliment.

Mackenzie eyed his guest. *So, he is trying for a landed title. Being married to one of the lord's sisters— his reward for successful past clearances—could not but help his plans.* "Well, don't forget me when you are a high-brow peer," the sheriff said. "You know I have ambitions myself beyond this job, though none as grand as your own."

They ate in silence.

The sheriff broke the quiet. "I heard about your recent clearances at Rosskeen. There was no trouble? The villagers went quietly?"

"Trouble is inefficient, Mr. Mackenzie," Gillanders said between bites. "No one likes it, least of all me. Legal action—firm legal action—that's the key."

The sheriff nodded and continued eating his plowman's pie and fresh-baked bread.

"But does it never bother you, laddie?" the sheriff asked.

"What?"

"The evictions, man. Clearing out the people, your own countrymen, for sheep." Mackenzie lit his pipe and puffed out billows of smoke. "Oh, I know the reasons behind the Improvements, as you call them. But what about the people?"

The factor shrugged. "Although a few clansmen have to be displaced, the whole region will gain from it."

"I am not opposed to the clearances," Mackenzie answered. "And you may be right, maybe they are what the Highlands need now. But I'm thinking about the clansmen. Sometimes a new policy does not work out like it is supposed to. I've seen the Glasgow slums, where many of the evicted clansmen wind up, heard them coughing from consumption, seen their poverty. I've watched children work twelve hours a day in sweatshops."

Gillanders didn't answer but watched in fascination as the sheriff's right eye drifted outward. He had to tear his gaze away.

The sheriff sighed, put down his pipe, and picked up the applications for the Writs of Eviction. He looked hard at the factor. "Do you think there will be trouble, Jamie?"

The factor shook his head. "There needn't be. I have a plan, one I've discussed with Alex Munro and the lord's lawyer. We all think it will work."

The sheriff leaned forward. "Tell me."

"What I propose is this. There are only four tenants on Alex Munro's rent rolls in Greenyards. They're the heads of the four principal families. Once they've been cleared, the rest will go without trouble. I am certain of it."

"Go on."

"You must act quickly and quietly, Sheriff. Send one deputy—just one, not a whole posse. And a witness. There has got to be a witness. Have them plan to arrive in Greenyards early morning, before the village is stirrin'. They should head straight to the four tenants' houses, deliver the writs, then leave before the rest of the village even knows it's been done." His riding crop cracked against his leg. "Before they have time to react."

The sheriff rubbed his chin, apparently in deep thought. "I like the plan. I must confess I don't like having to do the deed, but the scheme seems possible. It just might work," he finally said.

The factor nodded. "It will. And once the writs have been delivered, the law's requirement to give notice will have been satisfied. That's right, isn't it?"

"Aye."

"Good. After it's done, we'll sit back and wait awhile." Gillanders smiled confidently. "It will be a *fait accomplis* for the villagers. They'll accept their lot. They always have. In a few weeks they'll all be gone. Then we can tear down the houses and clear the land. There'll be no trouble. The key, Sheriff, is getting the writs delivered quickly and quietly."

The sheriff again appeared pensive.

Finally, Gillanders asked, "When will you do it, Sheriff?"

Mackenzie looked at the newspaper advertisement again. "Whitsunday. It says here the new leases are to start this Whitsunday. Hmm..." He tapped his pipe into an ashtray. "I'd better get going. The sooner the tenants get the notices, the more time they'll have to find other housing. I will see to it right away."

"Thank you," Gillanders said, rising to go. "The lord will be grateful. I'll be sure he knows of your cooperation."

The sheriff focused both eyes on him. "I hope your plan works, James. Remember, Ross Shire has a history of resistance, one of the few shires that does. Truthfully, I am not convinced the Greenyards' clansmen will allow themselves to be tossed out as easily as you think."

Gillanders seemingly ignored the warning. "Who will you send to deliver the writs? What about the regular constable who patrols there? What's his name, Macgregor? He'd not raise an alarm."

Mackenzie grunted. *A Judas!* He shook his head. "No, Ian Macgregor doesn't work for me, though I am sure his Superintendent would loan him for this task if I asked. But I want to keep him in reserve. He is well liked there. Sending him with the writs would destroy any future usefulness he might have. No, I'll send one of my own lads, a regular deputy sheriff. Probably Macpherson."

Gillanders nodded, tapped his riding crop to the side of his forehead in salute, and departed.

When he'd gone, Mackenzie refilled his pipe and recalled his first day as a law officer many years ago. A rookie constable, he'd stood before the elders of the village, removed his hat, and placed a handful of earth on his head. Then he swore an oath to serve Her Majesty the Queen, symbolized by his uniform and badge, and the people of this village, symbolized by the earth on his head. How long ago had it been? Now he would help clear out the very people he'd once sworn to protect. How times had changed.

He relit his pipe. A tobacco ember crackled out and fell on his uniform. He flicked it onto the floor, but not before it had burned a small, blackened hole in his shirt. "Damn!" He stared at a map of Strath Carron and the large red 'X' Gillanders had slashed through the village of Greenyards. "Bad business," he said softly. Guilt gnawed at his insides like a rat.

Catherine ushered Finn to bed, watched while he knelt and said his prayers, then tucked him under the covers with a good-night kiss.

As she turned to go, he said, "Momma?"

"Yes?"

"I like Mr. Macgregor. I like him a whole lot."

She smiled. "So do I, son. So do I."

But sleep wouldn't come. She tossed and turned in her bed, wondering if she cared too much for Macgregor and his shiny badge. Too much for her own good.

At his home across the river, Alex Munro tallied up the extra income he would get once Greenyards was cleared and the sheep farmers given their new leases. He made a note of new purchases he would make.

The homemade wine he sipped made him wince, then shudder. Not very good wine, he thought. He spat into the fire, which erupted with a devil's tongue of flame. Maybe the first thing to buy should be a hogshead of fine French claret. He moved it to the top of his expanding list.

He cackled, rubbed his hands together greedily, and continued writing.

Ian Macgregor paced restlessly around his small apartment. He tried to read, but his concentration quickly wandered, his mind drifting back to the beautiful, strong woman who lived in Greenyards with her son. The woman he was falling in love with.

When she'd asked him what he'd do if a confrontation occurred, he'd displayed no emotion, but her question had shaken him to the core. What if it did come to a showdown between his love for her and his sworn duty to the law? Between the lord's eviction plans and her and Finn? What would he do?

He drank some whisky and finally settled into his narrow bed.

Pray God it wouldn't come to that. Pray God he wouldn't have to make *that* choice.

Chapter Eight

Notice of the Greenyards clan meeting passed by word-of-mouth, first through the village itself, then down the paths on both sides of the river like wind rippling through the barley. Dinner dishes were washed and put away, peat fires smothered, and children gathered into the care of grannies or young girls.

Catherine listened to the murmur of anxious, fearful talk as small groups of her friends and neighbors clumped together and filed into the little schoolhouse.

Like other village dwellings, the schoolhouse was built of stone and thatch, but was nearly twice as large. Nestled among a copse of oak trees and mountain ferns next to the river, it normally held about sixty children of all ages in its one big room. Six rows of long wooden benches faced the teacher's small table at the front. Behind it, a bare piece of slate was mounted on the wall to serve as a blackboard. Chalk was so precious it was used down to a stub so small it could barely be fingered. On the back wall, behind the students' benches, a fireplace burned peats and an occasional stack of wood brought in by the teacher or a villager.

Mr. Henry, the itinerant teacher, was hired by the village for a few pounds a month. Three mornings a week he came from Ardgay and introduced many of the children to English for the first time. He'd been ill for several weeks, so the children were enjoying an unscheduled holiday.

Three-fourths of the adults at the meeting were women, all similarly dressed—long, dark woolen skirts reaching to the tops of their shoes; cotton blouses with ruffled sleeves and low-cut necklines which buttoned over their skirts; and long shawls in red tartan plaid, either wrapped about their shoulders or drawn tightly over their heads and across their breasts.

The men wore long trousers, high-topped boots, shirts and coats. Some, including Old Pete and Angus Macleod, were in traditional Highland dress—the long kilt. Getting into this yards-long piece of fabric wasn't easy. Catherine had watched her husband David do it many times and marveled at the dexterity it required.

First, the cloth was wrapped two complete turns, then secured at the waist with a belt, a sash, or a silver pin. The loose end was brought up over the left shoulder and down across the back, finally tucked into the waist on the right side.

A homespun shirt, leather boots, and a snappy bonnet completed the Highlander's outfit.

The wearing of the kilt had been outlawed after the Jacobite Rebellion of 1745, the revolt which had tried to put the young Stewart, Bonnie Prince Charlie, back on the throne of Scotland. In 1782 the law was repealed; though seldom seen in cities except on ceremonial occasions, they still wore the kilt regularly in Highland villages and countrysides.

The Greenyards elderly and a few other villagers took their seats at the students' benches. The rest lined the walls. Some had brought slabs of peat which they threw onto the fire, stirring it up from time to time. It was toasty warm. On any other evening, it would have been cheery. Tonight's mood was somber.

The few men present included Peter Ross—'Old Pete'—age 72, the clan bard and historian. He quietly spoke with Margaret Macgregor Ross, a widow with seven children. Catherine's Uncle John Ross stood with his wife Christy at the front of the room. Donald MacNair, a crippled veteran of the Battle of Waterloo, leaned on his walking stick.

Angus Mackay, the new minister, had been invited, his first community meeting. He helped some of the elderly to their seats. Angus Macleod, the moonshiner, had come down from his cave in the hills and shared a joke with Davey Macdonald, whose own father was away in one of the Queen's Highland regiments. A few other male teenagers accompanied their widowed or elderly mothers. But mostly it was a crowd of women and a few old men.

John Ross, now behind the teacher's table, prepared to call the meeting to order.

The new minister joined him, a puzzled look on his face. "Where are all the men?" he asked.

"They're gone, Mr. Mackay. Gone for soldiers. Ross Shire has been a prime recruitin' ground for British Regiments for decades. No, centuries."

The minister looked startled. "I never realized so many were missing," he said quietly. "Even at Sunday services, what with all the children running around, it never seemed so striking before."

"Take Margaret Macgregor Ross," John said, nodding in the widow's direction. "Her husband was a Royal Marine. Drowned at sea three years ago. Or Naomi Macdonald"—he pointed to another woman, young Davey's mother. "Her husband's in the 78th. Been in Egypt and India. Same place my niece Catherine lost her husband a few years ago."

He ticked off the names of more absent men, either dead or still in uniform, nodding toward each one's wife as he named him.

Mackay had never seen this face of the clearances before. They didn't teach that in the comfortable Edinburgh and Glasgow seminaries where he'd studied. A thin wedge of doubt drove into him.

"How can the lord even consider evicting women whose men are fighting for their country?" he muttered. "Or worse, have died for it?"

"Aye, that is the rub, isn't it, Mr. Mackay?" John answered grimly. "When the men signed up, they were promised their families would be spared eviction for as long as they served." He rubbed the stubble on his chin.

"Can you imagine the men comin' home from the Queen's Army only to find their homes, their wives, their bairns all gone. Their houses burned to the ground and sheep grazin' in what had been their livin' rooms."

Mackay could only shake his head.

John banged the table for quiet. The hum of conversation ebbed away and died. He held up the Inverness newspaper and pointed to the advertisement announcing sheep farms for lease in Greenyards.

"Many of ye already know about this," he announced.

Her forehead lined with worry, a woman from the back by the fire asked, "What does it mean?"

"If it is true," John answered, "it means the lord wants to turn our homes and farms into sheep walks. We are to be cleared out. Evicted. And soon." He slapped the newspaper with the back of his hand. "Accordin' to this advertisement, the sheep will be here by Whitsunday."

"The 'White Plague,' is coming to Greenyards," someone shouted.

"The 'four-footed clansmen,'" another said, his voice laced with bitterness.

"Worse than the black death!" a third said. It sounded like a curse.

Talk welled up across the room like a tidal wave. The Widow Ross started to weep. Several teenagers bowed their heads, some teary-eyed. Others looked grim, their fists clenched. Angry words, threats, and oaths drifted to the front.

"What shall we do?" John Ross asked. "What is the clan to do?"

The room hushed.

"Can they really do this?" Naomi Macdonald asked. A flinty woman, razor-backed from hard work, she was known to like her whisky neat and could swear with the best of the men. And when she could afford tobacco, she smoked an old pipe. "Can Munro and Gillanders just

73

boot us out like this?"

"Of course they can," John Ross answered patiently. "Ye know how it works. We four principal tenants collect rents from all of ye and pay the total rent due to the tacksman annually. We have never needed a piece of paper for it. Never been behind in payin' either, for as long as I can remember. We have done it this way since..." he scratched his head..."why, just about for-ever."

"And I know no one in this village is on the poor rolls," the minister said quietly. "The kirk is the first source of aid for anyone in such distress, and there's no Poor Tax needed here. The lord gives no charity in Greenyards."

"Aye. We take care of our own less fortunate ones," someone added, his voice tinged with pride.

"And we pay our own teacher, too." The speaker, Anne Munro, a stout woman from Langwell across the river, stood up. "Nary a penny comes from the lord."

"It has always been so!" shouted Helen MacIntyre.

"So, as far as I can tell," John Ross said, "the tacksman has no good reason to evict us. Nor the lord's factor."

"But that has never stopped them before," Naomi Macdonald said, anger contorting her words. "Not here in Strath Carron, nor anywhere else. They do as they please and call it 'improvements.'"

Voices, more full of anger than sorrow now, buzzed around the room like hornets.

Angus Macleod, the bootlegger, suddenly asked in a loud voice from across the room, "Catherine, what about that constable friend of yers? Does he know anythin' about this?"

"Aye," Naomi Macdonald added with a mischievous grin, playfully elbowing the villager next to her. "Ye seem to be on good terms with him, Catherine."

"Very good terms," someone snickered in the back.

Guffaws and cackles rippled through the room.

Catherine detached herself from the little knot of

women she'd been standing with along the wall, her cheeks heated. An image of Ian's handsome face flickered through her mind, then was gone.

"Constable Macgregor," she said stiffly, "suggests we talk with Mr. Munro before we make any decisions we might live to regret." Her eyes roamed the room. "Munro's our tacksman. Have any of ye heard from him? Has there been any talk of evictions from him? All we have seen or heard is that advertisement in the newspaper."

This caught the crowd by surprise. The room quieted.

"What are ye drivin' at?" asked Peter Mackinnon, a stonemason. His hands were heavily calloused, his hair flecked with granite dust.

"Yes, Cath, what do ye mean?" her uncle asked.

She stepped to the front. "Mr. Macgregor knows about the law—"

Giggles interrupted her.

"Go on, lass," her uncle coaxed. "What does the constable say?"

"That only the tacksman can sign the Writs of Eviction. That's the legal requirement. And since we have not heard from him directly, maybe the advertisement is a false alarm. Maybe the factor has jumped the gun before getting approval from Munro. Maybe there is still time to come to some sort of agreement with him to save our homes and land. Maybe..."

The buzz of conversation droned like a swarm of bees.

Catherine let them talk among themselves for a while, then interrupted sharply. "We should send someone to Braelangwell tomorrow and ask Mr. Munro directly if he has or has not applied for the writs? And what exactly are his intentions?"

The Waterloo veteran stomped the floor with his walking stick. "I don't trust him!"

"Nor his father before him." someone else hissed.

"Nor his father before that," Old Pete said. He was

whittling a piece of oak, its shavings piling up at his feet. "And I have known them all."

The room hushed. Finally, someone voiced all their fears. "But what if it is true? What if they do mean to clear us out?"

"Then I say we collect clubs and stones and prepare to stop 'em!" This belligerence erupted from the mouth of David Munro. A small crofter and a distant but none too friendly relative of Alex Munro, he stood in a corner with his arms folded defiantly across his broad chest.

Uncle John shook a finger at him. "Do not be foolish, man. The widow there has seven children. She canna risk them. Besides, the lords always get their way. They can use the police—even soldiers—to force us out if they want to."

"Violence is not the answer," the minister admonished.

David Munro's eyes still blazed. But he kept his tongue.

"Violence," the minister continued, "would be all the excuse the factor needed to call out the militia. Then people would be hurt for certain."

"Better to die on ye feet than to live on yer knees," someone grumbled from the back of the room.

"What do ye think, Cath?" Uncle John asked.

She'd considered the options. "I will listen to Munro, no harm in that," she finally replied. "But I will not be chased away like my own father was."

Many heads nodded in agreement.

Donald MacNair raised his walking stick. "I have a question."

John Ross pointed to him. "Yes?"

"Where will this new constable, this Ian Macgregor, stand if the evictions do come? Is he a friend of the village, or of the lord?"

All eyes turned to Catherine.

She brushed back a strand of hair. "I canna say for certain. I know him to be a man of honor who feels his duty keenly. But he is confused right now, not certain what his duty would be—or to whom—if it came to a confrontation between the village and the lord's men." She sighed. "He prays such a thing never happens.

The old veteran nodded.

"All right," John asked, "who shall we send to see Munro?"

"Yourself," someone said.

"And Catherine, she can speak and read the English."

"And the minister," someone else chimed in. "To keep a rein on Catherine."

Everyone laughed, the tension broken.

The crowd started to disperse.

"Wait!" shouted Elizabeth Gunn, a 26-year-old freckle-faced, red-haired beauty, her husband away soldiering. "Suppose the factor tries to deliver the writs before you see Munro?"

John Ross nodded. "She's got a point. Once the writs are delivered, we will have been given legal notice. The factor can come back with a posse anytime after that, evict us with force if necessary."

"We'll see Munro first thing in the morning," the minister said.

"That's fine," Elizabeth persisted. "But suppose they come while you're gone?"

"I will not be put out without a fight!" Naomi Macdonald exploded. "Not while my husband's still in the Regiment."

Mary Ross of Greenyards, the wife of another clansman who'd enlisted in the Army last year, was hot faced with anger. "Nor I," she said, that anger flashing in her eyes. "I stand with Naomi. I will fight them with my last breath."

The minister raised his hands for calm. "Friends, friends. Violence is not the answer," he pleaded.

When the hubbub died down, the old veteran Donald MacNair looked hard at the minister and said quietly, "Who said anything about violence, Mr. Mackay? We can resist without violence. It is called peaceful disobedience. It is our right as the Queen's subjects. We will just block delivery of the writs. We won't have to attack anyone."

"Aye, that is it," someone said. "We only have to prevent the writs from bein' delivered."

"It might just work," David Munro said with a grunt.

"It is worth a try," Old Pete said.

"But we'll need a warnin' that the writ servers are comin'. So we can be ready for 'em," Mary insisted. "How do we do that?"

"Erect a road block at the entrance to the Strath," David Munro suggested.

Catherine shook her head. "Ye canna do that." She'd moved next to her uncle so everyone could see her. "Ye canna block a public road. That would get the sheriff out here fast. No, we need to find another way. We need lookouts stationed to warn us if they can see anyone coming down the road from Tain."

"Ye think that's where the writ servers'll come from?" someone asked.

"That is where the courthouse is."

"Excuse me," sixteen-year-old Davey Macdonald said softly.

Nobody paid any attention to him.

"Excuse me!" he repeated louder, waving his arms for attention.

John Ross finally called on him. "What is on your mind, lad?"

"Sir, I was on Ardgay Hill not long ago. There's a clear view from there in all directions—west up the Strath towards our village, east toward Bonar Bridge, and south towards Tain. Even the route over the Great Pass can be seen from there, where it joins the Tain road at MidFearn."

John nodded vigorously. "Perfect! We will station lookouts there, on Ardgay Hill."

"But who?" his wife Christy asked. "We may have to keep watch 'round the clock for days, maybe even weeks or months. We all have work to do, and canna spare that much time away from our chores."

Davey cleared his throat for attention again. "We can do it," he said, "the lads and lassies." He was a thin boy, barely coming into manhood. He looked frail among all the adults, but his voice was strong and sure. "It would be like *sheilin'* time in the summer months, when we take the cattle up to the high pastures and camp out. We'll take blankets and food and tents to Ardgay Hill and build fires. But instead of keeping watch on the cows, we'll be lookin' out for lawmen."

"Now wait a minute," the minister spluttered, red in the face. "This is going too far. These are children! Surely you're not going to send children to do this kind of work. How will they manage up there by themselves?"

Catherine answered evenly. "These are Highland children, Mr. Mackay. They have been raised from babes with such responsibilities. If it would make you feel better, we can assign one or two adults to be with them. Each family will take its turn in rotation. And we'll all bring 'em food and blankets and peats for the fires. They will be fine."

The minister reluctantly agreed.

"All right," John Ross said, "now that's settled, how will they warn us? What's to be the signal?"

"Fire a pistol shot," Old Pete suggested. "There are still a few of us with guns."

"No, no," Catherine said with alarm. "We can't use firearms. That would give the sheriff an excuse to come back with a posse, claim there was armed resistance, disobedience." She had a frightening image of Ian as part of the posse ordered to clear the village by force. She didn't want it to come to that. She shuddered as an icy hand of fear gripped her. Instinctively, she reached into her pocket for the comforting feel of her mother's comb.

"How then?" her uncle asked.

She pulled an object out of her pocket. But it wasn't the comb. It was Finn's new whistle. "Here's how." She gave it a mighty blast. Those seated in front of her jumped. Others covered their ears.

Everyone laughed as the sound died away.

"We'll give all the children whistles like this. They are easy to make. Each family can carve one for itself and one or two extras. There is plenty of good birch wood around to make them, and their sound carries well down the glen." She gave another toot, more subdued this time.

Everyone clapped.

"That's it, then," Uncle John said, holding up his hands for quiet. "Let's get the lads and lassies up on Ardgay Hill this very night. And everyone start carving whistles. In the meantime, Catherine, the pastor and I will meet with Mr. Munro tomorrow."

As the meeting broke up, several villagers lingered to look at Finn's whistle.

The minister approached Catherine, nervously twisting the brim of his hat around and around with his fingers. He was of such small stature she had to look down to meet his eyes. "About our meeting with Mr. Munro," he began, "I've never met the man. What sort of a fellow is he?"

"There's not much to tell. We hardly ever see him around the village—except when our rents are due."

Mackay nodded. "Still, we must try to convince him not to agree to the evictions. I don't know how we might do that, but we must try every way possible. And if we can't persuade him, then we must all obey the law. It is our duty under God."

Catherine arched an eyebrow. "There'll be no trouble, minister. Unless they start it." She continued to stare at him. He fidgeted under her gaze.

Finally turning away, she began to restack the peats by the fire. Over her shoulder she said, "Pastor, at some point we all must decide where we stand. I have made my decision. What about ye? Are ye with us or no?"

Silence. She didn't have to look at the man to know he couldn't find the words. Clearly, his indecision had rendered him mute, nothing came out but a long breath. When she turned back, he'd turned on his heel and left.

Catherine followed him out with her eyes. She looked at Aunt Christy, shrugged and arched a brow.

Christy brushed back a wisp of hair and nodded grimly.

Chapter Nine

Ian Macgregor, his head bowed in thought, slowly cantered homeward along a narrow path through an eerily darkened forest. Returning from a day-long visit to nearby Strath Oykel, he'd taken a shortcut through the woods. He knew this trail would eventually meet up with the River Carron's north road, which he'd then follow east to his apartment in Ardgay. Or he could take the road west—to Greenyards. To Catherine. The image of her beautiful, honest face and her dark emerald eyes made his breath hitch.

He passed through a small copse of silver-black birch trees, ghostly apparitions in the dusky moonlight. A pair of curlews fluttered from the branches, their mournful, ululating cries echoing down the glen. Far off, high on the hillsides, a wildcat growled in frustration mayhaps at its failure to catch a red grouse, one of the few which escaped some sportsman's gun.

Ian rested one hand on his rough cord breeches, dug his square-toed boots into the stirrups, and urged his horse onward. He'd seen much today, had much to ponder.

As he emerged from the forest onto the river road, he passed several groups of villagers heading up the strath in the direction of Greenyards. They were courteous, respectful, and friendly.

"Headin' for the schoolhouse," one informed him. "To a meeting of the clan there."

"Good evening, constable," or "good evening, Mr. Macgregor," others said. The men doffed their caps, the women curtseyed slightly.

Ian knew many of their names and returned the greetings with a nod or a two-fingered salute to the brim of his cap.

When he cleared the last cluster of houses, he caught sight of Braelangwell and Alexander Munro's house high on the hill. It was the biggest house in the strath, the easiest one to spot.

He looked at the sky, so full of stars it made his head reel. He picked out Orion the hunter, high overhead on the meridian.

For no particular reason—or maybe because he'd strolled with her through the heather on many an evening such as this—his thoughts turned to Jenny Burns, his first love. It was two years since she'd thrown him over. He hadn't known that something not actually physical could hurt so much. Her image spread itself across his inner eyelids, then was gone.

He shook his head to clear it, nudged his mount onward, and continued down the road to home.

Ian had come face to face with the clearances in Strath Oykel today, up close and direct for the first time. A picturesque valley once teeming with people, the strath now was mostly empty of human inhabitants. A few hardy crofters who'd returned after the evictions to try and scratch out a bare survival from the soil, and the sheep farmers in their comfortable, spacious homes, were the only humans dwelling there now.

What had once been a land of thriving villages, with houses, sheds and gardens, now deserted. All gone with the north wind, save for an occasional chimney standing defiantly in a field of weeds, broken walls and burned timbers. Some houses were merely gutted. Others had been completely destroyed, their stone walls pulled down and thrown into piles—piles of rubble where people had once lived. The lonely chimneys, like silent pleas to the goddess of history, or like the ghost of Hamlet's father, seemed to cry out *Remember me! Remember me!* Forlorn apparitions, they were monuments—grave markers—to a dead land.

The only living creatures Ian had seen today were sheep, thousands of sheep, some grazing in the ruins of the razed houses, some clustered on the roadside to get at the sweet grasses growing there, others wandering freely through the valley. Fat sheep, thick with wool, they dotted the landscape like patches of dirty snow. A few lambs jumped aside as his horse approached.

Ian was deeply moved. For the first time he understood Catherine's hatred and fear of the clearances, understood her distrust of him and the authority he represented. This understanding wouldn't make his decision—if it came to that—any easier. But it made his choices clearer.

When he reached Ardgay, the moon had set and darkness enveloped him. He made his way home by gaslight, changed out of his uniform, and rattled around his sparsely-furnished apartment for a time. But he couldn't get out of his mind the images he'd seen earlier today. Worse, he recognized the mere threat of new clearances in Greenyards blew like a chill wind on his relationship with Catherine, which, up to now, had been blowing fair. The clearances threatened to destroy that relationship, just as they were preparing to destroy the village itself.

Pulled in two directions at once, he was caught in a hard place—wanting Catherine on the one hand, yet angry her stubbornness might force this dilemma upon him.

He suddenly stopped pacing, threw on some old clothes, and headed for the Red Deer Inn, a nearby pub.

When he got there it buzzed with activity—noisy, crowded and smoke-filled. He spied Jock Chisholm, an old pal, across the noisy room, paid for two pints of ale, and headed over.

"Good evening, Jock." He immediately noticed his friend's fine clothes and boots.

The other man stood, shook hands, and accepted the drink. "Ian, old chum, how are ye, lad?"

Ian and the other man had grown up together, attended the same school. But Jock had stayed in Culrain and taken over his father's haberdashery store.

They clinked mugs and drank deeply of the frothy dark brew.

"How long's it been?" Ian asked.

Jock laughed. "A few years, I'll wager. I hear ye are the constable here in Ardgay. Doin' well, too, they say."

Ian thanked him, then asked, "Do you ever see our old teacher, Mr. Mactavish?"

Jock roared. "That old bugger! He was the 'Old Nick' himself, and ye and I were his favorite targets, were we not? Remember how he'd get after us. Of course, we usually deserved it." He looked at the backs of his hands. "I wasn't sure which would last longer, his cane or my knuckles."

They talked and reminisced. Ian felt better. This was what he needed.

"Jock," he asked, "do you ever hear anything about... about...you know...?"

The other man tilted his head. "Jenny? Is that who ye mean?" He shook his head. "Are ye still carryin' the torch for her?" He ordered two more pints. "Forget her, laddie. She's long married. Her husband's an important man, a clerk of the court in Dingwall. She's got one babe already and another bun in the oven."

Ian wiped the foam off his lips. "The torch *is* out, Jock. Just curious is all." He looked at his friend. "How about yourself? What brings you down here?"

"Business, lad. I'm thinking of opening another store, maybe here in Ardgay."

"Business that good, eh?"

"Booming."

"Do you have a sweetheart?"

"A sweetheart! Why, I've had a right proper wife for over two years. And a wee one crawlin' about the house." He belched. "How about yerself, man? Do ye have a lassie?"

Ian blushed. "I've met a woman from Greenyards. In Strath Carron."

Jock snorted. "A farm girl, huh? There's no profit in that."

Ian ignored the barb. "She's a widow, has a young son. I care a great deal for them both."

They listened to the talk swirling around them. Jock leered at the serving girl.

Ian tugged on his friend's arm for attention. "Jock, have you heard any news about the clearances starting up again?"

His friend wiped his mouth on his sleeve. "I have. Up north, in Sutherland and Caithness. And I wish they would hurry down this way." His words were starting to slur. "I'm thinkin' of branchin' out. Why should I have to send to Edinburgh for my raw goods?"

"What do you mean?"

"I've got plans for a textile mill in Culrain. To make my own cloth—cut out the middlemen. I've already got financial backin' for it. But to make it really profitable, I'll have to lease some land for a sheep farm. Then I'll have a cheap and ready supply of raw material. I've got my eye on some property. The problem is, there's still two dozen tenant farmers and crofters on it."

"What will you do with them?"

Jock slammed down his mug. The ale slopped over the rim and sloshed across the table. "Why, they'll have to go, won't they? All of 'em. They can't be allowed to stand in the way of progress, can they?"

Ian tensed. "But they've done no harm. Broken no laws. Leave them a little parcel of ground to farm. You'll still have enough land for your sheep walk."

"This is business, Ian. I canna afford charity. I'm the one takin' a big risk. I've borrowed up to my knickers from the bank, and I'm puttin' up my own home and shop as collateral." He drank again. "Don't get me wrong. I mean the clansmen no harm. If it's not too costly, I'll help them resettle someplace else. But I can't afford to worry over them. My partners in this venture expect me to be firm."

"Suppose they do not want to go? Suppose the clansmen resist?"

The other man smiled. "Why, laddie, that's why we

have men like ye."

Ian felt the blood rush to his head. "I work for the law, Jock. Not for a group of greedy businessmen!"

Jock's voice hardened. "Listen, constable, I'm in this for myself. It's called 'capitalism.' That's the new religion now. I leave the care of dispossessed clansmen to others, like the kirk, or the Widows and Orphans Aid Society."

"How far will you go, Jock?" Ian balled his fists. He felt like the veins on his temple would burst. "How much force would you use?"

"As much as it takes!"

"Would you fire on them? Beat them? Drive them into the snow? That's been done, you know. Just how far would you go, old chum?"

The other man rose unsteadily and leaned across the table, his face pushed into Ian's. The room hushed. All eyes were on them.

Jock hiccupped. "Listen, my friend. Ye had better give some thought to yer job. Ye're paid to enforce the law. Ye've sworn an oath on it. Ye should..."

Ian took a breath to calm himself. "Sit down, Jock. I'll buy us another round."

But the other man straightened, pulled down his waistcoat with a snap, and said sharply, "No, thank ye. I'll find other company." He turned abruptly, elbowed his way past a knot of men, and staggered out the door into the night.

Ian paid his bill and headed for home and bed. The first doubts about his career since he'd put on the uniform and badge crept into his mind and churned through his gut. Would he really have to choose between love and duty, between Catherine and the Crown?

Just thinking about the dilemma gave him a headache. He rubbed his temples with his fingertips and longed for the clarity of earlier days. He closed his eyes and finally fell into a tormented sleep.

Chapter 10

Catherine arose early, washed her face, and selected a white blouse with a collar embroidered with bluebells. A perfect reflection of her mood...happy. Yes! Despite everything going on around her, she felt joyful. She had a new...well, what exactly was Ian? Not yet lover, but more than friend. Much more. And he'd given her reason to believe the evictions might be avoided after all. She'd find out soon enough, when she met with Alexander Munro later this morning. But all in all, there was every reason to feel hopeful.

In the midst of combing her hair, she suddenly remembered last night's dream. The memory so vivid, so startling, it made her stop combing. She sat back heavily on the bed. It'd been many years since she'd had that dream. But despite the passage of time, it was still the same. She bit her lip remembering the violent images.

She was surrounded by leaping flames, an ogre's breath licking at her, closing in on her. Her home was ablaze, everyone gone. The fire ring pressed her back inexorably. When she turned, a loch spread out before her. She'd swum in that water many times—it had always been cool and friendly. But not tonight. The surface roiled and thrashed. Then it subsided, and she saw the ghostlike faces of her family stretched out across the surface. Her mother, father, brothers, all of them, their mouths twisted in anguish or in soundless screams.

Back, back the fire forced her. Towards the loch. Towards her family. When her clothes caught fire and her hair was singed, she turned and leaped into the faces. Leaped into the water and disappeared beneath the surface.

Then she'd awakened, breathing heavily and sweating.

She slowly donned her blouse. What did it mean, this dream? She'd never understood it, or why it repeated itself. But it was always the same, never changing.

Once, her tossing and moaning had been so loud it had aroused Finn. She awakened to find him standing by her bed, crying and trying to shake her from sleep.

Dreams could be portents, couldn't they? Omens? Predictors of the future?

Icy fingers spread through her insides.

Margaret Ross arrived to look after Finn while Catherine made the trip to Munro's house at Braelangwell. She sat, and Margaret brushed her hair and tied it back with a heather braid. Catherine gave her cheeks and lips a hard squeeze to make them blush, then lined her eyes with a hint of blue.

"You look smashing, cousin!" Margaret said.

Catherine smiled, satisfied with what she saw in the mirror. The icy fingers began to melt.

"Are you nervous?" Margaret asked.

"About what?"

"Meeting with Mr. Munro?"

"Aye. A little." Icicles again.

"They say he's a grim man. And none too kind toward common folk like us. It's also rumored he's hard on women who do not know their place."

Catherine shrugged. "I'm going to represent the village. He will have to accept me." She checked the buttons on her blouse and took one last look in the mirror. "I notice ye and young Davey Macdonald are together a lot these days."

"He's a sweet boy," the girl replied without much enthusiasm. The emphasis on the word 'boy.'

Catherine frowned. "What are ye saying? He's yer own age, barely a few months younger. I think he's sweet on ye."

"Aye." She waved her hand impatiently. "He has plans to organize the children's camp on Ardgay Hill. He's definitely excited about it."

"Has he heard from his father lately?"

"No, not in a long while. He turns purple when he thinks about his mother and the little ones getting evicted while his dad's gone soldiering."

"Davey's a Highland lad. He'll do just fine."

Catherine gave her young cousin a final hug. "The minister has offered me a ride to Braelangwell. I'd better be getting out to the road." She kissed Finn. "Behave yerself, son." He grinned wide. It melted the last of the ice.

The mist from the peat bogs stood thickly all around while she waited by the roadside. The only sounds were those of the river cascading over the rocks, the larks and finches cooing and warbling, and the cattle lowing. The weather warmed and she removed her shawl, folding it over her arm.

The sound of hoof beats broke through the mist. A horse and carriage emerged and stopped directly in front of her. Uncle John sat in the back.

"Good morning, minister," Catherine said to the driver. "Good morning, Uncle."

Angus Mackay tipped his cap. "Good morning, Mrs. Ross. It's going to be a lovely day, I think."

She glanced at him. Perhaps she'd been too hard on him at the clan meeting last night. He did seem less of a stern moralizer than most kirkmen, who were all hellfire, brimstone, and vinegar faces. She'd never forget being scolded as a little girl for merely skipping down the road on a Sunday. But her own relationship with God was decidedly different from most of her neighbors. She believed in the Almighty, and in the moral teachings of Christ. But she felt God had given her free will to choose, a brain to choose with, and a backbone to stand up for those choices. She didn't need a preacher to interpret God's expectations of her. She may have been at odds with His kirk. But she loved Him.

She studied the parson out of the corner of her eye. He appeared to be about her own age, maybe a little older, and looked like a professor: smallish, slim, clean-shaven and slightly stoop-shouldered. He wore Ben Franklin glasses perched on a narrow nose. His sermons, at least the few she'd heard, matched his cerebral temperament—more intellectual than visceral.

The three travelers chatted pleasantly as the sunshine burned away the haze. They passed other farms and cottages and were greeted with friendly waves and hellos. Soon they'd cleared the western end of Greenyards and rolled and bumped through stands of birch trees and fields broken by peat bogs. Uncle John whistled his bagpipe skirl, some old clan tune. The village herd boy was just visible through the trees, flicking his stick at the rumps of his laggard charges. The pungent smell of peat was redolent in the still air.

"I hear your father's a minister like yourself," John said to Mackay.

The pastor laughed. "Yes. And my mother's a minister's daughter. I suppose it's in my blood. But the truth is, I'm not much like either."

"How's that?"

"Father's a member of the Old Kirk—a high official. There was quite a rift between us when I chose to join the Free Kirk instead. As you know, we are now the predominant sect in the Highlands, to his great discomfort."

"I never quite understood the difference," Catherine said.

"Ah," Mackay said, pushing his glasses higher on his nose. "The main bone of contention is over who should name the ministers. In the Old Kirk, they are appointed by the kirk hierarchy—the archbishop and bishops, usually with the blessings and support of the large landowners and wealthy merchants."

"And in the Free Kirk?"

"Each congregation names its own. Meaning they are more likely to be local men, free of influence from the rich and powerful."

John nodded. "Aye, that's right. I remember a few of us were asked to approve yer own appointment before ye first came here. Never done that before with our pastors." He looked rueful. "I only wish we could provide ye with a proper kirk."

Mackay pulled his spectacles back down again. "The little schoolhouse is just fine for Sunday Services. And when the weather's good, what could be better than holding them outside along the banks of God's own river."

John reached over and nudged him gently from the back seat. "I hear ye like to play the game of golf."

Mackay beamed. "My hobby, yes. A passion, really. I've just acquired a fine new set of clubs." He chuckled. "The grounds keeper at the manse is forever getting after me. Says my practice swings are tearing up the lawns."

John chuckled.

Catherine allowed a thin smile to part her lips.

The minister shook his head. "I've also learned more about humility and self-discipline on the Royal Dornoch Golf Course than I ever did at seminary!"

Like everyone else in the village, Catherine and Uncle John had heard the story of how a parishioner had come upon Mackay in his study, putter in hand, trying to roll a white ball across the carpet into a silver chalice. A silver chalice!

It was also rumored Mackay had a fondness for whisky. But the brands he preferred weren't available in the Highlands, so he always ordered a supply of his favorites whenever he travelled to Edinburgh or Glasgow. The story that spread was that once, while walking around Greenyards after such a trip, one of the villagers informed the pastor there was a wooden box addressed to him at the train station.

"Oh, yes, well," Mackay had stammered, "just a few

books I ordered from Edinburgh."

"Ah, well, then," the parishioner replied, "I wouldn't be overlong in gettin' 'em. They're leakin'."

Catherine recalled the first time she'd heard the tale she'd burst into uproarious laughter.

The threesome trotted on through Strath Carron, Mackay occasionally flicking the reins against the horse's rump.

They all looked up when a blur of color whizzed by— a scottish crossbill with a red chest, a cousin of the common house finch. Further down the road, they heard the sibilant call of the pulpit bird. It seemed to be lecturing them.

They approached what had once been a small settlement. Catherine and John grew quiet. Mackay looked puzzled, so she explained that this wasn't just Highland reticence. And when they neared the first ruined house, she told him this was all that was left of the village of Amat, cleared ten years earlier.

Catherine was thankful when Mackay slowed the horse to a walk. This was 'holy ground' to the clansmen.

Farther on they saw a shepherd boy talking with a well-dressed man—the sheep farmer himself, the one who'd purchased the land after it was cleared of people. The lad waved as they passed by. The man looked up, blinked, and leered at Catherine. She squirmed under his gaze until he finally turned away.

At Braelangwell, Alexander Munro listened with annoyance to his wife list all the new things she was going to buy with the extra money they'd soon be getting from James Gillanders, that fifteen percent— clothes, furniture, carpets, and more. Her droning gave him a headache. Though not yet noon, he'd already poured his first drink. He was into a second round when his son announced the arrival of a carriage.

When advised of the visitors, he asked irritably, "What? What do they want?"

"They want to talk with you, sir. They're quite

insistent. The new minister, Mr. Mackay, is one of them."

"Oh, well, all right," he grumped. "Show them into my study while I freshen up."

He splashed water on his face, dried his hands on his pants, and strode out to meet his visitors.

After introductions and a few pleasantries, Catherine unfolded the newspaper advertisement announcing sheep farm leases in Greenyards. She pointed to it and asked, "Does this mean we are to be evicted?"

Clearly Munro was caught off guard. "Where did you get this?" he demanded.

John stepped forward, hat in hand. "Peter Mackinnon, the stonemason, was in Inverness two days ago. He picked it up and brought it to me."

Catherine persisted. "Is it true?"

Munro's round face, of indeterminate middle age, was red from windburn. He had bushy eyebrows and a balding head rimmed with patches of graying black hair.

He handed back the newspaper, then walked to the minister and took him by the arm. He was close enough for Mackay to smell the whisky on his breath. In a half-whisper, but loud enough for everyone to hear, Munro said, "A *woman*? They've sent a woman? Aren't there enough able bodied *men* left in the village?"

Catherine snapped straight and clamped her jaw tight. She saw Uncle John's eyes darken like storm clouds over Bodach Mor.

Mackay appeared speechless, evidently unac-customed to such rough talk. He pulled back his arm.

It grew deathly quiet in the room.

Munro finally faced them all and shrugged. "I know nothing about this. Ye'll have to ask the factor, Mr. Gillanders."

The three visitors looked at one another, puzzled.

The minister was the first to ask, "You've no intention of evicting your tenants from Greenyards?"

"No." Munro stated.

"Ye are not planning to apply for Writs of Eviction?" Catherine repeated. She checked her pockets. Her mother's comb was still there, reassuring.

"I have no such plans." Munro stared at her hard, his black eyes full of malice.

The three envoys from Greenyards were prepared to argue with him, not to have him deny everything at the outset. They were at a loss about what to do next.

"Let me be sure I understand this," the minister finally said. "You and Mr. Gillanders have made no plans to clear Greenyards?"

"I've already said no," Munro replied sharply. "I've had no conversations with the factor on this matter."

Catherine looked at her uncle and the minister. This was too easy. Something wasn't right.

I smell a rat, she thought. "Will ye sign a statement that ye have no intention of evicting us," she asked.

"Of course." Munro loudly rang a small bell. A servant woman appeared. "Bring me paper, pen, and ink," he ordered.

The woman nodded to Catherine, managed a weak smile, then scurried away under the glowering gaze of her employer.

Munro took a chair beside a small desk. He didn't offer seats to his visitors. They all stood and waited in uncomfortable silence.

When the servant returned, Munro wrote out a brief statement acknowledging what he'd just promised, that he had no intentions of evicting his Greenyards tenants. He dated it, signed it, and started to hand it to John.

"Give it to Catherine," he said. "She's better with the English."

Catherine read the statement slowly, then re-read it. It was exactly what they'd asked for. She nodded to the others, folded the paper, and put it into her pocket.

"Well, are you satisfied?" Munro asked sharply.

Catherine and John nodded.

"Very well," Munro said. He pointed to the two men.

"Will ye join me for a drink?" He yelled for the servant to fetch it.

The men fidgeted while the serving woman left to get the refreshments. Catherine fingered her mother's comb.

When the servant returned with a tray full of glasses and a decanter, she tripped on the carpet and fell, whisky, glasses, and tray all flying.

Munro was on her in a flash. He grabbed a cane from beside the chair and stood over her, arm raised. "Ye fool!"

Without thinking, Catherine leaped across the room and stood defiantly between Munro and the cowering woman.

He glowered at Catherine, cane raised to strike.

Finally, slowly, he lowered his arm, turned, and walked to the front door. He opened it, and said, "Our business is concluded. Ye'll excuse me..."

Mackay muttered something under his breath as he went out. John looked straight ahead, as did Catherine.

From the corner of her eye, Catherine saw Munro lower his cane to trip her. If her uncle's back hadn't been just ahead to support her, she'd have fallen. She flushed, turned, and stabbed daggers at him with her eyes, her jaw muscles bulging.

Munro turned away and slammed the door behind them.

As they headed for their carriage, they heard yelling from inside the house. Then the sounds of blows being struck; a woman crying. Catherine started back. The others grabbed her arms and pulled her away.

Beads of sweat appeared along Munro's collar line, dribbles of it running down both armpits. His headache had returned. He could see through the door into the next room. His wife pretended to knit, but had been eavesdropping.

After the Greenyards trio left, she came into the room, surveyed the broken glass and the weeping servant. "Do ye think they know they're about to be evicted?" she asked her husband, ignoring the injured woman.

Munro poured himself a large whisky from another decanter on the sideboard, rubbed his arm, and said, "No, but they will soon enough." He drank deeply. "I'd like to be there when they get their comeuppance." He smacked the cane against the wall. The glasses on the sideboard trembled.

On the way home, Mackay turned his carriage eastward, heading for the Gledfield crossing of the Carron. Catherine took out Munro's statement and read it again.

"Do ye trust him, Cath?" Uncle John asked.

"Not at all. But we've got the paper. Maybe that will stop the factor."

They continued silently along the north bank, crossed the river at Gledfield, and headed westward again towards Greenyards. Catherine looked up to Ard-gay Hill, searching. She saw smoke rising straight up in the windless air and small figures moving about on top. She elbowed her uncle. He glanced up and nodded back. The children lookouts. They were on watch. Good lads and lasses!

When Mackay dropped her off at her house, Catherine waved goodbye. "Thank ye, minister."

She clutched Munro's signed paper. *A ray of hope? Maybe.* A gust of cold air lifted her shawl and crawled up her back. She shuddered and ran for the house.

Chapter Eleven

The next day started out like any other for Catherine—a litany of chores to be done. But this repetition of daily tasks was a balm for her troubled spirit.

First, there was milking and animal care duties, followed by housework. Then a noontime meal of tinned herring and boiled potatoes with freshly churned butter. Catherine looked out the kitchen window while she ate. A red deer came warily down the hill to explore the barren furrows of her garden, looking for any scraps she might have left unharvested last autumn.

Catherine placed an oily herring on a crust of bread and chewed. She thought about her near-brawl with Alexander Munro over his piggish behavior toward his serving woman. And about that servant herself. Though their life's experiences had been radically different, the two women shared the unspoken bond of poor and oppressed people, and of husbandless women, everywhere. When their eyes met, they'd made an instant connection, if only for a moment.

John Ross called the villagers back to the schoolhouse that evening to report the results of the meeting with Munro. News of the signed agreement raised the mood.

"What do ye want to do now?" he asked the group.

"Maybe the whole business is behind us," Naomi Macdonald remarked hopefully. It sounded like a prayer.

Others remained skeptical.

"Did ye show Mr. Munro the newspaper advertisement?" Old Pete asked. He'd whittled his branch down to a twig. It would soon be a toothpick.

"Aye," John answered. "He said he knew nothing about it. Denied it with both hands and all his teeth."

The crowd chuckled. This was the most emphatic denial a Scot could make.

"What about the paper he gave ye." Donald MacNair, the veteran asked, leaning on his staff.

Catherine pulled Munro's statement out of her pocket and read it aloud.

"Does this truly mean we won't be evicted?" The question came from Peter Mackinnon, the stonemason.

The room hushed as Catherine answered.

"This paper is only as good as the tacksman's word. It states he has no plans to clear us now, today. But that doesn't mean he won't change his mind tomorrow. This is neither a promise nor a guarantee. It's only a statement of his intentions on the day he signed it."

Christy Ross looked confused. "So, it counts for nothin'?"

Catherine faced her aunt. "No, I didn't say that. Maybe the writ servers, if they do come, will honor this piece of paper." She held it up to the group. "But I believe the lord and his factor will still try to have their way. They have the police and magistrates on their side. We all know that. No piece of paper will stop them."

"Then what should we do?" Naomi Macdonald asked. "Should we bring the children down from Ardgay Hill?"

Old Pete slapped his knee. "I recommend against it. Catherine may be overly gloomy. But I think she's more right than wrong. I don't trust any of those gentlemen. We should stay prepared."

Murmurs and nods of agreement rippled through the room. It was agreed the children lookouts would stay on the Hill.

Suddenly, Angus Macleod stood up and roared, "Well, let's have a drink on it then, ye old sourpusses. And I've got the drink for it."

Everyone laughed. A fiddler broke into an eightsome

reel while the bootlegger, with help from Davey Macdonald, hoisted a hogshead of whisky onto a bench and set about tapping it. Children held hands and danced around in circles on the side while adults pushed the school benches away to clear a space in the center of the room. The men drank their liquor, straight, the women diluted theirs with water.

Old Pete held his glass up to the light and smacked his lips. "There's two things a Highland man likes naked," he remarked to John Ross. "And one o' them's whisky!"

The clansmen were able to forget their troubles for a while, reveling in the *ceildh*. The women outnumbered the men almost three to one, but they danced with one another without a second thought. Catherine took her cousin Margaret for a partner, but young Davey could hardly wait his turn. When it came, he whirled the redhead around the floor until she cried 'enough!' Those who didn't dance, clapped or stamped their feet. Even the old Waterloo veteran tapped his walking stick on the floor in time to the music.

Catherine stopped dancing when her foot began to ache. She was content to stand on the side and watch. Out of nowhere, two arms wrapped themselves around her waist. She looked up. Ian, changed from his uniform into casual clothes, grinned down at her. She inched back into him, caressed his arms, felt his warm breath on her neck. When he stealthily slid one hand up to cup her breast, she slapped it away.

"Behave," she whispered, "or I'll send you over with the children."

When everyone grew tired of dancing, Old Pete was persuaded to sing a few Gaelic ballads. Although his rich tenor voice was now cracked around the edges, his passion and the richness of the Celtic images the songs evoked brought a hush to his listeners. After the piper played some rousing tunes, the fire crackling and spitting in the background, the bard plied them with stories of the clan's history and deeds.

The fire finally burned down to its last embers, and the last line of the last story was told. The room began to empty. Pete put his hand on Catherine's arm to stay her, then rumpled Finn's hair affectionately and shook hands with Ian.

Sensing the old man wanted a moment of privacy, Catherine nodded to Ian who gave her an understanding wink. "I'll go on ahead with Finn," he said.

Catherine patted her son on the behind as the two left, then turned to Pete. "Thanks for the songs and stories."

He nodded. "'Tis a difficult road ye're takin' lass, standin' up against the lord and the full force of the law. Do ye think we have a chance?"

"Aren't ye the one who's always telling the children there's virtue in the struggle itself? Not in whether ye win or lose?"

"Aye, there is that. And win or lose, mayhap some foolish old man like me will tell stories or sing songs about us when it's over." He looked at the floor.

Catherine sensed he had more to say but was reluctant.

"What is it, Pete?" she coaxed.

He moved closer and lowered his voice. "An old friend of mine, a tradesman from Tain just returned from Sutherland Shire, told me the clearances were startin' up there again."

"I'm not surprised."

"There's more."

"What?"

"One of the most vocal opponents to the evictions there, a cobbler from Helmsdale, was found dead in a ditch a fortnight ago."

Catherine's hand flew to her mouth, her breathing momentarily stopped.

"The authorities claimed the man had fallen from his horse..."

"But ye don't believe it?"

"He was covered with bruises. Both his arms were broken, and he was bleedin' from his head. I think he was beaten to death."

"Oh, Lord!" Her shoulders sagged.

Probably thinking she was going to faint, Pete reached for her.

But she snapped straight, balled her fists, and clenched her teeth.

"I don't care what the danger, Pete," she finally whispered. "I intend to stay. Until they throw me out... or worse."

He nodded slowly. "I thought as much. I just wanted ye to know what ye're up against."

She gave him a peck on the cheek. "Thank you, dear friend. Good-night."

He touched her arm and headed into the night.

Catherine didn't mention to her neighbors the death of the resistance leader from Sutherland. They'd hear about it soon enough through the grapevine. If Ian should bring the matter up in conversation, she'd ask his opinion on it then. She tried to let the matter drop, but it wouldn't drop from her mind. It weighed heavily on her. Now she knew the real risk she was taking; not just to her property, but to her life and limb as well.

But the days went by one after another in Greenyards. Except for Ian, no other constable appeared in the village. No writ servers showed up. No whistles were heard blowing from Ardgay Hill. A palpable easing of tension descended upon the community. The clansmen allowed themselves to believe that each passing day was proof their fears of eviction had been unfounded. They set about spring plowing and planting.

Nonetheless, they kept the children lookouts on Ardgay Hill.

April winds gave way to May showers. The snowline steadily receded up the hillsides, the days lengthening measurably. Foxes, mountain hare, roe and red deer, and badgers became more plentiful. White-barked birch trees sprouted new greenery to catch the warming breezes, gracefully bending and waving like a corps of ballet dancers.

Stands of scots pine became nesting places for cross-bills and crested tits. Red squirrels scrambled through forests of ancient oaks, hunted relentlessly by osprey, hawk and eagle.

The natural rhythm of life returned to Greenyards.

Catherine and Ian resumed their search for intimacy. They were observed everywhere together, carrying food to the children on Ardgay Hill or merely strolling along the road, Finn beside them. Margaret pestered her cousin for the juicy details. Catherine kept them to herself, although she was almost ready to believe she'd found another loving partner for herself and a caring and firm father for Finn.

One night, after tucking Finn into bed, she lay with Ian cuddled on the rug in front of the fire. She knew he wanted more physical love, his wandering hands silently demanding. His warm breath and soft nibbles on her neck sent electricity down her spine and ignited parts of her that had lain dormant for such a long while.

"I cannot help but want you, Catherine. You have come to mean a great deal to me and I've taken a big tumble and fallen deeply in love with you, lass," he whispered.

Her heart took flight as he spoke the things she longed to hear. She felt him shift beside her, his desire neither hidden nor unfelt.

"And my feelings are the same for ye, Ian. I'm not oblivious to your need. It is also my own." She prayed her embarrassment didn't enflame her cheeks anymore than their caresses and the actual fire had already done. "I know the physical way between a man and a woman and the happiness and pleasure it brings. But I don't think age or experience changes the right time for that to take place."

Catherine hoped he understood her refusal, though her resistance—sorely tested—waned. She wanted the passion of the embrace as much as he did. But it was not the proper thing to do, for she believed lovemaking before a marriage commitment was as unwise for a grown woman as it was for a young lassie.

A sudden gust of wind rattled the windows, startling them. But they dismissed it and returned to their quiet talk and tender touches.

But she *was* ready to believe—or at least to hope—that Ian was right about the evictions coming to Greenyards; that the newspaper advertisement had been a false alarm; that the village wouldn't be cleared after all. She didn't realize God was just holding His breath.

In Tain, unbeknownst to Catherine, Ian and all of Greenyards, Deputy Sheriff Taylor dined with some of his constables. He sipped Knockando whisky—much more peaty in taste than Angus' moonshine—and examined the four Writs of Eviction he'd just received from his boss, Sheriff Rob Mackenzie.

It was Taylor's job to see these writs delivered.

"As soon as possible," he'd been ordered. "And with no trouble," the sheriff had added.

Taylor formulated a simple, direct plan for getting the job done. He was now ready to put it into effect.

Across the river at Braelangwell, Alexander Munro, his own whisky tumbler in hand, gazed out across the strath from the bay window of his study.

"Soon," he muttered to himself, "it should be soon." He couldn't stand the waiting—and the lying—much longer.

Chapter Twelve

Two days later. Dawn.

The famously fickle Highland weather changed again. Warm sunshine was replaced with leaden clouds and a lowering sky. A steady, cold wind blew up the strath from the Kyle of Sutherland. Rain or a late snow-storm was in the offing. Here and there a ray of diluted yellow light found its way through the cloud cover. But mostly it was a gray and somber palette.

Two visitors rode slowly through this brooding landscape along the main road from Tain. Sheriff Officer William Macpherson and his witness Peter Mackenzie, a Tain constable and a distant kin of the sheriff himself. The two men passed through the town of Ardgay, then turned eastward into Strath Carron. Their destination was the village of Greenyards where they had writs to deliver.

Macpherson was irked he had to be up at such an early hour just to deliver some legal papers. But his boss, Deputy Sheriff Taylor, had been adamant. The orders, Taylor told him gruffly, had come directly from Sheriff Mackenzie himself. Still, there seemed no reason for hurry, and he and his partner rode along at a leisurely pace, talking quietly, their coats buttoned high against the weather, their blue hats pulled down around their ears.

Catherine prepared Finn's breakfast, automatically stirring the porridge and turning over the bannocks. Her conscious mind, however, was full of visions of Ian —his arms wrapped around her waist; the smell of his masculinity; his facial features, which she mentally traced with her fingertips across his forehead, down his cheeks, and around his lips. She pulled her arms to her side and trembled slightly as the image intensified.

Her daydreaming was abruptly shattered by a shrill whistle. And not from Finn this time. Lonely and far away at first, it was joined by others, then relayed closer by others, then by others closer still, until the noise seemed to come from everywhere, individual sounds blending into a general cacophony. It dissipated her thoughts of Ian like a strong breeze clears the mist from the river. It froze the wisp of a smile on her lips.

Finn thought it was some sort of game, until he saw his mother's face drained of color.

Catherine took a deep breath, calmed herself, and set the porridge pot down just as Margaret Ross, wide-eyed and breathless, burst through the door.

"It's the warning. From Ardgay Hill!"

Blurred figures hurried past her window. Neighbors heading down the glen.

Catherine said simply, "Let's go." She wrapped her shawl around her shoulders, took Finn by the hand, and hustled out the door.

At the main road, they met an excited crowd of ninety or so people, mostly women, all milling about and talking at once.

Uncle John grabbed her arm. "Should we wait for them here?"

Catherine swallowed, squeezed her mother's comb in her pocket for good luck, and took a deep breath to calm the butterflies in her stomach. "No. Let's head east. Meet them on the road and stop them before they get to the village."

Pulling her shawl over her head against the cold, she set out at a brisk pace, Finn half-running, half-walking beside her. The crowd fell in behind them. Most of the women were in front, about a dozen men and boys at the rear. Conversation ceased. The only sound was the moan of wind in the birch trees and footsteps marching along the dirt road.

Minister Angus Mackay was still asleep when the whistles aroused him. He didn't understand what was happening at first. He threw a robe about his shoulder, stumbled bare-footed outside, and looked in the direction of the sound—Ardgay Hill. Then he understood. With his heart turning over in his chest, he dressed quickly, hitched his horse to the carriage, and set off for Greenyards.

At first, the explosion of whistles almost deafened Officers Macpherson and Mackenzie. It startled their horses so badly they had to grip the reins tightly and use gentle words to regain control of the animals.

Macpherson looked up. "There!" he pointed. "Up on the hill."

Mackenzie's eyes followed his companion's outstretched arm. He spotted a little knot of children, and maybe one or two adults—the taller ones—running around the hilltop, blowing whistles and pointing... pointing down at them!

The witness, Mackenzie, was by nature a twitchy, excitable little man. "Well, that turned my stomach over. What's going on? What's happening?" he stammered. "Remember, Macpherson, I've been ordered only to act as a witness for you. I'd not bargained for this."

As suddenly as they'd begun, the whistles stopped. The knot of children disbanded, turned away, and disappeared over the crest of the hill.

Macpherson drew a deep breath and turned to his pale, shaky companion. "Steady, lad. I don't know what's going on. But we've got a job to do."

They spurred their horses into a trot and were soon well up the strath. About a mile farther on, the two lawmen encountered the crowd from Greenyards, wordlessly assembled across the road next to a peat fire they'd built. A few children huddled around the smoky fire trying to stay warm.

"What's the meaning of this?" Macpherson demanded. "Stand aside!"

No one moved.

Catherine Ross stepped out from the group and inspected the two lawmen. The one who seemed to be in charge was a handsome man with a bushy mustache extending well down past his lip line. The other was lean, clean-shaven and ashen-faced.

"What business have ye here so early, Officers?"

The mustachioed one looked around, his Adam's apple bobbing up and down as he swallowed. The bluster in his voice gone now, he mumbled, "I'm on the Court's business. Will ye not stand aside?"

Catherine stared at him unblinking. "What sort of court business?"

He hesitated, then said quietly, "We're here to deliver legal papers." He patted a leather pouch slung over his shoulder.

Angry voices whirled up from the crowd like a dervish. A few of the men moved menacingly towards the officers.

"Wait," Catherine ordered. "These two are just messengers. We want no trouble with them." She turned back to the two lawmen. "Let me see the papers."

The one in charge glanced at his white-knuckled companion, then pulled the documents from his pouch and handed them over.

Catherine turned her back on the lawmen and scanned the four documents. "It's what we feared," she said to Uncle John. "Writs of Eviction." She pointed to his own name at the top of one of the pages, then turned back to face the lawmen, pulling from her pocket a paper of her own.

"Officer," she said, extending her arm, "we have a statement signed by our tacksman, Mr. Munro. It says he has no plans to evict us." She held up the paper and pointed to the signature.

"Lass, I know nothing about that statement of yours," the man answered politely. "My orders are to deliver these writs, that's all. If you have grievances, you should present them directly to Deputy Sheriff Taylor in Tain." He paused. "Now if you'll let us pass..." He held out his hand for the writs.

"Cath, look at this." Uncle John, who'd been quietly studying the papers, pointed to a signature at the bottom.

Catherine recognized the name immediately. "Munro!" she cursed, and held the paper up to the crowd. "The tacksman," she said bitterly. "He's betrayed us. His name is on these writs, dated two days—*two days*—before he wrote his statement for us at Braelang-well. Even when he was signing our statement, he'd already applied for these Writs of Eviction."

She turned back to the horsemen, coldly furious. "Ye can inform the sheriff that the writs didn't get delivered." She tore up the papers and threw them into the peat fire.

The crowd cheered.

"Ye can go now," she said to the two mounted men. "Tell your sheriff we won't be evicted. We mean to stay."

The officer-in-charge shrugged. Both horsemen turned and cantered off down the strath.

The crowd watched them go, then watched the ashes of the burning writs rising on the hot air.

Catherine nudged her uncle. "The die is cast now."

"Aye. We've challenged the Queen's authority."

They took one last look at the retreating horsemen. Then, with Finn in tow and the rest of the crowd behind her, she started the long walk homeward.

On patrol across the river, Ian Macgregor had halted his horse and craned his neck for a better look. Filled with impotent anguish, he'd observed—from start to finish—the confrontation between the villagers and the blue-uniformed lawmen. He cocked his head to one side to catch snippets of angry talk wafting across the water. He easily spotted Catherine at the front of the crowd and bit his lip when she abruptly tore the papers to shreds and burnt them, to the cheers of the villagers.

When the crowd dispersed, he turned his mount toward the nearest river bridge and galloped off.

Not far away, Alex Munro watched the same scene from his front porch at Braelangwell. He could hear nothing of what was being said, but his spyglass captured Catherine's red face when she turned to the villagers, tore up, then burned the writs.

Munro smashed the spyglass down onto the railing, shattering the lens. "That damned woman!" he cursed, storming into the house.

He ordered his horse saddled immediately. "I'll see that woman evicted—or in hell!—if it's the last thing I do!" he yelled to his wife.

He threw himself into the saddle, whipped his horse and was gone.

Chapter Thirteen

Ian pounded down the road towards Greenyards. Towards Catherine. Clumps of bluebells scattered along the roadside sped past his stirrups in a blur. Butterwort and yellow bog ashpodel displayed their early spring colors, but he paid hardly a glance. Out of the corner of his eye he caught a burst of color from a vivid bouquet of pink rhododendrons challenging the bad weather by breaking through the ground. He ignored them also.

He gripped the reins and looked up to Ardgay Hill, his breaths coming in gasps, his heart beating so fast it felt like it would burst through his chest, and pounding as hard as his horse's hoof beats.

The children on the hill above stared down at him. Some waved, but Ian, grim faced, held on tight, looked straight ahead and kept riding.

When he cleared the Gledfield crossing, he met Macpherson and Mackenzie heading back to Tain from their failed mission. He reined in hard and stopped in a cloud of dust, both horse and rider winded.

"What happened back there?" he demanded.

"You saw it?" Macpherson looked around, puzzled. "Ahh, you were across the river?"

Ian ignored the question. "What was it all about?"

"We were ordered to Greenyards to deliver some writs," Macpherson answered casually. "Creep in quietly, we were told." He pointed upward. "But children on that hill sounded the alarm. A mob blocked the road before we could reach the village. Would not let us pass." He shrugged. "I protested, but they seized the writs and burned them—"

Ian cut him short. "Who was their leader? Was it that tall, black-haired woman in front?"

Macpherson whistled. "I dunno if she's the leader. But she's a real corker! Fearless, she was. Straight as a ramrod. Never blinked."

"Someone called her 'Catherine,'" Mackenzie volunteered. "Catherine Ross, I think. I know her uncle, John Ross."

Ian abruptly spurred his horse into a full gallop and set off again, passing groups of villagers who jumped out of his way. He arrived at Catherine's house, his horse in a lather, as the first cold drizzle of rain began to fall.

She greeted him stony faced at the front door, invited him in, and motioned him to a seat at the table. She served him scones and still-warm milk, waiting quietly for him to say something.

His breathing slowed. He munched a scone and looked out the window, seemingly oblivious to her presence.

Still she waited.

He didn't know where to begin. His feelings were all jumbled. Fear for her safety, but relief as well, relief she and Finn were all right. And anger. Definitely anger. Anger that she'd placed herself in harm's way. But he was driven by an equally strong urge to take her in his arms.

He exhaled a long breath. "So, Munro betrayed you?" was all he managed to say.

She walked to the window, hands on her hips, then whirled around, her face distorted with rage. "Munro! That oily bastard. Even when he was assurin' us he had no plans for our eviction, he had already applied for the damned writs. Probably cooked the whole plot up with Gillanders even before we met with him."

Ian looked away. "Still, you should not have blocked the writ servers. That's obstruction of justice. And then you burned the writs. That's a crime as well."

"We hurt no one," she snapped back. "And we were

very respectful to the two of them. As for destroying the documents...pshaw!" She threw up her hands. "They'll just draw up more tomorrow."

"That's right, they will," he shot back. "They'll return again and again until they win. Don't you get it? Power is on their side and you're going to lose."

She glared at him. "So, we should just roll over?" She stamped her good foot. "Put our tails between our legs and slink away?"

He stabbed the air with a finger. "I'm telling you, you cannot win this fight. And now, because of what you've done, they can arrest you on charges of inciting a riot."

They were both yelling.

"That is ridiculous," she said. "There was no riot. Just a bunch of clansmen tryin' to save their homes and land."

He pointed at her. "You've been identified as the ringleader. *You.* One of the men has your name. It will be *you* they come after next. Think what could happen to you. And to Finn." He lowered his voice so the boy wouldn't hear. "I think you should leave Greenyards. You and Finn. Just pack up and go. I'll help you relocate. For your own safety."

They were toe to toe. Her face was red, her jaw set, eyes blazing. "Go? Go where? We have nowhere to go."

Ian saw further discussion would serve no purpose. Her mind was made up. He rose from the table, turned, and crossed to the door. "I'll keep my eyes and ears open, see what I can find out. See what they plan to do next."

He paused at the portal, nodded wordlessly, then left.

Catherine didn't even have time to say goodbye. After he'd gone, she sat on the edge of a kitchen chair. Her chest felt like someone was sitting on it, her heart in her throat.

She sank back into the seat, doubt creeping through

her mind. Was he right? Was she about to lose her home—and him too? Was it all futile? And dangerous as well? What about Finn? Who would take care of him if she were arrested and imprisoned? Or worse?

She put her elbows on the table, hands steepled together, closed her eyes, and began to pray. She drifted off. A vision etched itself on her eyelids, a replay of her recurring nightmare. A ring of fire again forced her toward a ghostly lochan, the water surface roiling and thrashing. The geography of the lake slowly evolved into a face. Ian's face. His countenance stared back at her, its eyes agape, its mouth contorted in pain.

She awakened with a gasp, blinked several times to clear the horrific vision, then shut her eyes tightly and with more determination resumed her praying.

Her anguish was interrupted by the sound of a carriage outside. She blew her nose, wiped her eyes, and went to the door. The minister walked toward her house. Startled by the timing of his arrival, coming as it did in the middle of her prayer, she thought it more than mere coincidence. But she welcomed him in, put on the kettle, and sat across from him at the table.

Surely he could tell she'd been crying.

"Are you all right?" he asked.

"Aye."

"I heard the whistles from the children on Ardgay, but arrived too late to be of any help. I am sorry."

She nodded and patted her eyes with a corner of her apron.

"I passed your uncle on the road. He told me what happened. You shouldn't have torn up the writs."

She stiffened. *Not again. First Ian, now the minister. She wouldn't be scolded.*

"It was instinctive, minister," she said gruffly. "I was so angry at Munro's treachery that I could not help myself."

He loaned her his handkerchief. "I know, I know. But you broke the law." He fiddled with one of the spoons on the table. "I'll pay a call on Mr. Gillanders.

See if I can persuade him to hold off his efforts to clear the village until we can work something out."

"Minister, I know ye want to help. If it will make ye feel better, go ahead and talk with the factor. But I think it will do no good."

"I am simply trying to prevent violence, prevent the villagers from getting hurt. Or arrested. Openly disobeying the authorities is not the answer."

She breathed deeply. "Mr. Mackay, ye don't know these men—the lords and their factors—like we do. They understand only two things. Strength and resolve. They understand and respect only those two things."

Mackay kept silent. After a while he said, "I wish you would put more trust in God. Have more faith He will find a way."

She wiped her face. "Isn't it written somewhere that heaven helps those who help themselves?"

"Aye. So it is written."

"I will take any help He is willing to offer. If He can soften the factor's heart or give the tacksman more humanity, that would be wonderful. A miracle." Her jaw muscles tightened. "Until then, we mean to stand our ground."

He stayed long enough to drink a cup of tea, then left. When he reached the road, he yelled back from his carriage. "I hope to see you at services this Sunday!" He flicked the reins and was off.

At the courthouse in Tain, Alex Munro angrily paced back and forth like a caged animal. Clearly, he'd ridden hard from Braelangwell. Sheriff Mackenzie, when informed by a speedy messenger from Deputy Sheriff Taylor that Macpherson had failed to deliver the writs, had rushed there as well. James Gillanders, also notified by Taylor, arrived close on the heels of the others.

Munro eyed the sheriff. "Not only has my reputation been sullied," he shouted, "but I've nothin' to show for it. The damned writs still have not been delivered."

Mackenzie raised his hand for quiet. "Settle down,

settle down, Alex. Nothing's to be gained by flyin' off the handle."

Munro huffed. "That's easy for you to say, all snug in your bed at Dingwall. What about me? I am the one in the fire."

Mackenzie puffed on his pipe. He didn't like Munro, an arrogant man, cruel toward common people. And he'd heard rumors of despicable behavior toward a new servant. Alex Munro was no gentleman. He sighed. But boorishness wasn't a crime. And Munro *was* the village's legal tacksman. He'd have to be tolerated.

Gillanders slapped his riding crop into his palm. "What about it, Sheriff? Those writs are duly signed court orders. Now that your ploy to have them delivered on the sly has failed, what do you intend to do?"

Mackenzie turned to his deputy. "What say ye, William? What should we try next?"

William Taylor was a stout man, with a loud voice and a face like a bulldog. He had no sympathy for lawbreakers. "I say we round up some of our own lads, go back there tomorrow, and show them that the Queen's Writ extends even into Strath Carron."

The sheriff chewed on his pipe stem.

Munro glowered from the corner.

Gillanders looked out a window.

Taylor leaned back in his chair.

Mackenzie finally announced his decision. "I'm an officer of the court, and these are in fact court orders. It's my job to see them executed. But how I do it is my own business. I'll see to it in my own time and manner."

Munro started to protest, but was cut off with a withering look and a stab of the pipe.

The sheriff next pointed his old briar towards Gillanders, the real power in the room. "Now the clan's riled up. Mad as hornets. I will not risk stirrin' them up further just yet."

The factor remained calm and cool. "Very well, Sheriff. But remember this, I have promised the sheep farmers the land would be available by mid-May. Even after the village is cleared, I need another week to get it ready for the sheep walks. The clansmen have to be gone no later than the first week in May. You're right. How you do it is your business." He slapped his crop on a chair. "But it must be done by then."

The sheriff nodded. "Fine. But there's no harm waitin' a few more weeks. Let tempers cool down." He leaned back and blew a perfect smoke ring. "In the meantime, why don't ye talk with some of the villagers, especially that woman—what's her name? She seems to be the leader."

"Catherine Ross?"

"Aye, that's it. Invite her to lunch." He grinned. "Lay the famous Gillanders charm on her. Make her an offer. See if you can't work out a compromise."

Gillanders slapped his crop again and gave a stiff nod.

Mackenzie next turned to Munro. "And ye, sir," he said sharply, "I want ye to keep low. Ye're like a flame to dry tinder for these villagers. The less they see of ye the better. I'm orderin' ye to keep to yer home 'til this is over."

Munro glared at him, but wisely said nothing.

Mackenzie next faced his deputy. "William, part of this job is knowin' when to use force and when not to. Diplomacy—negotiations, bargainin', compromise—will often get the job done faster than brute strength. Like my father used to say—bless his dear departed soul—'don't use an axe to break an egg when the back of your knife will do.'"

"Exactly what does that mean, Sheriff?" Taylor asked irritably.

"Talk to their own constable, that Macgregor fellow. He's well received there. See if he can persuade them to accept the writs."

The deputy nodded. "Ian is rumored to be sweet on that Ross woman. Maybe he can influence her. I didn't want to use him before. But maybe now's the time."

"That's the idea." He turned back to Gillanders.

"And ye, James, why not talk with that young minister. The kirk has been helpful to ye before. Maybe ye two can find a way out of this without startin' another riot." He lit his pipe then grinned. "Take him to play golf. I hear he's mad for it."

Gillanders nodded. "All right, I will. I'll invite him to my club at Dornoch. But remember, Sheriff, the lord expects his property to be ready for his new tenants by Whitsunday. If these efforts don't work—"

"Yes, yes," Mackenzie said, brushing a cloud of smoke away with the back of his hand. "I'll use the rod if I have to. But first the honey stick."

Chapter Fourteen

The Ides of April came and went. On the forest floor, yellow gorse and creeping lady's-tresses showed first buds as May Day drew closer. At higher elevations, alpine plants like saxifrage and clubmoss began layering rocks and tree stumps with garlands of pale green. The good days, the warm, sunny ones, increased exponentially over the bad ones. Spring had come to stay in the Highlands.

The villagers of Greenyards returned to their daily routines as though the incident with the two writ servers had never happened. But just below the surface, left unspoken, they felt the Sword of Damocles hanging over them. And it showed.

The changes were subtle and not easily detected by strangers. They were little, seemingly unimportant things, like neighbors keeping more to themselves. Though not inhospitable, they retreated from one of their favorite pastimes, social intercourse, the simple pleasure of talking and laughing with one another along the roads or over garden walls. The tension was apparent in other ways as well—faces lined with worry, curt answers to simple questions, the hoarding of food and fuel. Like a prize fighter, the village was rising onto the balls of its feet, ready to receive the next blow, or preparing to strike one itself.

Catherine had neither seen nor heard from Ian since their last, angry parting. No one in the village had. It was as if he'd been swallowed up by the mist which swirled over the peat bogs.

His silence gnawed at her. Was it a signal their relationship was over? She scolded herself for not at least having said goodbye to him the last time they were together. She considered sending Davey Macdonald to Ardgay with a message inviting him to supper. But she ended up following her Aunt Christy's advice:

"Do nothing for now. Let time heal. If left alone, a deep enough river will find its true course."

To take her mind off her cares, she stayed busy with chores.

One day, when the sunshine stabbed through the morning clouds and turned the river a gemstone green, she loaded her uncle's horse with food, blankets, and creels of peat. With Finn perched atop, she set out with Davey Macdonald and Margaret Ross for a trip to the children's camp on Ardgay Hill.

Davey led the horse, while Catherine and Margaret walked along. Finn, forbidden to play his whistle for fear of raising a false alarm, pestered Davey to play a game. Catherine saw the young man, his long, straight hair almost covering his eyes, his freckles sprouting in the sun, was more interested in watching Margaret than in entertaining the boy. But the two finally played 'cloud shapes' for a time. Finn spotted a rabbit's outline in a cumulus, Davey a deer's.

When the lad lost interest, Davey snatched up a dandelion head, blew away the puffs with one breath. She watched him count the ones left. It was an old folklore omen. The number of puffs remaining predicted the number of years until he and his true love would marry. She knew his sights were set on Margaret.

Halfway to Ardgay Hill a carriage silently pulled up. It wasn't the usual old cart, the kind common to the strath, with wobbly wooden wheels and creaky sides. This was a fancy surrey, with spoked metal wheels, upholstered seats, and a brocade top. It was pulled by a handsome horse liveried in shiny black tack. There were two occupants in this wonderful conveyance, a man and an older teenage boy.

The moment he looked at her, Catherine recognized

the man. The sheep farmer from up the glen, the one who'd leered at her when she and the minister had passed by on their way to Alex Munro's house.

"Goodday," the man said, ogling her.

She squirmed under his gaze.

"I am Samuel Howard. This is my son, Roddy. We're neighbors. Would you like a ride, there's plenty of room?" He winked and patted the seat next to him.

Politeness forced her to look at him. She saw a ruddy-faced man with a paunchy midriff even his fine waistcoat, frilly shirt, and woolen pants couldn't hide. His leer revealed tobacco-stained and missing teeth. With short, scruffy hair receding at the sides, bushy muttonchop whiskers, and a bulbous nose, he couldn't have been less appealing.

Though repulsed by his looks, she tactfully refused his offer. "Thank ye, but we'll manage on our own."

She looked around for the others. Finn had hopped down from the cart and was exploring the surrey, stroking the horse, touching the wheels, running his fingers along the frame. Davey, head down, held Catherine's horse, kicking at the dirt and scowling whenever he looked over at Margaret.

Catherine suddenly saw why. The girl was engrossed in conversation with Roddy Howard. Well-dressed and lean, with reddish-brown, immaculately coiffed hair, the younger Howard appeared around seventeen or eighteen, if the sparse chin whiskers and few acne skin blemishes were reliable indicators. He had young Margaret's hand between his own and gazed cow-eyed at her. She blushed and laughed gaily at his witticisms. When she brushed a strand of hair out of her eyes, only to have it settle back, he reached out casually and cleared it away.

Davey, clearly upset, had to look away.

Catherine cleared her throat. "Margaret, we must be going."

The lassie came over with the young Howard in tow.

"Could we not ride with them?" she asked, her eyes

pleading. "There's plenty of room. We can tie the horse to the back of the carriage."

The young man doffed his hat to Catherine, smiled, and bowed deeply. "It would be our pleasure."

Catherine wavered; the ride would make the trip much faster and take the pressure off her sore foot. But she thought better of it. "No, there really isn't enough room, Margaret." She tugged on her cousin's arm. "We don't want to delay the gentlemen."

The girl persisted. "Please. I have never ridden in such a fine carriage."

Catherine shook her head. "No, now let's be on our way."

Margaret nodded reluctantly and obeyed.

The young Howard blew the girl a kiss as the surrey set off. "Come and see me. We'll go for a ride together," he shouted back to her.

For the rest of the journey, Margaret couldn't keep quiet about her new friend. She'd learned that the family hailed from near Stirling. The elder Howard had recently acquired the farm lease up the strath from Greenyards, and Roddy was to attend the University at Edinburgh later in the year, studying to become a doctor.

Catherine said nothing. She looked back. Davey lagged behind, a hang-dog expression on his face. He kicked at the rocks and twigs in the road.

Finn acted bored.

There were two routes up Ardgay Hill. One approached it from the east, south of Gledfield, winding its way up in a gentle counterclockwise direction. The other way, south of the town of Ardgay, twisted up the hill clockwise.

Catherine chose the former road, the closer one. As they neared the crest, the hilltop itself rose slightly higher to the right. At the base of this little summit mount was the collection of tents and fire rings which made up the children's camp. She counted twelve children and two adults.

Peter Mackinnon, the stonemason, and Anne Munro, were the two adult volunteers today. While the children unloaded the horse, they gave Catherine a tour of the camp and showed her the lookout site. It had a good vantage point—the countryside all around was clearly visible.

Catherine panned the horizon and nodded her approval.

"We call this the 'observation post,'" Anne said. "It's always occupied. Night and day, around the clock. It's where we first spotted the writ servers comin' from Tain."

Catherine sat on a make-shift bench and shared a cup of tea and a few minutes conversation with the adults.

"I am so proud of the children," she said. "They've proven my faith in them was well placed."

Anne Munro wore a man's cord pants, frowned upon by most. "Some are as young as eight," she said. "But they're gettin' along well. The older ones lead them in games to pass away the time and share the cookin', clean-up and laundry chores. They all pretend it's *sheilin'* time. Old Pete was up here yesterday and spent the day tellin' stories and leadin' songs. Even Mr. Henry, the teacher, came by."

"He's feeling better?"

"Aye. He hopes to resume regular classes soon at the village schoolhouse. He was amused by our little camp. But he made the best of it and took the children into one of the bigger tents for a lesson."

"The whole clan's behind ye," Peter Mackinnon told Catherine. A big man, his hands were gnarled and scarred from years of working granite, marble and alabaster.

Catherine called the children around her. "I am proud of ye for helpin' out. For stayin' here in tents when ye could be home sleepin' in yer own beds. For puttin' up with the cold and the rain. Stay alert. I expect there'll be more visitors on the road from Tain any day now."

The children waved goodbye as the visitors, Finn now on the garron's bare back, headed down the hill towards home. Catherine dawdled, hoping to meet up with Ian. But no luck. Her slow pace only delayed their arrival at the village, where lengthening shadows and growling stomachs signaled suppertime.

She set three places at the table and fed Finn immediately. Though she waited until a full moon had risen overhead and the candles on the table had guttered out, no visitor knocked on her door. She finally smothered the fire and retired with an empty stomach.

She'd never felt so lonely.

Chapter Fifteen

Ian Macgregor was nowhere near Catherine's house in Greenyards. He was fifteen miles away in Tain, at the tolbooth. He'd escorted a prisoner there and been ordered to remain on hand to testify about the case—which meant he'd have to spend the night in Tain and appear before the magistrate in the morning.

But his mind wasn't on the criminal, a petty little thief. His thoughts were of Catherine, and he was impatient to get back to Greenyards, back to try and patch things up between them.

His partner on the escort detail, Charlie MacNab, was a constable from nearby Bonar Bridge. Unlike Ian, MacNab didn't mind the wait. A jolly, easy-going fellow a few years older than Ian, Charlie had a wife and three children. Billeted at an inn across from the jailhouse, the man viewed the detail as something of a holiday at government expense.

For Ian, the hours dragged by, boredom increasing as the wheels of justice ground on at a snail's pace. He fussed and fumed to Charlie, "I need to be getting back." But he didn't tell him the real reason, his longing for Catherine, made greater by worry about their heated argument the last time they were together. Their separation was all the more maddening because he couldn't even get a message through to her, could find no one heading for Greenyards to deliver it.

After a supper of fresh sea bass, potatoes, and rhubarb pie on their government expense vouchers, he and Charlie headed to a local pub popular with lawmen and other government officials. It was in high gear when they arrived, noisy and crowded. A pall of tobacco smoke floated like a gossamer curtain below the ceiling. They found a seat near the bar, ordered drinks, and looked around. Ian knew many of the patrons, mostly constables and sheriff officers. Some were still in uniform.

As he drank, Ian listened to a small clot of men having a noisy time at the bar. MacNab wasn't bothered by it, but Ian, who'd hoped for a quiet time with his partner, found the rough talk irritating.

At the center of the group was an Excise Tax collector named Dugald MacCaig. Ian had heard about the man through numerous complaints from Ardgay merchants. They said he was often drunk, obnoxious, intimidating and crude when he came to collect the taxes. Ian didn't like the man by reputation. Seeing him in person for the first time, he cared for him even less.

A big, swarthy fellow, heavily-whiskered with a scruffy black beard and a shock of unruly black hair, MacCaig stood well over six feet tall and looked to weigh about 17 or 18 stones—much of it flab. His loud booming voice sprayed a fine mist of spittle when he spoke, which kept his listeners at a respectful distance. His right eye, infected as a newborn, was dead, clouded over and yellow. Ian found it hard not to stare. According to the local merchants, he had a reputation as a wife beater.

Normally, Ian would have paid no attention to the loudmouth and his noisy pals. But he was edgy tonight, and the man's crudeness was getting to him.

MacNab must have sensed his growing anger. "He's an ass," he said. "Everyone knows it. Ignore him."

But when the talk turned to the recent confrontation between Sheriff's Officer Macpherson and the Green-yards villagers—the entire region abuzz over it—Ian was instantly alert. No longer content simply to eavesdrop, he turned in his chair for a better look.

"Macpherson!" MacCaig said to one of his friends. "What a sissy. Stopped by a bunch o' women. What kind of man is that?"

"What would you have done, Dugald?" someone asked.

The braggart puffed out his chest. "Me? Why I'd have cleared them away, ridden right through them." He squatted slightly, pretending to ride, then slashed right and left with a deputy's baton he must have found somewhere. His friends all laughed.

Ian had heard enough and abruptly stood, his anger boiling over. "You have no idea what you're talking about. Why don't you shut up?"

The room hushed.

MacCaig put his glass down, wiped his mouth on his sleeve, and squared off to face Ian from about ten feet away. "Well, now, who have we here?"

One of his associates whispered in his ear.

"Ahh, the Greenyards constable is it?" He took a few steps forward, his coterie trailing behind like a dress' tattered train.

MacNab tugged at Ian's arm, trying to restrain him.

But Ian pulled away. "Macpherson did exactly the right thing," he said with cold fury. "The responsible thing. For God's sake, man, there were women and children there!"

"I could care less for those snotty-nosed bairns," MacCaig shouted back, spittle flying. "Or their miserable mothers."

Other patrons shook their heads and began to move away.

Ian tensed, fists clenched, nostrils flaring. "Let's get out of here, Charlie," he said in disgust.

But MacCaig wouldn't leave it alone.

Another of his companions whispered something to him.

"Is that true?" He looked at Ian. "Robby here says you've got a woman there yourself." He winked lecherously at his friend then turned back to Ian. "Plowin' a fresh field there, eh, Constable."

That was the last straw. "You fat sack of dung!" Ian

shot back. He took a step toward him.

With a bellow, MacCaig was on him.

Though he outweighed Ian by 5 stones or more, the bigger man was no match for him. Ian now saw the advantage of keeping in shape, his body lean. He easily blocked MacCaig's slowly circling fist, then drove inside and delivered a short jab to the man's gut. The bully folded over like barley in a hailstorm.

That would have ended it, and Ian was prepared to leave, but one of MacCaig's friends blind-sided him with a cheap shot to the head, catching him squarely in the eye. He almost went down, but recovered and threw a vicious uppercut to the man's jaw. It lifted the man off his feet and sent him crashing to the floor.

MacCaig was up again and rushed at him, arms out, roaring like a bull. Ian stepped aside at the last minute and stuck out his foot. As the man went flying past, Ian delivered a chop to the back of his neck, sending him sprawling across the table in front of Charlie MacNab.

Ian turned quickly back to face MacCaig's cohorts.

The pub owner came over, holding a huge club. "That's enough, by God! You're supposed to be lawmen. What kind o' behavior is this?"

Ian glared at him, mad and challenging. But he cooled off quickly and looked at his partner. "Charlie, I think we've had enough entertainment for one night. We'd best be going."

The two men walked through the crowd. As they passed through the open door, MacCaig shouted, "This isn't over, Macgregor! We'll meet again, by God!"

Chapter Sixteen

As the weather continued to improve, the roads and paths of Ross Shire began to dry. Increased numbers of tradesmen, merchants, salesmen and other travelers were seen bustling about on business and pleasure. At the Ardgay, Culrain, Dornoch and Tain market places, booths and stalls were set up for the sale of food, furnishings, farm implements and other wares. Farm animals were also offered for auction at the Tain and Dingwall Fairs.

One of these travelers, twenty-nine year old Robert Baillie, headed for Strath Carron on a sleek chestnut mare. The son of a prosperous sheep farmer from Glenelg, a cool, misty glen about 75 miles south by west of Strath Carron, Robert was, unfortunately, the second son. Second in line for an inheritance. When his father died a year ago, his older brother became lord and strongly hinted it was time for Robert to leave the nest. But Robert had learned how careful management of a sheep farm could prosper. His father had developed the Glenelg land into a great estate, worth many times more than he'd paid for it.

Robert paid a visit to his lawyer to discuss his financial future.

"War in the Crimea is imminent," the lawyer said.

"I know. I read the papers. War with Russia. But what's that got to do with me?"

"The Army will need mutton. Lots of mutton for the troops."

Robert understood where the man headed.

"And uniforms," the lawyer added. "The soldiers will need uniforms. That means wool. Lots of wool. And that means sheep. Sheep to serve the Queen's Army."

Robert smiled. "Sheep might just be the answer to my problem as well."

The lawyer nodded. "I think they might."

"If I can find some affordable land and turn it into a sheep walk..."

"You'll make a killin'."

Robert set out immediately to find land for sale or lease. But no one near Glenelg was selling. They could read the tea leaves as well as he could.

"Go east, northeast," the lawyer suggested. "You might find somethin' there."

Robert next tried Strathglass, the glen near Loch Ness. Acreage *was* available there. But every other sheep farmer had bid on it, and prices had quickly escalated above what he could afford. He was disheartened.

Then his lawyer showed him James Gillanders' advertisement in the Inverness newspaper:

'LAND FOR LEASE IN GREENYARDS'

"Where the hell is Greenyards?" Robert asked.

They had to pull out a map to find it.

"I'll wager that land is still unimproved," the lawyer said, stabbing the newspaper with a finger.

"If I can get there before others discover it..."

"You might get a lease on it at a good price. A very good price."

"I can afford about three hundred gimmers," Robert said. He'd already done the calculations.

The lawyer nodded. "With a dozen or so tups to get started, you could be in the black within a few years."

Robert smiled to himself and daydreamed: *A landed gentleman! I could look for a wife. The right sort of wife. One with ample breasts and a dowry to match.*

He saw the lawyer watching him. "It all depends on gettin' the land at a good price. You'll have to hurry."

Robert had set out for Strath Carron the very next day. He stopped briefly at Dingwall Fair to check the prices for Cheviot sheep. They were about what he'd expected, right in line with his financial plans. In good spirits, he left the fair. The sunshine raised them even higher. He hurried along toward Greenyards.

Catherine had received no word of Ian, not a word, for two days. When she could stand it no longer, she asked Davey Macdonald to take a message to him. She found the lad loading a creel with supplies for the children on Ardgay Hill.

He tucked the message into his shirt. "When I am finished on the Hill, I'll stop in Ardgay and find your constable."

Catherine had a second thought. "Have ye seen Margaret lately? She hasn't been by to see me in days. That's not like her."

The boy's smile faded. He kicked at the ground and muttered something inaudible.

"What?"

"She's with him," he yelled. "With that fancy-pants farmer's son, Roddy. I have seen her sneakin' up to his house in the mornin', dressed up in all her best clothes. She doesn't come home 'til late."

Catherine was aghast. "She is spending that much time with him?"

Davey nodded. "Yesterday, I walked part way with her, just to be friendly. She hardly said a word to me, shooed me away as we got close to the Howard house. Later, I saw them together in that expensive surrey, his arm around her."

He roughly hoisted the creel onto his back, spilling some oats. "I must be off."

Catherine wasn't worried about Davey. He'd get over being jilted. But Margaret's headlong rush into this new romance was worrisome. She resolved to speak to her young cousin at the first opportunity.

When Robert Baillie finally arrived at the entrance to Strath Carron, he noticed the children on Ardgay Hill eyeing him. He waved. A few waved back. Baillie cantered into the strath, humming a popular ballad as he rode.

He liked what he saw—plenty of water; a narrow valley to provide good winter shelter for the Cheviots; and grassy areas on the flatlands, perfect for sheep walks. But he was puzzled. He'd seen no sheep as yet, none at all. At least not any real ones, any Cheviots. Only a few of the scrawny native beasts and a smattering of black cattle scattered along the braes.

As the road emerged from a copse of trees, he was met by a good-looking lad loaded down with a heavy pack.

"*Failte duibh,*" the boy said.

Robert, who didn't understand Gaelic, couldn't return the greeting. Instead he asked, "What's your name, lad?"

"Eh?" The boy put down the creel.

Robert repeated the question.

"Ahh!...aye." The young man spoke in English and tipped the beak of his cap in polite salute.

"How far to Greenyards?" Robert asked.

"Thirty minutes ahead by horseback." Apparently grateful for the respite, the lad unshouldered his creel and wiped his brow. "Anyone in particular you're lookin' for? I know 'em all there."

"No, no. Just looking over the land. I may be bidding for a lease on some of it."

The young fellow's eyes widened, his jaw dropped, clearly speechless. When he spoke again, he spluttered, "You...you're a sheep farmer?"

Surprised by the boy's response, Robert's fists clenched. He nonetheless stuck out his hand in a friendly gesture. "Robert Baillie, Esquire. Of Glenelg. At your service."

By now, the boy's face had turned scarlet. He glared at Robert, who remained mystified.

They stared at each other for a few moments. Abruptly, the boy took a birch whistle from his pocket and started blowing it at the top of his lungs. Robert's mare reared, almost throwing him. Suddenly, whistles screeched everywhere. People came running from their homes and across the fields and bogs. Many had shovels and hoes held high like weapons.

A crowd of fifty or more quickly surrounded Robert. The boy spoke to them excitedly. Robert didn't understand a word of it. But he was frightened.

The crowd started toward him. Two women held his horse so he couldn't get away.

Robert's heart pounded. Panic rose in his throat like bile.

Abruptly, the crowd parted. A dark-eyed woman pushed through. She talked briefly to the boy who'd started it all, then looked up at Robert and raised her hands to quiet the crowd. The noise subsided, the weapons were lowered.

Robert's breathing slowed.

Catherine studied the terrified young rider. He looked soft. No calluses on his hands, no worry lines around his eyes. A gentleman, unaccustomed to work and the rough ways of common people. Of medium height and heavy-set, he was a curly-haired redhead with an engaging smile. Fine clothes. Well dressed in thick woolen pants, high-topped leather boots, a sheepskin coat, and a costly brimmed hat, he appeared in no hurry.

Now she understood how he'd managed to get this far without the whistles being blown. Evidently, when they'd seen he wasn't a lawman, they'd paid him no further attention.

"Good morning, sir. What is your business in our strath?" she asked.

"I-I just came to look over the land." Robert dug into his coat pocket, pulled out a newspaper, and held it out to her. "I came about this."

She took the paper and recognized it instantly—Gillanders' advertisement for sheep leases.

This fool, she thought, *from some far away place,*

has no inkling of what is going on here, or why he's stirred up such a hornet's nest.

"We usually greet visitors more hospitably than this," she said. "But the land in that advertisement is not just empty fields. It's our land. Our homes. We live here. And before ye and yer sheep can come here, we'll have to leave. And we don't want to leave..." She folded her arms. "We don't *intend* to leave."

"I-I didn't know. I didn't realize," he said. "I thought the land had already been—"

"Cleared? No, not yet. And with God's help, it won't ever be."

She turned back to the crowd and spoke in Gaelic. "This man is not our enemy. There's nothing to be gained by barring his way."

Davey continued to glare at the visitor until Catherine tugged on his arm. "Thank ye for your vigilance, lad. But the emergency's over."

To the crowd she said, "Let us all go home."

They began to disburse. Naomi Macdonald, Davey's mother, walked up to Robert, stroked the horse's mane, and gave the man a smile. Then, her arm around her son, the two of them turned and left with the others.

"Greenyards is straight ahead," Catherine said to Robert. "Ye'll come to no harm."

She and Finn joined John and Christy Ross for the walk home.

Robert wheeled about and headed out of the strath at a fast trot, counting himself lucky to have escaped in one piece. He didn't return to Glenelg, but went instead due south to look for James Gillanders. He found him at his home at Highfield Cottage.

The factor listened to his story in silence, then asked some questions.

"Were you injured in any way?"

"No."

"Did anyone lay hands on you?"

"No, not really."

"Were you frightened?"

"Well...yes."

"For your life?"

"Well, maybe."

"The newspaper advertisement instructed you to contact the Ground Officer at Bonar Bridge first," Gillanders said. "You were not supposed to go wanderin' into the strath by yourself."

Robert said nothing.

"Write me out a statement about the incident," the factor ordered. "And emphasize the menace of the crowd and the fear for your safety."

Robert sat down at a small desk, put pen to paper, and handed the finished statement to Gillanders.

"Please come back in a few weeks for another look. The strath will be empty by then. I promise you."

"I don't think I'll be back this way." Robert headed for the door. "Ever."

After he'd gone, Gillanders slammed his fist onto the desk and gulped down two whiskys. He wrote a sharp note to Sheriff Mackenzie in Dingwall summarizing the business with Baillie and requesting an immediate meeting. He sent it off by his fastest courier.

He called for his horse to be saddled. As he mounted and headed down the road at a good pace, he began to wonder where the sheriff's loyalties truly lay.

It was time to build a fire under him. A big, hot fire!

Chapter Seventeen

Catherine cooked the evening meal, occasionally glancing out her kitchen window as an orange-red sun settled toward the western horizon. Magenta hues laced fluffy clouds. A lazy breeze ruffled the aspens, their leaves dancing to the soundless tune. The soothing slap and slosh of the river rushing over ancient boulders lulled her senses. It was eerily serene. Even the village sounds were hushed except for the lowing of the cattle. It was unreal. Time seemed to stand still.

She heard the clip-clop of a horse nearby, then a whinny. But she paid it little attention, unwilling to let go of this moment of tranquility in what had been a stormy past few days.

The hoof beats drew nearer, then stopped. A soft knock on the door.

Ian.

Finn rushed past her to greet him noisily. She held back, arms folded sternly across her chest.

He tousled the boy's hair, then raised his head.

She gasped when she noticed his left eye. It was swollen black-and-blue.

"What happened?" She reached out to touch it.

He gently pushed her hand away. "It's still a wee bit tender."

"Were you in a fight?"

He shrugged. "A minor scuffle. Let's not talk about it. I'm sorry I haven't been here the past few days. I was on a detail. Couldn't get away any sooner."

He stood in the doorway, waiting.

She took his arm. "Please come in. Will ye stay for supper?"

He smiled. "I'd like that."

She led him to a seat at the table and set an extra place.

They ate in strained silence, heads bowed, the only sound the scraping of utensils across plates. Even Finn was unusually quiet, concentrating on the chicken stew and scones.

Between bites, Catherine glanced up. "I hope I was not the cause of yer...yer...minor scuffle." She smiled to let him know she'd forgiven him. "I feared ye had come to harm. Or worse."

"Worse?"

"That ye hadn't wanted to see this thing through."

He put his fork down. "What thing?"

"Us. I thought maybe ye had chosen just to walk away. That it was becoming too hard for ye."

"Och, lass!" He reached for her hand. "How could ye think that of me. Of us. I thought of nothing but you while I was away." He touched his left eye, winced, and chuckled. "Even when I was gettin' this."

She laughed and patted his hand. "Well, don't be gettin' any more of 'em."

Finn looked from one to the other, shrugged, and continued eating.

The tension ebbed like salt water in a rip current.

"Your neighbors gave me the cold shoulder when I rode up," Ian commented.

"I am sorry. Everyone is so tense and sharp with one another now. Ever since the incident with the writ servers..."

"Aye. I understand. That sort of thing would set anyone on edge." He sipped some of the whisky she'd poured. "But their coldness today seemed different, something new. It was deliberate and personal, aimed directly at me."

She heaped another ladle of stew onto his plate and sat back down to her own meal. "They're startin' to put ye on the other side, the side with the lord and the tacksman. They fear they might have to face ye across a line in the road some day. They don't want to be friends with someone they might have to fight."

He stopped his fork in midair. "But I have never done anything to make them feel that way."

"Ye don't have to. It's yer uniform. And that badge. And what they represent. If ye want their friendship back, ye will have to take them off."

"I can't do that. It's my job and I have sworn an oath. 'Tis a matter of honor."

She didn't answer.

Finn looked on the verge of tears.

Ian sipped more whisky and changed the subject. "I heard about your encounter with the young sheep farmer from Glenelg today," he said.

"Oh?"

"News travels fast."

"I was frightened, Ian. I thought the crowd was going to attack him."

"Truly?"

"Aye. They were angry beyond anything I have ever seen. So was I." She wiped her hands on her apron. "I don't like what's happening to us here in the village. That's not the Highland way to treat a visitor."

"I'm glad you were there to stop it. If he had been harmed, the sheriff would have been back here with a posse. There would have been real trouble then."

"I know."

After supper, with Finn snugly tucked in bed, they sat in front of the fire. Ian had gathered and chopped a few pine logs. Still wet, they snapped, crackled and spit as they burned.

Ian finally broke the silence. "That incident with Macpherson and this latest one with the sheep farmer give the factor the excuse he needs to demand harsher measures to have the writs delivered."

"Have you heard about calls for a posse? Or the militia? Is there any talk of troops coming here?"

"No, nothing like that. Sheriff Mackenzie is a good

man. He won't thrash about blindly. But you know the factor. He's heartless. He'll be after the sheriff to do more."

She moved closer, hooked her arm through his elbow. "I am frightened. I don't know what's waiting for us around the bend, but I fear it won't be good."

His eyes widened. "Frightened? You? You are a pillar of strength."

"I'm shaky as a kitten."

"You hide it well. That's real courage."

She smiled up at him. The fire was warm and cozy. That feeling came over her again. What was it? Contentment? Security? Safety?

She repeated the question she'd asked before. "Ian, suppose ye were ordered to be in a posse sent to clear us out by force. What would ye do?"

There it was—the dilemma he most dreaded. He took a long time answering. "I would be caught in a hard place. I could never hurt anyone in this village. You should know that by now."

"Then quit. Take off yer uniform and badge. Come live with us here in Greenyards."

"And how would I make a living? I'm no farmer. This is the only job I know. Besides, I'm more optimistic than you. I don't believe the clearances will come to Greenyards. I think men like the sheriff and that new minister will find some way out of this. Some compromise allowing use of the strath for sheep, but letting the clan remain here as well."

They clung to one another for a moment in the doorway. "Yer heart's here, Ian," she whispered. "Yer badge and yer office may be in Ardgay. But yer heart's here in the glen."

He started to leave, then turned back, took her in his arms, and kissed her on the lips.

She tried to push him away, but relented and pulled him closer. When they stopped for a breath, she started to speak.

He put a finger to her lips. "Shhh, lass. Leave the moment alone. Words'll only spoil it. There'll be time for us soon. I know there will. We'll be together soon."

He mounted his horse and, with a final wave of his cap, started down the road.

Chapter Eighteen

The days passed by slowly in Greenyards, days bright with sunshine, scattered clouds, and light, re- freshing breezes. The villagers went about their daily chores, finding comfort from an uncertain future in the routines they had followed for generations.

Catherine, sleeves rolled up, stood over an old wooden butter churn outside her door, slowly turning the white cream from the brown cow into yellow butter. She had to laugh. Pleasant thoughts of Ian kept her company while she worked. Finn, pleading not to go, had been sent to school anyway, a battered primer under his arm.

Naomi Macdonald stopped by for a chat. Catherine was glad for the respite.

"Where's yer son been these past few days?" she asked Naomi. "I've not seen him around the village."

"Och! He's been with Angus Macleod in that cave of his. Angus told me the boy now plays an active role in the distilling process: mixing, pouring, roasting the barley—whatever's required."

Catherine arched an eyebrow but said nothing.

"Angus even allowed him to experiment with a small batch of his own, from start to finish."

"Doesn't seem like a promising trade," Catherine commented.

"It's not. The boy's just brokenhearted over his unreturned affection for Margaret Ross."

Catherine nodded. "I've seen that myself. But can all this moonshinin' do the lad any good?"

Naomi shrugged. "Angus just lets him talk, listens to his complaints about the fickleness of women, puffs his pipe, and nods wisely."

After Naomi departed, Catherine returned to her churn. When she deemed the butter ready, she carried the churn into the house and began to scoop out the contents.

She was startled by sudden noise bursting through the door and Davey Macdonald's appearance. His clothes smelled of yeast, peat and raw whisky. His coat was wrapped around a pitiful creature with disheveled hair, blouse dirty and torn.

"Och, my God!" Catherine screeched when she recognized the creature as her cousin Margaret Ross.

Aghast, she led the girl into the kitchen, Davey trailing behind. She tried to remove Margaret's coat, but she wouldn't allow it. Catherine quickly saw the reason why—one of her breasts was sticking through a gaping hole in the blouse.

"Lass, lass, what happened?" Catherine whispered.

The girl remained mute, her eyes red-rimmed and glazed, her face scratched and bruised, her dirty hair matted with pieces of hay and oats. Her only response was to draw her coat more tightly around her.

Catherine looked at Davey.

The boy spread his arms, his face ashen. "She's said not a word since I found her like this across the river, wandering through a field near Croick."

Catherine wrapped the girl in a hug and stroked her hair until a long sigh signaled an ebbing of tension. Margaret went limp and put her head on Catherine's shoulder. Huge sobs wracked her body. Catherine let her cry. Davey stood off to the side, hands in his pockets, staring at the floor.

When she thought the time was right, Catherine ordered the boy to add some fuel to the fire. "And put the kettle on for hot water. I'll get her cleaned up."

She led Margaret into her bedroom and gently but firmly removed her dirty clothing. Blood stains covered her skirt, dried blood on her thighs and legs.

Davey knocked on the door. "The hot water is ready.

Should I fetch her mother and father?"

"No, not yet." She took the pail from him. "Have a seat for now. We'll be out shortly."

She bathed Margaret and bandaged one or two deep scratches on her legs. "Here's a cloth and some water," she said. "To clean yourself down below, your private parts."

Tears shone in Margaret's eyes. "They're not so private now."

When Margaret had finished washing herself, Catherine dressed her in clean clothes and repeated her question, "What happened to ye lass? Who attacked you and did this?"

The girl smoothed her skirt. "May I have something to drink? I'm very thirsty." Her lifeless eyes peered straight ahead, not meeting Catherine's gaze.

Catherine helped her to the kitchen table, brought glasses of milk and plates of scones for the three of them. She sat next to Davey and waited.

Margaret stared into her milk. "I always dreamed it would be beautiful, you know...love-making. That it would be gentle and soft, slow and romantic. Not...not like this." She dissolved into tears again.

Catherine gave her a handkerchief. "Go on, lass. You're doing fine. Tell us what happened."

"Roddy Howard and I went for a carriage ride. The weather was warm, the sky blue, so blue... We picked dandelions, blew off the puffs, then lay on our backs in the heather and told one another all the shapes we saw in the fleecy clouds." She stopped to blow her nose.

Catherine eyed her patiently.

"We went back to his farm. To the barn, then up to the loft. He had a bottle of whisky hidden there and started drinkin'. I had a few sips, too. At first it was wonderful. The spirits went to our heads and we started kissin'."

Margaret turned toward Davey and lowered her eyes. "We'd kissed before, but never passionate like this. Before I knew it, his hands were all over me, everywhere. Pushin' at me, pokin'."

Catherine looked at Davey. *Should he hear this?* He was staring at his shoes. Margaret seemed oblivious to his presence. "Go on, lass," she urged. "Let it out. Let it all out."

Then, in what Catherine considered an act of sheer courage, Margaret looked straight at Davey. "I was frightened. I pushed his hands away and told him to stop. That only made him mad. He called me a tease and other names I'd never heard before. He tore at my clothes. I tried to get away, but he pulled me back. I scratched his face. That only infuriated him. He started hittin' me with his fists."

The girl nibbled on her bottom lip. "He got on top of me and pinned my arms. When he pushed his way into me, it hurt so much." She returned her eyes to her cousin. "Is it supposed to hurt like that? I screamed, but he covered my mouth. He kept pumpin' and clawin' at me."

She sat straighter. Catherine knew getting that part out had been the hardest for her. Margaret dried her eyes, took a drink of milk, and went on, more easily now.

"When he was done, he rolled off me and went to sleep. I must have gotten away. That's all I remember, 'til Davey found me."

"She wouldn't let me take her home," Davey said, his hands balled into fists, his eyes ablaze. "Made me bring her here."

Catherine lifted her cousin's face. "Listen to me, Margaret. Lovemaking *is* beautiful. This wasn't love. This was an abomination. This was rape, pure and simple. Don't judge the barrel by one bad apple."

The girl managed a weak smile.

Catherine lifted Margaret's head and wiped her tear-stained cheek. "It's now time to tell yer mother and father."

The girl grabbed her arm, panic stricken. "My father will kill him, I know he will. Couldn't we just say I fell, that's how I tore my clothes? How I got the cuts and bruises?"

Catherine considered the request. "Is that the only reason ye don't want them to know?"

Margaret didn't answer.

"Are you afraid they'll be ashamed of ye?"

"I know now I was foolish for throwin' myself at Roddy like that. And I have paid for it. Do they have to suffer as well?"

"Don't underestimate John and Christy Ross. They love ye, lass, and they'll understand. They'll be hurt, that's for certain. And angry. But they'll get over it."

Davey asked, "What about him?"

"Roddy? He'll be punished. But that's a job for the authorities." She helped Margaret to her feet. "I'm going to take her home now. I want ye to ride to Ardgay as quick as ye can, Davey. Take my horse and cart. Find Ian and bring him to John and Christy's house. We'll wait for ye there."

The lad started for the door. Margaret reached for him. "Thank you, for all your help. You're a good friend." When she kissed him on the cheek, he blushed crimson and raced out.

Catherine's predictions proved correct. Christy Ross, after the initial shock, calmly took her daughter into the bedroom to attend to her.

John Ross was enraged at first and bellowed oaths of revenge. But Catherine finally persuaded him to wait for the constable. To wait for Ian. To let the law do its work.

"Her mother and I knew she was seein' the Howard boy," he admitted. "I didn't like it, her takin' up with one of them. But her mother said to leave it be. What was the harm of it? After all, his father is supposed to be a gentleman. Reluctantly, I agreed." He looked into his hands. "We were both wrong."

When Ian and Davey arrived, they found the four of

them seated at John Ross' table, Margaret's head on her mother's shoulder.

The girl was pale. Ian could plainly see the bruises and scratches. "How is she?" he asked. "Does she need a doctor?"

"She'll be all right," Christy answered. "There's been no permanent damage, thank God. Not to her body, at least."

"Amen." Catherine muttered.

Ian nodded, his face crinkled with concern. "The lad here told me what happened. But I need a written statement from her—from the lassie herself. Catherine can write it out for her to sign. Leave out nothing. When it's done, she'll swear an oath, and I'll sign it myself as a witness. It will be a proper affidavit."

Margaret looked anxiously at her mother.

"Don't be embarrassed, lass," Ian coaxed. "You must tell it all if you want to see justice done."

When the three women had moved to a corner of the room to draft the statement, John Ross demanded, "What are ye goin' to do about him?" He pointed a bony finger in the general direction of the Howard farm.

"Arrest him. As soon as I have the affidavit. As soon as the girl signs the complaint."

John rose to get his hat. "I'm comin' with ye—"

Ian interrupted and held up his hand. "No, you're not. This is my job. Yours is to stay here and comfort your daughter."

"What about me, can I come?" Davey asked. He was as eager as a hunting dog on point. "I want to see this."

"No, laddie, I can manage myself."

When the women returned, the papers all properly signed, Ian put his signature on them and tucked them into his pouch. "He'll be in jail by suppertime," he promised, heading for the door. "And arraigned before the magistrate in the morning."

He motioned to Catherine. Out of earshot of the others, he said, "If she feels up to it, the girl needs to be at the courthouse in the morning. The prosecutor and the magistrate may have some questions for her."

Catherine looked alarmed. "She'll have to face the boy again, so soon after?"

"I'm afraid so. Will you see she's there?"

"Aye. But this will not be easy. To hear it said in public, in front of strangers... It will take all her courage."

He kissed her on the cheek. "Courage is one thing you Ross women seem to have in abundance."

Catherine looked dubious.

"You'll see," Ian said confidently. "The law will take its course. The boy will be properly punished."

An hour later, at the Howard estate, Roddy stood sullen-faced next to his father as Ian read the complaint against him.

"You're under arrest, lad."

His father was furious. "The boy told me all about it," he fumed. "He and the girl were foolin' around in the barn. One thing led to another. She wanted to do it as much as he did."

Ian drew his truncheon. "If that's true, how do you explain those scratches and bruises on the boy's face?"

The man jerked his son's head first right, then left. "These? Why that's just passion." He winked. "The rougher it is, the better some o' them like it."

Disgust contorted Ian's face. "Sir, your son is coming with me. I've seen and talked with the girl and have her complaint. If you try to interfere, I'll take you in as well." He pulled the boy out the door by his shoulders and marched him off.

"Wait," the elder Howard pleaded. "At least let me take him in the carriage." His voice had lost its thunder. "It's a long ride down the strath."

Ian saw no harm in it. "Very well. We'll avoid Greenyards by crossing the river at The Craigs and return to Ardgay along the north bank. The villagers won't take kindly to seeing your boy right now."

He tied his horse to the surrey and sat in the back

with his prisoner. He hadn't seen the boy's mother and didn't ask about her.

Ian kept his promise to Margaret Ross. Before the sun set that day, Roddy Howard was locked up in the two-celled jail at Ardgay. He was equally confident of his other promise, that justice would be done.

Roddy's father threw open the front door. "We're not finished here. I'm off to find a solicitor."

Chapter Nineteen

Ian was up early the next morning as sunshine dappled his apartment in lemon drops of light. Today was judgment day for Roddy Howard, and he was certain his faith in British justice would be vindicated.

He put on a freshly-washed uniform for the occasion —sharply creased blue pants, a blue, high-buttoned jacket, and a blue cap. He looked at the image staring back from the mirror. Except for the silver badge and black truncheon, he was blue from head to foot.

"Blue Boy!" he chuckled.

He began his official business at the office of Simon Greebe, the Queen's Prosecutor for Ross Shire. A bony man, with sharp elbows, a long nose and a pinched mouth, Ian found him at his desk reading Margaret Ross' statement and taking notes. He squinted and drummed his fingers as he read. Ian knew little about the man, other than the rumors that he was in line for some high court position; which is to say, some high political position. Maybe even a seat on the Queen's Bench in Edinburgh.

Greebe put down his papers and cocked an eye at the constable. "You know who Samuel Howard is, don't you? The boy's father?"

Ian shrugged. "A sheep farmer. He's new here, just acquired a lease up Strath Carron from Greenyards."

Greebe threw down his pencil. "Ha! He just happens to be a personal friend of the lord himself. His family is well-connected, has extensive holdings near Stirling. He plays golf with James Gillanders every week, and I hear he may be bidding on the new Greenyards leases himself."

Ian didn't like the direction this conversation was taking. "This case isn't about the father and his political connections. It's about the son. It's about rape. The boy, not the father, called the tune. Now the boy, not the father, must pay the piper."

Greebe drummed on the desk. "Hmm. The boy and this girl were well-acquainted, isn't that right?"

"Yes."

"Did the girl's parents know what was going on between them?"

"They knew she was seeing him."

"And there were no witnesses?"

"None. But I saw the girl myself shortly afterwards. Cut and bruised she was, a sorry sight. Her clothes were torn and bloody."

"Hmm. I wonder what the other side of the story will be." He cocked an eye at Ian. "There will be another side, you know. There always is. Even a flat bannock has two sides. These cases are never black and white." He drummed one last measure and rose. "Let's see how dyspeptic old Alisdair Chisholm is feeling this morning." He wrapped his robe around his shoulders, slapped a dingy, gray wig on his balding head, and led the way into the courtroom.

It was a courtroom in name only. In reality, it was a converted large office, the 'bench' merely an elevated worktable and chair. Another high-backed chair placed next to it served as the witness dock. Facing these, on opposite sides in front of the bench, were tables and chairs for the prosecutor and for the defendant and his barrister. Behind these was the bar separating the official court from the rows of chairs for the spectators.

Ian stood against the wall next to the bailiff and swept the room with his eyes. It was packed. Designed for no more than twenty people, there was standing room only. Roddy Howard was at the defendant's table with his counsel, Trevor Bannerman, a foppish-looking man in a shiny robe, an elegant wig, and Ben Franklin spectacles. Roddy's father sat in the front row of spectators, directly behind the defendant's table. Other well-dressed men and women—friends and supporters of the Howards—took up most of the chairs, including Alex Munro, who risked the sheriff's ire by leaving his house. But he wouldn't have missed this for anything.

Greebe entered the room, signaled to the clerk, and took a seat at his table.

Ian scanned the crowd of villagers from Greenyards, who stood at the back of the room or lined the walls along the sides. They were easily distinguishable from the other ladies and gentlemen by their rough clothes, mostly homespun. They stood respectfully, hats in hands, talking quietly in Gaelic. Ian smiled encouragement to Margaret Ross, standing between her parents, nodded to Davey Macdonald, who stared daggers into Roddy Howard's back, and winked at Catherine, who smiled back. He watched the minister enter the room and make his way over to Margaret Ross. He took the girl's hand, patted it comfortingly, and spoke briefly to John and Christy Ross.

The bailiff thumped his staff once, then twice more. Everyone sitting rose and all conversation ceased. The bailiff announced the arrival of the Magistrate. Court was now in session. British common law—the envy of all God-fearing people—was about to be dispensed.

"Here we go," Ian said under his breath.

Alisdair Chisholm, an old, frail-looking, half-bent over man, his robes hanging off him, shuffled across the floor to the bench. A Parliamentary appointee, Chisholm had been given the judicial position as a reward for years of faithful service to the political establishment. His disposition, prickly to begin with, had worsened with the recent passing of his wife.

He banged his gavel, ordered everyone to be seated, and waited while the clerk of the court read the charges.

He looked at the Prosecutor. "Mr. Greebe?"

"If it pleases your Lordship, this is an arraignment hearing to determine if Master Roddy Howard should be bound over for trial on a charge of forcible rape. Here is the complaint, the victim's affidavit, and the arresting officer's report." He motioned to the clerk to take the documents to the bench.

The judge glanced through them. "Yes, yes," he said, then looked at Roddy Howard. "How do you plead, young man?"

The boy's lawyer approached. "Your Lordship, my client pleads not guilty. Also, we wonder why we are wasting the court's time today. There's little enough evidence here to warrant a trial."

"I'll decide that." The judge turned to the prosecutor. "What about it?"

"The girl's complaint alleges forcible rape," Greebe answered. "In the opinion of the investigating officer, there was enough evidence to arrest and hold the boy. The constable also examined the girl's injuries and torn clothing and deemed they were consistent with her story."

Chisholm looked around the room. "Is the girl in court today?"

"Yes, your Lordship." Greebe pointed out red-haired Margaret Ross in the crowd of villagers.

"Come here, girl," the judge said. "Let me look at you."

Margaret cringed and shrank back into the crowd.

Catherine put her arm around the girl's shoulder and gently led her to the front.

The judge's brusqueness didn't help. "Let me see you, lass. Take off your plaids."

Catherine started to remove the girl's shawl, but Margaret clutched at it desperately. Catherine stroked the lassie's hair, and Margaret, keeping her gaze riveted to the floor, reluctantly removed the tartan, pulled back her hair, and slowly turned her head from side to side to reveal the cuts, scratches and bruises.

Chisholm's tone softened. "How did you get those, girl? Who did this to you?"

Still unwilling to look up, Margaret stretched out her

arm and pointed behind her in the general direction of the defendant's table. After a nod from Chisholm, Catherine led her back to her place in the crowd of villagers.

"Your honor," Roddy's lawyer was on his feet. "We don't challenge that the girl has been injured. That's plain enough to see. But we *do* reject the charge that my client forcibly raped her. In fact, how do we know she's even *been* raped. Has she been examined by a doctor? Is there a medical report?"

The judge looked at the prosecutor.

Greebe shook his head.

Howard's lawyer continued. "Your Lordship, we contend this whole matter is a misunderstanding. A lover's quarrel, nothing more."

The villagers began to stir and grumble.

"No, that's not right," one said. "What does he mean, a lover's quarrel?"

"The girl was raped," yelled another.

The judge gaveled for quiet. Then he turned to Bannerman, "Explain yourself, sir."

"I shall. The girl and my client were known to be romantically involved. It was common knowledge. They'd been seen showing affection to one another on several occasions. But the girl's interests, it seems, were more than just friendship. She wanted marriage, talked about it all the time. Master Howard wasn't interested in matrimony. He decided to tell her it was over, that he would be leaving for the University soon, and it would be best if they ended it now."

He paused while Roddy whispered something to him.

"Well, well! What else?" Chisholm demanded.

"The girl became hysterical, flew into a rage. She leapt at him, scratching for his eyes." He held the boy's face up and pointed to scratch marks as proof of his claim. "What could he do? She was a wild woman, out of control. He tried to calm her with words, but she wouldn't listen. He tried to restrain her, but she broke free. He had to defend himself, and in the process caused her some injury. Regrettably. But it was only in self-defense."

From the back of the room, Davey Macdonald raised his hand in a fist. "No! That's not it. That's not how it happened." He pointed at Roddy. "He did it."

"Order!" Chisholm banged for quiet. "Order. Or I'll clear the room."

Several villagers grabbed Davey and managed to shut him up.

Ian glanced at Margaret Ross. She'd turned as white as a sheet.

The judge pointed to the prosecutor. "Well, Mr. Greebe, what do you say to that? A lover's quarrel? Hellfire from a woman scorned? Is this a matter for the court?"

Greebe's response was dry, matter-of-fact. "Her affidavit is before you, your Lordship, witnessed by the constable. She also alleges he deflowered her. And violently so. Her injuries and torn and bloody clothes give credence to her story."

Trevor Bannerman tugged smugly at his lapels. "Circumstantial evidence. Circumstantial at best. The Queen's Prosecutor has yet to produce one shred of direct evidence to support the charge of rape against my client. And as for the girl being deflowered, I can produce several young men who will testify that Master Howard was not the girl's first, nor her second lover. Nor even her third."

"No. She's not that kind of girl!" a villager yelled out.

"These are lies." John Ross, the veins popping out on his neck, started up the aisle.

"Order, order!" the judge yelled. "Bailiff!"

The bailiff drew his truncheon and started toward the crowd. Catherine and Angus Mackay got hold of John Ross and pulled him back. The bailiff returned to his spot next to Ian and reholstered his weapon.

Judge Chisholm shook his gavel at John Ross. "One more such outburst and I'll clap you in jail!" To the other villagers he threatened, "Any more from the rest of you, and I'll clear the courtroom." He adjusted his wig and turned back to Roddy Howard's lawyer. "Now, then, sir, you may continue."

"Thank you. I repeat, there were no witnesses to the alleged attack. All we have is her word against his, and I invite the court to look at the character of the accused and of the accuser. Many local gentlemen are here in this courtroom who will testify to Master Howard's good character. He is from a highly respected family. His father is a gentleman, very active in the High Kirk of Scotland."

He whirled suddenly and pointed at Margaret Ross. "And what of the accuser?" he said, his voice like thunder. "An illiterate farm girl, desperately seeking a man of wealth and position, like many Highland women nowadays. And willing to do anything to get one."

He turned back to the bench. "Which one, your Lordship, which one is to be believed?"

The villagers were stunned into silence.

Margaret Ross, her eyes wide with shame, her face white as a birch tree, sobbed and put her face in her hands. Her shoulders hunched, her body shaking with grief, she collapsed into the arms of her father, who stroked his daughter's hair and glared at Bannerman.

But Bannerman wasn't finished. "I beg your Lordship, do not besmirch this young man's—and his family's—name by dragging him through a public trial, a spectacle, on the flimsy claims of this girl." He bowed to the bench and sat down.

The crowd found its communal voice again, rising to Margaret's defense. One voice rose above the others. Diminutive Angus Mackay shouted and held up his hands to the bench for attention.

The judge recognized him and motioned him forward. "Mr. Mackay, if we cannot trust you to speak the truth, who can we trust? What is it you wish to say?"

The minister half-turned to the audience, but spoke

directly to the judge. "Your Lordship, I know nothing of the facts of this case beyond what I've heard today. I was away when the...the..." he groped for words.

"The alleged rape," Chisholm said helpfully.

"Yes, when the alleged rape took place. And I am sorry for not being there to comfort the girl. Nonetheless, I bitterly resent that man's"—he stabbed a finger at Bannerman—"scurrilous slander of Margaret Ross, and his derogatory innuendo about Highland women in general. Without hesitation, I can testify they are all God-fearing women of high moral character. If Mr. Bannerman thinks poverty alone leads to low morals, he knows nothing about the life of Christ."

Mackay leaned forward. "Furthermore, while Highland lives may not be as refined as others here, I have found their love and compassion for each other—even for those not of their clan—to be truly Christian. Do not be deceived, your Lordship, by money or fine clothes. Neither is a guarantee of good morals. In truth, Your Honor, I'd stack the character of these poor villagers against that of these gentlemen any day."

Applause and hoorahs erupted from the back wall. The villagers pulled him into their ranks and slapped him on the back and shoulders. Catherine gave him a peck on the cheek. When Mackay turned in his direction, Ian thought the expression on his face was as close to rapture as any he'd ever seen.

Chisholm banged for quiet, then motioned Greebe and Bannerman to approach. After a brief discussion, out of earshot of everyone else, both men returned to their seats.

The courtroom hushed as Chisholm announced his decision. "After carefully weighing the statements from both sides, I find there is insufficient evidence to hold the defendant for trial on a charge of forcible rape. That charge, therefore, is dismissed."

The villagers protested loudly.

Chisholm had given up on the gavel, or he was simply too tired to wield it anymore. He waited for calm, then nodded to the prosecutor.

Greebe stood. "Your Lordship, we accept the court's decision on the matter of rape. We will, instead, charge the lad with simple battery."

Ian nudged the bailiff. "They've cut a deal."

The bailiff nodded. "Aye, so it appears."

"Master Howard, how do you plead to this new charge?" Chisholm asked.

After a look from the lawyer, Roddy spoke his first words of the day. "Guilty, your Lordship."

Without a pause, the judge continued. "Very well, your plea is accepted. You are sentenced to a fine of twenty pounds or twenty days in the tolbooth. Court is adjourned."

Chisholm banged his gavel one last time, quickly rose and left the room even before the bailiff had commanded the spectators to 'all rise.'

It happened so fast the villagers didn't realize it was over.

"What?" someone wondered aloud.

"What does it mean?" another asked.

"He's not going to jail?" a third asked angrily. He smacked his fist into his palm.

"A slap on the wrist," Ian said to the bailiff. "Twenty pounds! Less than the price of one of his fancy coats."

First Roddy, then his father, pumped Bannerman's hand who then slapped the boy on the back and led him out of the room. His gentlemen friends formed a corridor between them and the villagers. Roddy couldn't suppress a smirk as he passed down it. His father was busy counting out the fine to the clerk of the court.

Ian stared across the emptying room. Catherine eyed him. There was no animosity in the look, no accusation. Just an unspoken and grim expression. 'What did you expect?' it asked.

He had to turn away.

Ian followed Greebe back to his office and grabbed him by the arm. "Is this an example of British justice?"

Greebe looked at Ian over his half-spectacles. "Watch it, Constable!"

But Ian had no intention of curbing his anger. "How can you expect these people to respect the government and its laws when they see injustice like this? You wonder why there's disobedience in the land. If their grievances are unmet by the law, what other recourse do the clansmen have?" He stabbed a finger in the air. "The real crime wasn't committed yesterday in Greenyards. It was committed in this courtroom today."

Greebe slammed a book onto his desk. "The law is the law. It serves accused and accuser alike. That's why we have courts and magistrates and prosecutors..." He paused. "And constables like you. To see the law is carried out. That's your job, isn't it? Read your oath of office again."

Late that afternoon, Ian headed for Greenyards. He'd bathed, shaved and donned his best civilian clothes. On the way, he stopped at an Ardgay store and purchased a small toy for Finn and some sweets— chestnuts covered in brandied sugar—for Catherine. He was fearful of the look he'd seen in her eyes and wanted all the help he could get.

He took the north river road past Hilton and Braelangwell. Alex Munro was on his porch, watching him go by. Neither offered the other so much as a nod in greeting.

When he reached the bridge south of The Craigs, Ian spotted Davey Macdonald ahead, a pack on his back, heading into the hills. He considered saying something to the lad, but decided Angus Macleod and his cave could probably comfort him more.

After crossing the river, he quietly slipped into Greenyards and knocked on Catherine's door. To his relief she greeted him with a welcoming smile. Finn, his delight at seeing him an unchanging constant, took the new toy and sat before the fire to play with it.

Catherine served him a light supper. "Ye did yer best," she said. "It was not for want of yer trying that the boy got off."

"I have let you down, let the whole village down."

"Ye haven't. Ye wanted to show us all how justice works here in the Highlands. Or at least how it's supposed to work. What we got instead was injustice. But it was not yer fault."

"How's the clan taking it?"

"As you might expect. If the boy had gotten what he deserved, its faith in the law might have been restored. But after today, there's little chance of that."

"They're determined to continue resistance to the evictions?"

"More than ever."

They watched Finn play with his toy.

"How's Margaret taking it?" he asked.

"She's devastated. It took all my persuasion—and her mother's—to get her to court. She expected to see Roddy put on trial for his crimes. But she was the one on trial. *Her* credibility, *her* virtue were tested. Not his."

"I feel badly for her."

"Let's talk about something else."

"What did you think of the minister today?" Ian asked

"I was amazed. Never seen him so passionate. Maybe I have misjudged him. Perhaps he's on our side after all."

"And what about ye, Ian?" she asked later when they were snuggled in front of the fire. "How is it with ye?"

He sighed. "My faith in the law was sorely tested today. I'm not sure how much further I can go with it."

Catherine inclined her head and kissed him.

They silently held each other.

"I've a long day tomorrow," he finally said. "I must go." He turned at the door for a parting word. "Today crystallized it for me. What I have been fearin'."

"What?"

"That I'll soon have to choose between justice for this village, and the law. Just as you said I would."

"Why not do it now?"

He shook his head. "Not yet. There might still be some good my badge and uniform can do."

Catherine blew him a kiss goodbye.

Chapter Twenty

Two days later

Factor James Gillanders and Pastor Angus Mackay met on the first tee of the Royal Dornoch Golf Club as the early morning sun began to evaporate the heavy dew from the greens. A light breeze rustled the leaves of the birch trees lining the course. Stray cattle on the fairways were quickly driven off by attendants.

The men wore wool knickers, wool socks and tweed coats. Both carried their clubs in brown leather bags

"A pleasant spring day." Gillanders removed his driver.

"Aye, that it is." Mackay answered.

Gillanders' big booming drives carried far. But today's breeze and a life-long slice only drove them farther out of bounds.

Mackay, in contrast, worked at his game with maddening concentration. His drives were diminutive, but went straight down the throat of the fairways, or as they said locally, 'up the kilt.'

"I'm searching for a compromise." Mackay teed up his ball and hit a low drive which rolled and bounced two hundred yards, straight as an arrow. "The Greenyards tenants are prepared to pay you a ten-percent increase in their rents if you'll halt the evictions. The four principal tenants would continue to collect the rents from their sub-tenants and make the total payment annually to Mr. Munro. Just as it's done now. He'd be accountable to you for the corresponding increase to the lord."

Gillanders' shot topped the ball. "Damn!" He winced. "Sorry Reverend." He hit again. "I'll have to take the offer to the lord, but I can tell you renegotiating the rents was not part of his instructions to me. They were to clear Greenyards by Whitsunday."

Mackay hit a whistling five iron, landing fifteen yards short of the green. It bounced twice, and rolled on.

Gillanders' second shot found a wet sand bunker to the left of the green.

The minister sized up his putt. "Suppose I make a trip to London and talk with the lord himself."

"You're free to do as you please, of course." The factor dug his heels into the wet sand. "But the long journey there and back will only be a waste of time. The lord will defer to my judgment. He always has." It took him two strokes to get out of the trap.

Mackay two-putted for a par four.

Gillanders also two-putted, but for a double-bogey six.

The factor then played the first verbal shot of a scheme he'd been hatching all morning—to lure the four principal Greenyards' tenants to a meeting, then surprise them with the Writs of Eviction. Once they were served, the sheriff would be required to see them carried out. Gillanders had done that at other settlements in the shire, and it had worked perfectly. The trick was to find a way to get the unsuspecting tenants away from the village, then spring the trap.

"The lord is not without feelings," Gillanders began. "Perhaps an increase in rent would appeal to him, as a humanitarian gesture, if only for one more term." He looked down at his ball. "However, I would have to meet with the four principal tenants themselves to conclude any such negotiations." Not looking at Mackay, he kept his eye on the ball and hit.

The next hole was a par three. Gillanders selected a three iron from his bag. He paid little attention to his drive and hit the ball with barely a glance. It was a perfect shot, landing with a smack on the wet grass and holding dead still on the green. No one was more surprised than he.

"Good shot," Mackay said. He took time with his own drive. Then he said, "The four principal tenants are reluctant to meet with you directly, given your...uh...er ...past performance."

The factor one-putted for a birdie.

They're onto me, Gillanders thought. *The villagers know my game. Have to come up with another way.*

He did have another idea. "If those four are reluctant to meet with me, then I'll meet with someone else. I'm told there's a woman there, someone who has the village's confidence. Perhaps...?"

The minister rubbed his chin. "Aye. Catherine Ross, that's her name. And, yes, she's become the village spokesperson." But Mackay clearly wanted to play the negotiator and offered a suggestion of his own. "I would be willing to act as go-between for you and the villagers. If you have an offer, I'll be pleased to convey it to them."

But that wouldn't do, would it? Gillanders thought. What he had in mind would require a face-to-face with this Mrs. Ross. "Thank you. But I think it's time I spoke directly with this woman. I'll invite her to my home at Highfield Cottage."

Mackay shook his head. "I don't think she will meet with you."

"Could you not persuade her?"

"Even if I could, I am not particularly disposed to."

"What harm could come from it?"

The minister shrugged.

Gillanders tried to harness his frustration. *Another dead end. And with the sheriff unwilling to use force, what could he do now?* He considered the lie of his ball. Then he straightened up and considered his opponent. Mackay, he'd discovered, was exceedingly proud of his golf game. Golf and whisky seemed the minister's only vices. And both, in limited quantities, were usually harmless enough. *But mayhaps...*

"Mr. Mackay, would you accept a friendly wager?"

"Huh? What's that?"

"A simple bet on the outcome of the next hole."

"I do not wager for money. It would be unseemly."

"No, sir. It would not be for money."

"Oh?" Mackay appeared suddenly interested. "What did you have in mind?"

"One hole only. If I win, you will use your good office to persuade Mrs. Ross to meet with me privately. Nothing more. Just a meeting."

"And if I win?"

"I will cease all efforts at...uh...negotiations and allow the law to take its course."

"Very well. One hole. No handicaps. We play the ball where it lies."

"Agreed. And since you won the last hole, it is your honor to hit first."

Mackay teed up and hefted his trusty wooden driver. After a few practice swings he hit a poor shot, barely 100 yards into the left rough. "By Christ!" he said, apparently before he could stop himself.

Gillanders smiled and played his tee shot. Straight and long, 225 yards toward the green on this par five hole.

They walked up to Mackay's ball. Gillanders waited respectfully off to the side while the minister struck a solid three iron. The ball hopped along for good yardage, though it still ended up 175 yards from the pin.

The factor's next shot, a long iron, was pin high, albeit to the left of the green. He couldn't see the ball, but he knew this course well—no sand traps around this hole. A chip shot and a two-putt should give him a par. Maybe even a birdie. He whistled as he walked toward his lie.

Mackay's next shot was a short iron. It brought his ball to the 'frog hair' on the fringe of the green. But he was still one shot behind. He walked up to his ball full of doubt about the wisdom of the wager. Had Gillanders set him up? He acknowledged the folly of his earlier thoughts. *I can beat this man,* he'd said to himself. *And it would get the factor off the villagers' backs. And even if I lose, what harm could there be in a meeting"*

"Ye God!"

The factor's cry startled Mackay. When he walked over to see for himself, he understood the reason for the outburst. Head back, he roared with laughter. The factor's ball was an almost perfect lie. Pin high and barely five yards off the green. An easy chip shot. Except for one thing. It was embedded in a huge mound of steaming cow dung.

"Mackay," the factor spluttered, "surely you don't expect me to play the shot from there?"

"Thank you, God," the minister whispered. To Gillanders he said, "That was our agreement. Play the shot where it lies. If you don't, I'll consider the wager forfeit."

"And if I take a drop?"

"By Club rules, you lose a stroke."

Gillanders looked over his predicament for a full minute. Finally, he removed his coat, rolled up his sleeves, and selected a wedge from his bag. Standing wide legged, he hit the cow manure with a splat, sending the ball and a large knot of dung flying. Not all of it sailed toward the green. The factor's waistcoat, knickers and shoes were smeared with cow shit, some even splattered on his face. It took all Mackay's concentration not to burst into laughter again.

Muttering curses, the factor wiped himself off with a kerchief, and the two men turned in unison to see where the shot had gone. It landed squarely on the green, a makeable putt away from the hole.

Mackay swallowed and finished the hole with a two putt for a par. The factor holed his putt for a birdie, his only good hole of the entire round. Mackay had been had. Fickle fate or divine intervention? He couldn't be sure.

They finished the round. The minister carded an eighty-six, the factor a ninety-four. But as far as Gillanders was concerned, that one hole made up for everything. They cleaned and rebagged their clubs in silence.

"Very well," Mackay finally said. "I'll arrange the meeting. But I must insist it be held at my manse. Much closer for Mrs. Ross, who has a child and a home to care for."

"Neutral ground, eh? What is this, minister, warfare? But all right, your manse it is. Shall we say two days hence? Around noon?"

They parted with a handshake.

Chapter Twenty-one

Ian knocked on the door. It was late in the afternoon, but Catherine didn't answer. He rapped several more times. Still no answer. He finally gave up, walked around the side of the house, and peeked in through the kitchen window. No one in sight. Even Finn was nowhere to be found, probably still at school.

Worry crept over him. He looked around the entire perimeter of the house. Still nothing. He headed for the shed. As he neared it, he heard weeping but couldn't see where in the darkened building it was coming from. He followed the sound across a floor dappled with shadows and finally spotted her crouching in a corner next to the cow's stall. With his hat in his hand, he slowly approached her.

When Catherine saw him coming, she turned away and hurriedly wiped her eyes with her apron. She did not want him to see her weak and vulnerable like this.

But he rushed to her anyway, lifted her up, and wrapped his arms around her. She sagged into his chest, sobbing uncontrollably.

He stroked her hair. "Shhh, lass. What is it?"

She drew a breath and sighed. Her body shuddered. With a last sob, she became still for what seemed an eternity in the hushed surroundings, where the only other sound was a whisper of wind which had found its way into the shed and swirled a pile of oats on the floor.

He pushed her out to arm's length, wiped a droplet from the corner of her eye, and waited.

"Ian, I am so frightened."

"Of what?" He grabbed her shoulders. "Has something else happened?"

"Of everything. Of losing my home and land, my friends and family. Of being arrested, and what will happen to Finn if I am? Of losing...of losing whatever future ye and I have together..."

Worms of doubt crawled through her mind, like when she'd lost David and was for a time lost to herself. Had she the strength to carry on *this* time? Could she recover again? Giving in to the creeping doubt was so tempting

Ian carressed her cheek. "We'll get through this, lass. He wiped her eyes with his thumb, his eyes and soft smile full of reassurance. "And when it's over, we'll have our time. I promise you that."

"Do ye think so?" She put her face against his chest, allowing his strength to flow into her.

"We'll make it so."

She stepped back, took another breath to steady herself. "Minister Mackay just left. The factor wants to meet with us."

"Us?"

"With me."

"Where?"

"The minister's manse."

"That seems safe enough."

"I don't trust him."

"What harm can it do?"

"What good can it do?"

"Maybe you can come to terms with him."

"Terms?"

"An agreement of some sort. Something favorable for the village. At least hear him out."

She looked at him for a long time, vulnerability and misgiving chiseled across her face. "It will probably be a waste of time," she said, "but..."

She arrived at Mackay's manse the next day just as the sun crossed the meridian. High noon. She found the minister practicing chip shots on the front lawn, digging up large divots of wet sod with every stroke. His gardener stood off to the side, arms folded, sour-faced, shaking his head.

Mackay held up his club. "My new niblick," he said with pride. "Care to try it out?"

She hefted it, balanced it in her hands. "'Twould make a fair weapon, eh?"

He was startled...until he saw the twinkle in her eye. Then he laughed and led her into the house.

Gillanders kept them waiting more than an hour, with no apology or explanation when he finally arrived. After terse introductions, Mackay excused himself, left the room, and closed the door behind him. Catherine sat in one of the comfortable, high-backed, upholstered chairs. She fingered her mother's good-luck comb in her pocket. Gillanders paced the room, stopping to examine the paintings on the walls and *objets d' art* on the sideboard.

The silence grew into a test of wills.

The factor's broke first. "Have we met before, Mrs. Ross? You look familiar."

"You have a good memory. I was younger then, by ten years or more. I lived in Glencalvie."

"Ahh! Yes, I do recall it. The rest of your family emigrated to Canada. Yet you stayed in the strath." He slouched into a chair and draped a leg over one of the arms. "Still tender about Glencalvie, are you?" he asked.

"Highlanders have long memories." She sat straighter in the chair and kept her chin high.

"And sharp tongues. It would have been better for me if you had gotten on that ship with your mother and father." He cocked an eye at her and grinned. "And I could easily arrange it for you now..."

She said nothing.

Gillanders shifted in his chair. "Let me get to the reason I asked for this meeting. The lord, my employer, has instructed me to improve Greenyards..."

"Improve?" Catherine laughed. "Ha! You mean evict us. Clear the land of every living soul."

Ignoring her outburst, he removed his leg from the arm of the chair and leaned forward, his hands steepled. "I must complete this task soon. Several sheep farmers from the south have already bid on the new leases. They expect the land to be ready by Whitsunday."

She crossed her arms and held his gaze steadily. "I know all that. And I won't appeal to yer sense of humanity to allow us to stay. Glencalvie proved ye're sorely lacking in that quality. But ye asked for this meeting. What is it ye want from me?"

"I don't want you or any of your clansmen to be harmed or arrested. I want you all out, but I don't want to have to resort to force to do it. You're one of their leaders. If you were to talk to them, tell them to cease their resistance, I would let them remain another thirty days...so they might find other accommodations, other employment. That's cutting it as close as I can. And I'd be willing to provide a few horse-carts to help them move their possessions. That's more than reasonable. The sheep farmers will just have to wait a bit longer."

She grunted. "Ye're toooo kind, sir!" she said, sarcasm dripping from the words. "But we're not going anywhere. We've done fine so far. And I bet the sheriff has little stomach for a full-scale battle against women and children."

Gillanders' face turned beet red. He rose and paced around the room. His stomping reminded her of a toddler. It appeared he was trying to rein in his anger. Unsuccessfully.

"That land *will* be cleared. If I have to, I'll ask for troops from the Commander at Fort William." He stopped and glared at her. "But I want to avoid bloodshed." Softening his tone, he continued, "You must believe this. I'm not the heartless villain you think." He paused. "If you're not concerned about your fellow clansmen, think about yourself. As their leader, you risk certain arrest and imprisonment if you continue urging resistance."

"I'll take my chances. So will the rest of them. Some

of us still believe there's justice to be found in Scotland."

"What about your son? He doesn't need a *martyr*. He needs a *mother*. And a home. And a chance for an education." He approached her and continued in a half-whisper, clearly having saved the best for last. "I have an estate at Rosskeen. I could provide you with a house and a few acres of good farmland. It would be rent free the first year, a reasonable charge thereafter. With a long-term lease. You'd never have to worry about being evicted again. I'd help move your possessions and animals." He smiled—one of the fakest ones she'd ever witnessed. "I'd even throw in some cash to help you get started. All you have to do is leave Greenyards. Without you, the others will go peacefully."

But this, she hadn't expected. She'd been prepared for the stick, not the carrot. Oh, it was tempting. Very tempting. It could be a new beginning. Ian could keep his job, and they'd have a fine income. Most of all, they'd have security. It'd be a good way to start their new life together.

After a brief hesitation, she answered. "I'll accept yer terms if you offer the same to all the others."

He slapped his riding crop against the table. "Not bloody likely!"

She glared at him. "Did ye think me to be a Judas? That I could be bought so cheaply? These are my kinsmen. I would never betray them!"

"Not even to save yourself?"

"Especially not for that."

"Then be damned! Your stubbornness has condemned you—you and your clan. Prepare yourself. The future is coming. A four-footed future. It will sweep you and your old ways aside like a new broom."

With a final flick of his crop, he turned and stomped out with a tight-lipped, "Good day."

Riding home in her uncle's horse-drawn cart, Catherine pondered the factor's offer. The pros and cons of it tugged at her like feuding terriers. On the one hand, her duty to the clan seemed clear; after all, she was the one who'd raised the banner of resistance in the first place. But the security and comfort Gillanders' offer promised were as tempting as the apple in the Garden of Eden. Maybe she was just being stubborn? And stubbornness for its own sake was no virtue—it was folly. Maybe both she and the village would be better served if she relented.

By the time she reached home, she'd cleared her head of doubt. The course she'd charted for the village was the right one, she was sure of that. Honor and loyalty to the clan were more important than creature comforts and financial security. She'd not trade those for any price.

She stopped at John and Christy's to return the cart, hugged Finn, and described her meeting with Gillanders. She left out his attempt to bribe her. There was no point inflaming things further.

She lingered awhile to talk with Margaret. "How are ye, lass?"

They carried two old wooden chairs out the front door and placed them close to the house. The sun was still warm. Finn chattered and played nearby.

Margaret's hair was unkempt, her clothes rumpled from sleeping in them. Dark circles highlighted eyes red-rimmed from crying.

The girl exhaled a long breath. "It's been quite a lesson."

"Aye, lass? And what have ye learned?"

"First, what matters are not riches and worldly things, but the love and care of your family and friends. In the end, they're what count most."

Catherine took out her comb and drew it through the girl's hair. She smoothed the tresses and caressed her cousin in the doing. "We all know ye're not the kind of girl those evil men tried to say ye are."

"I've also learned not to follow my heart so readily. To be ruled more by my head."

Catherine chuckled. "Then ye've learned much. And

ye're right, passion alone is never enough. It must be tempered with judgment. Emotions can be very fickle. Many foolish girls, and grown women I might add, never learn this. Remember the day ye told me to 'look beyond the badge'? The same thing applies to clothes and station in life."

Margaret chewed on this for a while, then abruptly changed the subject. "Davey was wonderful in court, wasn't he? Standing up for me."

Catherine looked into the young girl's eyes. *She is a quick learner, this one,* she thought. "Aye, he's a stout lad. I'd match him against any of the young dandies in that courtroom."

"I've not seen him lately. Is he on Ardgay Hill?"

"I think not. He's probably with Angus Macleod, at that beloved still of his."

"I've treated him badly, haven't I?"

"Ah, lass, ye were blinded by that scoundrel Roddy. But now yer eyes are open. A word of kindness from ye is what he lives for."

The gloamin' of the evening—the soft Highland twilight—settled upon them. Streaks of pink filtered through puffy clouds.

Catherine relaxed for the first time that day.

Chapter Twenty-two

The sun dropped to the horizon, followed by a misty twilight which cleared away the last vestiges of dusk's pink aurora. Village sounds and quiet conversations around dinner tables stitched the purple-hued air.

Catherine combed Margaret's long hair, each stroke a caress for the lassie's troubled soul. Christy Ross sat next to them in another rickety chair on the porch. No one spoke.

Catherine's thoughts drifted back to her life with David, to those wonderful mornings of love-making after they'd fed Finn his breakfast and shooed him outside. Then she imagined Ian in her bed. Over the last several weeks, the mental transition was now easy, natural.

Though Ian was not yet her lover, it wasn't for his lack of trying. He'd made it clear in both words and actions how much he desired her. But he'd not yet given her that final thing which would get him into her bed—a commitment to their relationship, the ultimate commitment of marriage. She still doubted where his loyalties truly lay. And until he resolved that conflict in his own mind, she was resolved the two of them would remain friends—close friends, indeed—but not lovers.

As she gave Margaret's hair another ten strokes, she indulged herself in fantasies of how their love-making would be some day. His strong arms around her, her lips exploring his body, his male strength filling her with pleasure. She sailed away on this mental pleasure boat, the images becoming progressively more vivid, more erotic. On a rare trip to Dingwall Fair, she'd seen sexual drawings depicting naked men and women in various love-making positions. The crimson blush had extended even into her hands then. But she remembered them now and imagined she and Ian as the ones in the pictures.

Fantasies flirted with mental images of him standing before her naked. She'd felt his arousal against her thigh when they'd lain on the floor in front of the fire. She'd been so young when she married David—so shy. But she wanted to experience more with Ian.

The quiet—and her own romantic daydreaming—was suddenly shattered by Aunt Christy tugging at her arm. "Catherine, are ye all right, lass. Ye appear to be running a fever, ye're so flushed." The look on her aunt's face one of concern.

"Uh...I'm fine, Aunt Christy, really."

"Well, look! Up the strath! What is that?"

An orange glow, just visible in the darkening sky, brightened even as they watched. Small tongues of flame licked at the night sky, growing bigger by the minute.

Catherine took Finn by the hand and walked briskly toward the flames. Others rushed past them. She tried to keep up, Finn pulling at her to go faster. But her limp only worsened. She had to slow down.

She caught up with the rest of the villagers about a mile ahead. They were lined up across the road and into the fields on either side. A barn was totally engulfed in flames, the heat so intense that even at fifty yards some had to shield their faces from it. They could see, clearly silhouetted against the fire's glow, Roddy Howard, his father, two servants, and a small woman frantically trying to control a terrified horse and move a fancy surrey away from the blaze. They soon gave up on the surrey, but did manage to lead the horse to safety.

The villagers remained rooted in place, the pain of Roddy Howard's court hearing and Margaret Ross' humiliation still fresh in their minds. They watched unmoving as the Howards struggled with buckets of water drawn from the Carron. Ignoring the barn, they tried instead to douse embers falling on the house.

Peter Mackinnon, the stonemason, stood beside Catherine. "For all the good that's doin'," he observed "They might as well be pissin' on it!"

Catherine heard a sound behind her. Davey Macdonald, unseen until now, had joined them. His hair was burnt, his eyebrows singed, his clothes reeking of peat and raw alcohol. His gaze was wild and frightening. He was transfixed by the fire.

When he turned toward her, he grinned broadly, almost laughed out loud. She gasped when she realized what he'd done. But she said nothing and turned back to watch the spectacle.

Like the other villagers, Catherine was drawn by a compassion to help a neighbor in distress, a value ingrained into clansmen since childhood. But she was also tied to the ground by a baser desire, a secret pleasure at this form of punishment for the Howards.

Finally, the better angels of her nature won out. She started for the house. Wordlessly, her neighbors followed, some running back to Greenyards for more buckets, the rest forming a line snaking down to the river. Everyone pitched in, passing buckets of water hand-over-hand, concentrating on the roof of the house. But the heat from the barn was too intense. It drove them back. Soon, embers falling onto the roof remained unextinguished, quickly gaining a foothold. Before long, they had coalesced into a crackling blaze.

The Howards and their servants made several attempts to get their possessions out of the burning house. But it was an effort in futility. They were driven back as well. Defeated, they withdrew to the roadside to watch the conflagration.

When it was over and only embers remained, the villagers were genuine in their sorrow. They attempted to convey this to the Howards...in Gaelic, of course.

The Howards understood none of it.

The next morning, Catherine and a few others

drifted back up the glen, back to the site of the fire. She found more of her neighbors already there, standing or sitting, quietly talking. The ruins of the house and barn still smoked. Only the stone walls and chimney remained standing.

"Looks like what was left of Glencalvie after it was cleared, don't it," someone whispered.

"Aye," another answered in hushed tones. "It's not as much fun when the shoe's on the other foot."

The Howards had salvaged an old cart, hitched the horse to it, and loaded the few things they'd managed to save.

Davey Macdonald was still there, seated on the same rock, in the same clothes he'd had on last night.

Catherine saw a blue-uniformed figure picking through the ashes of the barn. Ian! She watched as he held up and examined a large metal flask. To her horror it looked identical to ones she'd seen at Angus Macleod's cave. He walked over and showed it to Samuel Howard. They talked, pointing back toward the barn, but Catherine couldn't hear what was said. After Ian strode off, still carrying the flask, the elder Howard slammed his fist against the side of the cart. He turned and spoke animatedly to his family, then pointed an accusing finger in the direction of the clansmen.

Catherine turned away and headed back to the village.

She set the table for breakfast, placing an extra bowl for the guest she knew would soon be coming. It wasn't long before a sharp rap on the door announced his arrival.

Without even so much as a greeting, Ian stepped past her into the room. He held the battered, soot-covered metal flask she'd seen him with earlier. He didn't remove his hat. His eyes were as dark as a Highland loch.

She chased Finn to his room, still clutching his steaming porridge bowl and protesting loudly. She returned to face Ian, her arms akimbo, her jaw set.

He stood stiffly erect. "The fire was deliberately set. Arson, I am sure of it. I showed this container to the elder Howard. He was certain it didn't belong to him." He held it up to her. "Ever seen it before?"

She studied it, but couldn't meet Ian's eyes. "I've heard bootleggers often carry their whisky in flasks like that. I may have seen one or two like it before." Lying and subterfuge were not her forte. She was failing miserably at being nonchalant about it.

"I'll wager you have. We both have. Probably at the same place you get the moonshine you serve me."

Her anger surged. "Ye like it well enough!"

"I'll also wager you know who set the fire."

"Why would ye say that, Ian? I don't know who set it. I might have a suspicion, but I'm definitely not sayin'."

"Probably the same one I have. But I've no proof, so I won't arrest the boy. Howard, however, says he'll be going to the sheriff."

They stared at each other, the air as taut as fiddle strings.

"Is this your idea of Highland justice?" he demanded. "An eye for an eye?"

"I don't condone it. I would have stopped it if I could. And since the barn went up first, it's probably safe to assume whoever did it, didn't intend the house to burn as well. The barn alone was the target. A bad miscalculation."

He took off his cap. "After this, how can you speak of justice? If lightning had struck the Howard barn and set it on fire, that would have been justice. This was revenge."

She could read the pain on his face, his mouth open, his eyes wide—like the face in the loch of her nightmares. He shifted his weight from foot to foot and played absentmindedly with his cap. Then he looked up, staring at her grimly.

She kept her patience, though she felt heat spreading across her cheeks, her muscles tense. She straightened and faced him, forcing her arms to spread wide, her hands to open in a gesture of conciliation. "Now, I'm not saying this is the case, but if so it was the work of a bitter and foolish boy," she said slowly. "Don't condemn us all for it. Did Howard not tell ye the whole village turned out to try and save his house? That we formed a line passing buckets down to the river and back up to the house? That some of us got burned in the process?"

He relaxed. His voice softened. "No, I didn't know. I'm not surprised, though. I would have expected it."

The tension ebbed, replaced with fatigue.

She sat wearily. "Och, Ian, I know this doesn't help our cause."

The knot in his stomach began to unwind. He put his arms on her shoulders. "Events are beginning to take on a life of their own," he said sadly. "When you first started this, you thought you could control it. But it's like pushing a boulder downhill. Once it begins, you never know where it will go, no matter how well you aimed it at the start. I believe you're right, the fire was the rash act of one person. But even though his anger was justified, his actions were not."

She leaned against his arm.

"The clan's put up a stout defense of its rights," he continued. "Hasn't honor been satisfied? Haven't you done enough? Why not accept the writs now, while there's still time to plan your departure and look for other land, other work, other shelter? Don't wait to be forcibly evicted."

He searched her face for an answer.

After some time she spoke, shaking her head. "I couldn't stop it now, even if I wanted to. Every day I walk through the village and ask people what they want to do. There used to be differences of opinion. But no more. They speak with one voice now. Resist! They're determined to play out this hand, if only for the satisfaction of it. Ye've said I'm their leader. That may have been true at first, when they took strength from my resolve. But no more. I'm just their spokesman now."

She got up to serve him breakfast.

When she returned with the porridge, scones and milk, he said, "I'll not report my suspicions on the arson, though the Howards undoubtedly will. And I still think you should get out before there's more violence. But I fear you've made up your mind to resist to the end. I won't break any laws to help you, but neither will I enforce any that are unjust. In return, I want you to do everything you can to cool the passions here. Talk with Davey and any other hotheads you know. Convince them rash actions only work against your cause."

He looked at her, his eyebrows narrowed, his jaw taut. "Agreed?"

She hesitated, weighing the pros and cons of his offer. She moved to the window and stared out, her heart as heavy as one of her iron pots. For the first time, she understood her mother's actions during those terrible first clearances. Tears formed as she wished she could take back the misplaced anger and shame she'd directed towards her mother and clansmen at that time.

In the end, she saw Ian was right. "Agreed," she said, and stuck out her hand.

He gently pushed it away and wrapped her in his arms tasting the salty tears and kissing them away.

Chapter Twenty-three

Sheriff Rob Mackenzie puffed on his pipe in his Tain office and eyed James Gillanders pacing around the room. The factor appeared to have ridden hard for Tain the day after his failed meeting with Catherine Ross. He was overtaken on the road by a messenger bringing news about the fire at the Howard farm in Strath Carron. Deputy Sheriff Taylor, arms crossed and stony faced, sat across the desk from Mackenzie.

The factor had huffed and fumed, relating the events.

The sheriff glanced out the window, letting him vent his rage. A full moon rose in the east, casting silvery light through the barred windows on the tolbooth. Oil lamps captured dust motes and ribbons of gray tobacco smoke in their flickering light.

Gillanders stopped pacing, turned about and faced Mackenzie. "Sheriff, when are you goin' to see the writs delivered? The lord's exceedingly displeased with the snail's pace of your progress. Whitsunday is almost upon us, and Greenyards is still full of clansmen, not sheep."

Mackenzie grunted. The factor was right. The lord had recently sent him several personal notes, each one more critical than the previous. Why hadn't Greenyards been cleared? What was holding up the improvements there?

Gillanders continued. "I've already had one potential client—Mr. Baillie from Glenelg—driven off in fear of his life. If this is how legitimate sheep farmers are goin' to be treated in Strath Carron, I'll never get the land rented." He glared at the sheriff. "The lord is not happy his plans are being held up by a mob of unruly clansmen." He pointed his crop. "And by a sheriff who refuses to take firm action!"

"Come off it, Jamie!" Mackenzie retorted. "We both know Baillie was treated gently. He suffered no real harm. What he did was foolish, a complete stranger wanderin' around in the strath like that, then stupidly announcin' he was a sheep farmer come to look over the land. It only served to stoke the fire. Ye and I agreed to try and get the job done quietly. Not cause a big fuss. Baillie's stunt was idiotic. It's raised the clansmen's ire further. Now their backs are up, and their determine-ation to resist as well."

"I'm not responsible for Baillie's stupidity." Gillanders waved his arms. "If he'd come to me first, or to my agent at Bonar Bridge, we'd have found a less visible way for him to look over the land. But he chose not to. Nonetheless, he does have a right of free passage in that strath, doesn't he? A right to look at land he's thinkin' of leasin' before payin' for it?"

Deputy Taylor chimed in. "Rob, this is no longer just about sheep leases. It's now about law and order. And whether the Queen's Peace is still in force in Green-yards. And whether honest citizens can travel public roads in this shire without bein' accosted."

Mackenzie said nothing, his jaw clamped tight on the bit of his pipe. He knew the clansmen. He knew from experience what their tempers were like once stirred up. He was determined to prevent another sheep riot.

But Taylor was insistent. "It's time to form a posse, Rob. Time to go back in there, with overwhelmin' force this time."

"And kill or wound how many?" Mackenzie threw back. "Why don't we just shoot them all, William? Wouldn't that be easier?"

Taylor seemingly ignored the sarcasm. Like a bulldog with blinders, he kept at it, kept chewing away. "Sheriff, you've read Macpherson's statement about the mob that stopped him. It was probably the same bunch that threatened Baillie. Macpherson's papers were torn up and burned. He, too, said he feared for his safety. Are you goin' to let them get away with that? It's a slap in the face to all of us who've taken the oath and wear the badge."

Mackenzie shook his head. He suspected Macpherson had exaggerated the story. The man had appeared before him, shaken but unharmed. Mackenzie looked sternly at his deputy. "A little less outrage and a little more common sense is what we need now, William."

But Taylor wouldn't let it go. "There's more. There was a fire in that strath last week. It was deliberately set. Arson. A prominent family, the Howards, were burned out…"

"Do ye have proof it was started by a Greenyards villager?"

Taylor shrugged. "No. But it seems more than coincidental it happened so soon after the Howard boy was cleared of a rape charge on a Greenyards girl."

Mackenzie nodded. "The Howards are a powerful family, with powerful enemies. There's many with a grudge against them."

Gillanders evidently had heard enough. "Sheriff, I've done everythin' you've asked of me to clear the village peaceably. I've met with their minister and one of their leaders. I've tried trickery, persuasion—even bribery. Nothin' has worked. It's time for you to do your duty."

"Aye," Taylor growled, "no more talking or shilly-shallying." He drew his baton. "It's time for this!"

Mackenzie sighed and put down his pipe. "Gentlemen, Greenyards is a powder keg right now. Any spark will set it off. Force will be met by force, with bloodshed a certainty." He pointed to some newspapers on the desk. "Have ye read the letters in these papers recently, Jamie? Do ye know what they're sayin' about ye and yer lord's improvement policy? Not very flatterin'. There's many sayin' the clearances should be halted. And not just common folk, but people of good quality as well. The tide's turnin' against ye. A riot now, with blood spilt, would play into the hands of these reformers."

Gillanders bit his lip. "So, you'll do nothin'?"

"Not yet. Let's wait a couple of days until tempers have calmed. Then maybe we can catch them off guard. Besides, what's the rush?"

"The rush, as you call it," the factor said, "is that I've got two prospective tenants ready to sign. But they're demandin' to see the land up close first. After Baillie's experience, they're afraid to go in there."

"Patience, Jamie. Ye'll get your precious leases signed. But this is not the time for force. I know a better way."

He turned to his deputy. "William, wait a few days until everything is quiet there. Then send a couple of men with the writs along the North River road. Start them at Culrain in the wee hours of the mornin'. They can breakfast at Munro's house at Braelangwell, then cross the river at The Craigs. That way they'll come at Greenyards from the west, under cover of darkness, not past Ardgay Hill and the sentries there. They should be able to get into the village undetected by first light, serve the writs, and be gone before the clansmen know any better."

Taylor scratched his beard. "It might work. The lookouts on Ardgay Hill won't see 'em comin' from that direction. No chance to warn the village." He nodded. "I'll give it a try."

"Good lad. Here are some new writs to replace the ones that were burned." He put the papers on the desk and looked at Gillanders. "James?"

The factor was clearly dubious. "Have it your way, Sheriff. For now. But if this doesn't work, I am goin' to ask the commander at Fort William for troops myself."

The sheriff was the first to leave. Next, Deputy Taylor escorted Gillanders toward the front door. They passed through the squad room, an open bay with several desks used by sheriff officers and shire officials to prepare reports or work on other administrative tasks.

Dugald MacCaig, the excise tax collector who'd gotten into the barroom fight with Ian, sat there chatting with a couple of friends when Gillanders and Taylor passed through.

The factor stopped suddenly and smacked his riding crop down on an empty desk. The room hushed.

"Good God, Mr. Taylor," he stormed, "what's it going to take for me to get these writs delivered? Isn't there anyone with the courage to do it for me?"

Taylor put his hand on Gillanders' arm, then led him out the door.

When they'd gone, MacCaig looked at his two friends. "How do ye think a man like that would show his gratitude for gettin' his papers delivered?"

"He'd be very grateful, I'll wager," one of them said.

"Aye," said the other. "Maybe tell the lord himself. Maybe offer a reward to the ones who done it."

"How difficult could it be?" the first one asked.

"Och, there's just women, children and old men left in Greenyards. We'd put the fear into them by just showin' up," MacCaig boasted.

He looked around the room. It was empty now, except for the three of them. He walked quickly into Taylor's office and returned a few minutes later. Furtively, he showed his friends some papers stuffed into his shirt.

"The writs for Greenyards," he whispered. "We're goin' to deliver them ourselves."

"We'll be heroes," the first one said.

"We might get a reward," said the other.

"It'll be a romp," MacCaig boasted.

They headed to the nearest pub to plot their strategy.

Chapter Twenty-four

The following day dawned gray and somber. A thick blanket of cold foggy air covered most of Ross Shire, tendrils of mist creeping inland from the Kyle of Sutherland all the way to Greenyards and beyond. It was a good day to stay at home.

But Dugald MacCaig and his two friends, all three in their excise tax collector uniforms, met at the Ardgay Inn as planned. After a leisurely lunch, and fortified with several bottles of wine and shots of whisky, they reeled out of the Inn, somehow managed to get mounted, and laughing and joking headed into Strath Carron to deliver the Writs of Eviction and put the scare on the womenfolk there.

The children lookouts on Ardgay Hill were on their toes. They sounded the whistle alarms at the first appearance of the three horsemen. MacCaig and his friends had heard about these lookouts, now common knowledge throughout the shire. But they'd forgotten about it in their drunken state. The whistling continued, different levels and pitches echoing and re-echoing off the sides of the strath and up the glen.

"Stop it! Enough!" MacCaig roared. The piercing sound hurt his ears and his head had started pounding him with a ferocious headache. He shook his fist at the nearest children, spurred his horse threateningly toward them, then rode hard past the hill to get some relief from the racket. His two companions followed close behind. Soon the whistling stopped, and the three men regained some of their confidence and swagger.

Halfway to Greenyards they were stopped short by a crowd of women standing silently in the road, their red tartan plaids pulled tightly around their shoulders. A thin, red line of defiance and determination.

Catherine and Finn had been visiting Christy and Margaret Ross when the whistles sounded. The three women froze at first, but soon began to move, though with less urgency this time. They'd been through it twice before.

"Margaret, please fetch Finn for me," Catherine asked her young cousin, her words pinched. Then she strode off with Christy to pick up Uncle John, who was working by the peat stack. The four of them walked briskly down to the main road.

What could it be now?

When they caught up to the crowd, they found sixty or more clansmen gathered across the road about a mile east of the village. Catherine sensed a different mood this time. Even from a distance she'd heard laughter. And she noticed immediately none of her neighbors carried a stick, a stone, or any other weapon, or even held a garden tool raised in anger. Just the opposite. They were smiling and standing easy. All of them. Puzzled, she looked at her aunt and uncle, then pushed through the crowd. That's when she got her first look at Dugald MacCaig and his companions.

MacCaig's eyes were red from drink. But there was fear in them as well. His words were slurred, and when he mixed them with what little Gaelic he knew, it produced such strange language the crowd roared at each fractured sentence.

The other two were equally inebriated. One of them swayed in the saddle. Two young girls pretended to flirt with him, raising their skirts and acting coy. The man's efforts to concentrate—staring hard, trying to focus— brought peals of laughter from the crowd. One of the girls came near, stroked his leg suggestively, then backed off when he tried to return the touch. He ended up falling off his horse, which broke up the crowd even more.

A number of children from Ardgay Hill, including Davey Macdonald, had joined the group.

"What's going on?" Catherine asked.

A villager explained. "These three at first said they were sheriff officers come to deliver writs. But when we stopped them, the big ugly one there said they were really only excisemen from Tain. We demanded to know what they were doing here. He confessed they'd just come to play a little joke on us."

Catherine looked up at the larger man. "Is this true? Ye're not sheriff officers?"

The crowd quieted.

He grinned wide and hiccupped. A tooth was missing. The rest were yellowed by tobacco. "The name's MacCaig. We were just havin' a spot o' fun. *Hic!* A little joke. *Hic!* Dinna mean no harm by it."

She took several steps backward to avoid the spittle spray, but grabbed the horse's bridle when the man tried to leave.

She winked at the crowd. "How do we know ye're who ye say? An exciseman wouldn't play a trick such as this on poor country folks, would he now?"

MacCaig's brows furrowed. "What are ye saying? Of course I am an exciseman," his words came out slurred. He fumbled in his trousers for proof. The crowd roared when he turned his pants pockets inside out and came up with nothing but lint. His unhorsed companion struggled to remount. Two of the women helped him up, and when they pushed he practically flew off the other side of the saddle.

MacCaig was too drunk to appreciate the tables had been turned on him—he was now the butt of the joke.

"Listen," he said, pulling something from his pocket. "Here's money...a few pounds. Take it. Ye can have it if ye'll let us go." He held it out to the crowd, but was shaking so badly he dropped it in the dirt.

Catherine ignored it. Instead, she spied the writs sticking out of his shirt, reached up, and grabbed them before he could stop her. He tried again to spur his horse away, but she held firm.

Panic rose in MacCaig's throat. Then anger. He took stock of his situation. Here he was, stopped by a bunch of women, a crowd of children, and a couple of men. He'd be the brunt of endless jokes at the station house. To redeem himself, he had to get those writs back and deliver them as planned. He played his last card. He drew his pistol.

The clearly astonished crowd moved back a pace, a cry of horrified surprise coming from its communal throat. Then silence.

The woman still held the bridle in one hand, the writs in the other.

"Damn ye, woman!" MacCaig spat out. "Give me back my papers."

She handed them over.

"Now let go of me. We aim to continue on to Greenyards and deliver these writs." He was feeling better. His bluster had returned.

But she kept a tight grip on the horse.

MacCaig cocked the gun, pointed it at her head. "Let go, I said. Or by God, ye'll pay!"

The crowd gasped and stepped back farther.

But the woman wouldn't let go. She held his gaze as steadily as the horse.

After what seemed like an eternity, a lad suddenly jumped out from the crowd and drew a rusty old revolver from his pocket.

"You'll be puttin' your gun away, sir," he said calmly, "or you'll be answerin' to your Maker."

MacCaig quickly took the boy's measure. He eyed the old gun in his hand, his thoughts as plain as day on his face. Was it loaded? Where had he gotten it? It looked ancient. Would it truly fire? Would the boy really use it?

The tension mounted. No one breathed.

A sudden shout pierced the silence. A familiar voice

demanded, "What's going on here?"

All heads turned.

Ian Macgregor raced up the road toward them in a swirl of dust. He reined in his horse beside the crowd, leapt to the ground, and quickly sized up the situation.

Though weaponless except for his baton, he walked straight up to MacCaig and barked, "You damned fool! What do you think you're doing? Put that thing away."

The bully stared at him for a few seconds then blinked. He slowly reholstered his weapon and smiled tightly. "Easy, constable, I would not have used it."

Ian jerked the bridle out of Catherine's grip. "Get out of here," he ordered MacCaig. "You and these other thugs." He swatted the horse's rump to get it moving.

MacCaig started back down the road with his companions. But he hadn't gone very far when he turned in the saddle, raised his fist, and shouted, "Don't be thinkin' this is the end of it. It's not over yet. Not by a long shot."

The crowd lost sight of them where the road passed through a stand of trees.

The villagers hadn't moved. Even after the three horsemen were gone, a hushed stillness remained.

Ian put his arm around Catherine. "Are you all right, lass?"

He could feel she wasn't. Her teeth were still clenched, her body as tense as a drawn bow, her eyes blazing. Gradually, the muscles unwound. She took a few deep breaths, recognized him for the first time, and smiled weakly.

The villagers finally moved, some directly towards their homes, others to cluster around Catherine and Ian. A few offered quiet words of praise, others expressions of relief. John, Christy, and Margaret Ross, with Finn in hand, lingered behind.

John shook Ian's hand. "Thank you, constable. You prevented another injustice. Maybe even a murder."

But Ian had seen something else today, a side to the resistance he'd not witnessed before. Something very disturbing. Something very dangerous.

"Now you know what the stakes are if you continue to resist," he said firmly. "Violence, injury—even death." He swept his arm around. "Are you sure these few acres of earth are worth it?"

"Constable, ye've proven yerself a good man, and a good friend, on more than one occasion," John said. "But ye're not one of us. Ye can't feel what we do for this land." He looked around him. "Everything we are—or ever will be—is right here in this glen."

Ian pressed his lips to Catherine's head. "Then I have a question. Are you not concerned by what this struggle is doing to you and your kin? One of you is an arsonist." He eyed Davey Macdonald, standing off with his mother. "And I thought for sure the lad was going to shoot that fool MacCaig. Either on purpose or by accident. What's next? Armed rioting? More arson? Murder? Where will it all end?"

John answered. "As long as it's for a right and just purpose, I believe God will forgive us what we're doin'."

Davey, surrounded by his family, joined them. His mother was at one moment scolding him for his rash act, the next beaming with pride at his bravery.

Catherine said to the boy, "Yer father would have been right proud of ye, lad. But I fear ye gave your mam a great fright. Ye'll be hearin' about it for a long time to come."

Davey grinned sheepishly. "Do you think that man would have shot you?"

"I canna say. But I wasn't going to get out of his way. Wasn't going to let him pass."

Ian took the revolver from the boy and turned it over in his hand. "Where did you get this?"

"Da had it for years. He kept it hidden, even from my mam. When he went off to the Army, he showed it to me. Sometimes, I take it out and look at it. It reminds me of him. I started carryin' it around about a week ago, when all these troubles started."

"Would you have used it on MacCaig?" Ian asked.

He opened the chamber and burst out laughing.

"What?" Catherine asked.

"It's not loaded!"

Davey shrugged. "I have no bullets. Never have."

"Well, thank you anyway, young sir," Catherine said. "For standin' up for me. Ye've shown true Highland courage. We'll get Old Pete to write a song about ye and sing it at our next *ceildh*."

They started back for the village. Catherine had Ian by one hand, Finn by the other. She noticed Margaret Ross, her eyes full of admiration, had slipped her arm through Davey Macdonald's for the walk home.

Chapter Twenty-five

Dugald MacCaig and his two friends continued their wordless ride back to Tain. They passed Ardgay Hill again, going the other way. No whistles this time. Only a group of children watching them. Some grinned. A few laughed outright.

MacCaig's humiliation worked on him like a thorn. That woman, that dark-haired devil! Catherine Ross' face burned itself into his brain. He'd have his revenge on her, by God. And on that boy, too. He was pretty sure the gun hadn't been loaded. Even if it had been, it looked so old it most likely would have blown up in the lad's hand if he'd fired it. But the nerve of it. Pulling a pistol on him. And he'd get even with that constable, that Macgregor fellow, if it was the last thing he did.

When the three excisemen arrived in Tain, they made their report to Deputy Sheriff Taylor. It bore little resemblance to what had actually happened.

"We were attacked by a mob of at least three hundred people," MacCaig said, raising his right hand as though swearing an oath.

The one who'd fallen drunkenly from his horse claimed he'd been pulled off by the crowd. "And here's a fresh bruise to prove it." He pointed to his right hip.

"The villagers all carried weapons," the third one said. "One of them even had a gun. I feared we were about to be murdered."

"Hmm." Taylor raised an eyebrow.

"And they took my money," MacCaig added. "At least twenty pounds. Maybe more." He turned his empty pockets inside-out for emphasis.

Before leaving, MacCaig said, "If there's to be a

posse, me and the lads want to be part of it."

Taylor dismissed them with a wave of his hand.

"We'll settle the score back there," MacCaig vowed to his friends on the way out. "Or be damned!"

Taylor licked his lips in anticipation. This new evidence of riotous behavior in Greenyards would force Sheriff Mackenzie's hand.

Deputy Taylor penned a note to the sheriff asking for an emergency meeting in Tain. Another note to James Gillanders, informing him of recent events.

"Forget about any more tricky stuff or stealth," he wrote to the factor. "It's time to clear out Greenyards. With a posse and in force. And I'm the one who'll lead it."

The next day, the unflappable Sheriff Mackenzie propped his feet up on a desk in Taylor's office and fired up his pipe. "William," he said to his deputy, "ye asked for this meetin'. Let's get on with it." He eyed James Gillanders, but said nothing to him.

Taylor recited the details of the 'lawlessness' in Strath Carron. The seizing and burning of Sheriff Officer Macpherson's papers, the mobbing of Robert Baillie, and, finally, the armed resistance to Dugald MacCaig and his friends.

"What the hell was MacCaig doin' there?" Mackenzie asked gruffly. "He's an exciseman, for God's sake, not a sheriff's officer. Not even a constable."

"Officer MacCaig was simply trying to deliver the writs while on his regular duties," Taylor said, his face flushed. "He's an officer of the court and duly empowered to serve them. The other two men were acting as witnesses."

"Hmm." The sheriff shook his head. "I hear they got drunk and went in there to have some fun, that's all. When the crowd, mostly women I might add, put up a determined resistance, they turned tail and ran."

Mackenzie could imagine the fat exciseman being

routed by such a small group of people. He suppressed a smile. "I seriously doubt the clansmen robbed him. He probably lost the money in his haste to get away—or did something stupid like try to bribe them." He took his feet off the desk. "Have you talked with the villagers? What's their side of the story?"

Clearly, Gillanders was growing impatient. He stood before Mackenzie, hands on his hips, a fierce look on his face. "Sheriff, the details of this incident are unimportant. What matters is that twice now—*twice*—officers of the court have been prevented from delivering their writs. And a client of mine was roughly driven off. Now they have firearms in Greenyards. All of us want to know what you are going to do about it."

"All of whom?"

"All the law officers. All the local gentlemen. Anyone who is a law-abiding citizen. What are you going to do?"

Gillanders slapped his crop and waited. When Mackenzie didn't answer, he continued. "It seems they also know how to use moonshine whisky for something other than drinking. The smoking ruins of the Howard house and barn are proof. About one-hundred proof, I'd say! I want the ones who did it arrested, and the rest of them cleared out. If you won't do it, I'll do it myself, by God, with my own men."

Mackenzie heated with anger. No one talked to him like this in his own shire! He pointed his pipe at the factor. "As soon as I have *definite* evidence of who started the fire, I'll send men to arrest him. Until then, ye'll keep to yerself about it and let me do my job."

When he'd calmed, he asked the factor, "Jamie, what are ye going to pay the villagers as recompense for clearing them out?"

"The usual. Each household will get ten pounds in cash. And if they wish to sell, I'll buy their animals at fair market value. They can also take along their roof beams to start a new dwellin' with."

"And where exactly would they do that?" Mackenzie said with sarcasm. "Are ye offerin' them other land in exchange?"

Gillanders answered patiently. "There's no other land available. It's all been leased. However, if any wish to emigrate to another country, the lord will contribute half their passage fee."

Mackenzie put down his pipe. He was tired. If he didn't act now, Gillanders and the lord's lawyer would doubtless appeal to the Lord Advocate in Edinburgh, maybe even accuse him of dereliction of duty. There would be a long investigation. In the end, the factor would get his way. He always did.

"All right," the Sheriff said reluctantly. "I agree something must be done about Greenyards."

Gillanders held out a sheaf of papers. "There's no point in delivering the writs to just the four principal tenants this time. I've prepared applications for new writs for them all—for the tenants-at-will, all the sub-tenants, and the crofters as well. I want them all delivered, all at once. A clean sweep."

"I'll see to it. But mind you this, James, this is still a matter for the proper authorities. I want ye and yer men to keep out of it."

Gillanders nodded stiffly.

"Now please leave us alone. Taylor and I have work to do."

"How long, Sheriff?" the factor demanded. "How long before you act?"

"I'll let ye know. Goodbye, James."

When Gillanders departed, Sheriff Mackenzie gave Taylor his marching orders. "Ye'll lead the posse, William. It's in yer jurisdiction. I am gettin' too old for it."

Taylor nodded. "Should I ask the military for help? We could probably get a company of soldiers from Fort William. Maybe a troop o' the 'Black Watch'."

"No, no, that won't be necessary. Plenty of our own lads are available. I want the posse big enough to do the job, but no bigger. I'll ask Superintendents Cumming at

Fort William and Scott at Dingwall to assign some of their own constables to ye."

The sheriff looked hard at his deputy. "I'm placing ye in command. I expect ye to control the men. Keep good order and discipline at all times. Firearms are not to be carried. Batons will be a sufficient show of force. Those are unarmed villagers in Greenyards, despite what that fool MacCaig says."

Taylor nodded again.

"If they resist or try to block ye, for God's sake read them the Riot Act first before arrestin' any of them. Then they can't claim ye didn't give them fair warnin'."

Taylor was taking notes.

"How long before ye're ready?" Mackenzie asked.

"A week, more or less."

"Keep me informed, and let me know when ye've set a definite date. Plan it carefully, William. A disciplined, determined show of force will intimidate them. Ye'll have no trouble if ye prepare it well."

Chapter Twenty-six

In Greenyards, many a chest was puffed out with pride.

"We've won!" John Ross said, his face beaming. "Three times. We've stopped 'em three times."

"Aye," David Munro, the crofter, agreed. "Three victories."

"I'm beginnin' to think we really can beat 'em," Elizabeth Gunn said, smacking her fist into her palm. "I never would have thought it possible."

"Thanks to the children on Ardgay Hill," Christy Ross added. "For warnin' us."

"And thanks to Catherine," Old Pete said. "For standin' up to 'em." He did a little dance with his cane and one good leg.

The villagers were beginning to feel invincible.

"Keep alert!" Catherine warned. "This isn't over yet. There could be another attempt. Gillanders will surely try again."

Catherine's turn to supervise the children on Ardgay Hill came the next day. She brought Margaret Ross and Davey Macdonald along with her. The two were practically inseparable now. They carried backpacks, even Finn, loaded with food, blankets and peats. Arriving atop the hill late in the afternoon, they found shelter in an empty tent and laid out their camp site.

Catherine went for a walk before supper, stopping near one of the lookouts, not really searching for anything. One of the children, a freckle-faced little girl, suddenly grabbed her by the arm and pointed to a figure on the road below. It was a man. A man astride a horse. A man in a blue uniform. A lawman. And he was heading for the strath!

"Look! Look," the girl cried. "An officer comin' to deliver the writs. Quick. Sound the alarm."

Heart pounding, Catherine fumbled in her pockets, finally pulling out the whistle. But as she put it to her lips, the girl grinned and grabbed her arm to stop her. Then she heard laughter all around. She turned to see a crowd of children gathered behind her. It was only a joke.

"See," the small girl next to her said, "it's only Mr. Macgregor, our own constable. You can tell by the way he rides."

Catherine looked harder and saw it was indeed Ian. She exhaled in relief. He lifted his hand in a general way toward them, must have recognized her, and waved more vigorously. She waved back and motioned him up.

They waited for Ian at the top and greeted him warmly, the younger children clustering around him. He knelt down so they could touch his uniform and feel his badge. Some of the older boys wanted to inspect his baton. Made of hard ash and painted black, it was a formidable-looking weapon. They passed it around gingerly, as if it might explode.

One of the boys pointed to the initials etched into it. "What's 'VR'?" he asked.

"Victoria Regina," Ian answered. "The Queen."

The boy nodded solemnly

Ian retrieved his truncheon and followed Catherine to a seat by the campfire. She served him tea in a tin cup, then warmed it with a red-hot poker. He threw more peats onto the fire, which crumbled into flames and shot clouds of embers into the crimson sky.

Catherine stirred her tea. "Ye have an easy way with the children, Ian. They like ye."

"Och, I've always had a soft spot in my heart for them. If I'd had more schooling, I would have been a teacher." He grinned. "What could be better than filling those empty little heads with knowledge?"

"Ye'd have made a good one."

He sipped his tea. "I'd like to raise one myself someday. Teach him or her about right and wrong—and how to tell the difference. Watch him grow. See her eyes light up with the wonder of discovery." He looked at a small group of kids playing a game of chase. "Like Finn, there. I swear, that boy can find pleasure in a mud puddle, hear magic in an old bull frog's croak."

She laughed. "And ask a thousand questions."

"Like, 'how does a whistle work'?"

"Or, 'why does fire burn'?"

"Or, 'what's at the bottom of the sea'?"

They both laughed.

He reached for her hand. "What about yourself, do you think Finn would like a brother or sister?"

She caught her breath, not sure how to take the question, finally staring back into the fire. "I believe he would," she whispered. "I would like one for him."

"Your face is all red," he said.

"Is it?" She touched her cheeks. They were indeed hot. "Must be the fire."

He smiled.

They kept silent, listening to the wind rustle the branches of an old oak tree. Finally, he put his arm around her and whispered, "It would be a right bonny child. Just like its mother."

He imagined being a new father, pressing a baby son against his naked chest, watching the wee lad suckle at his mother's milk-full breasts, guiding the boy through his first shaky steps...catching him when he fell.

And oh what joy it would be making that little tyke. Making love to Catherine had been at the forefront of his mind these several weeks. When he awoke, and especially when he went to bed.

The subject of his musings interrupted his thoughts with a quizzical look. He struggled to remember what they'd been talking about. Ah!

He laughed. "Me, a father! I can hardly believe such a thing." His eyes narrowed. "Born into our struggles, he'd have to be a tough one. Thick skinned. Well supervised and seen to..."

"You'd be a wonderful father," she murmured. "Equal parts love and discipline."

He gazed into those dark green eyes. They glistened with moisture. "Do you think so? Truly?"

Her answer was to bury her face in his chest.

For supper, Catherine served chicken stew and clapshot—a mixture of turnips and mashed potatoes. Later, they piled the fire with peats and huddled around it wrapped in blankets and plaids. The sky was so full of stars they couldn't count them all, though some of the children, as a game, tried.

Old Pete filled them with stories. Catherine hugged Finn, who sat in her lap stirring the embers. Ian pulled two children, both about Finn's age, down beside him, wrapped them in a blanket, and told a spooky campfire story of goblins, demons and ghosts. Catherine had never heard him as a storyteller before. He was good, the children wide-eyed with attention.

After the children were put to bed, Ian turned serious. "I have to tell you about the posse that's forming. It's the talk of all the local constabulary."

"I knew it wasn't over," she said bitterly. "It seemed too easy."

"They're recruiting from as far away as Inverness and Fort William."

"Fort William!" The blood drained from her face.

"Easy, lass. Not the military—there'll be no soldiers. Only constables from the town itself."

"When?"

"No one knows for sure. Except Taylor, and he's not saying. About a week, most likely. Taylor himself will lead it. He s a rough man. Some say he's in the pay of the landlords."

"What about ye?" She looked into his eyes, searching. "Will ye be part of it?"

"I've not been ordered to. They probably doubt my loyalties by now. But I'll find a way to be there anyway. Whether they like it or not."

"Why not stand with us? That's where yer sympathies are. Ye've said so yerself."

"Because there's still a chance this matter can be resolved peacefully. And I'm not ready to throw away everything I've worked so hard for until I see how it turns out."

She looked at the sky, searching. "I feel like an ant on a blacksmith's anvil. And the hammer is poised to fall."

He nodded and said gravely, "It appears the moment of truth will soon be at hand."

She faced him again. "Aye. For all of us."

He put his arms around her, drew her to him and kissed her forehead. She shuddered and lay her head on his chest. "We'll get through this," he whispered. "Ye'll see. We'll get through it and be the better for it."

Chapter Twenty-seven

It was the middle of May—almost Whitsunday—by the time Superintendent of Constables Archibald Scott and a handful of his men left the town of Fort William at the south end of the Great Glen. Scott had spent his entire career in law enforcement, most of it as a constable. Now middle-aged, with salt-and-pepper hair, hard eyes and a scar running from below his left eye to his jaw, he was the chief policeman for the growing town.

Scott's final destination was Strath Carron. His mission, he'd been told, was to restore law and order in the village of Greenyards.

This first fifty-plus mile leg of the journey would take him and his men only as far as Inverness, a two-day ride by carriage and horseback. Keeping the looming shadow of Ben Nevis to their right, they passed the ruins of Fort Inverlochy, one of the two original forts built at either end of the Great Glen in the seventeenth century to control the Highlands. The fort had been rebuilt in 1690 and renamed Fort William, though it was still called in Gaelic, *An Gearadsan*—The Garrison—indicating its original purpose. It was now home to companies of the Black Watch.

Fifty years earlier, Fort William had been the principal port of departure for tens of thousands of Highlanders forcibly evicted from Glengarry, Argyll, Ross and Inverness. Many were sent to the North American colonies of the Earl of Selkirk. One was at Prince Edward Island on the east coast of Canada. The other, the Red River Colony, was on the plains of Manitoba.

In those earlier days, Constable Scott had been part

of many a posse where physical force had been required to prod unfortunate clansmen—men, women and children—aboard ships leaving for foreign shores. They were often consigned to quarters little better than those on slave ships. Scott's own truncheon was nicked and stained with the blood of these, his countrymen, whom he'd helped herd into the poisonous holds.

Scott's carriage bumped and swayed through the heart of Lochaber on the way to Invergarry, where the waters of Glen Garry emptied into the loch. The men paid little attention to the sheep grazing up the glen, now virtually empty of people. The riders continued along the bank of Thomas Telford's Caledonian Canal, built in 1822 as the missing link to a continuous waterway between Inverness on the Moray Firth—and, thus, on the North Sea—and Loch Linne in the south, the exit to the eastern Atlantic.

Scott and his men spent the night at Fort Augustus, halfway up the Great Glen. They started out again early the next morning, riding along the west bank of Loch Ness past Urquardt Castle, the twelfth century structure built on the ruins of an old Celtic fort. Had they detoured west up Glen Urquardt a few miles, they would have come to Strathglass. It had been roughly cleared of several thousand people by the lord of Clan Chisholm in 1801. It was an empty land now. Except for the sheep.

The men looped around the northern end of Loch Ness, where the lake narrowed and flowed into the bucolic River Ness. Fishermen were pulling fat trout from the river's tree-lined banks as they passed. They continued into Inverness, where Scott saw the banner headline on the local newspaper, 'WAR DECLARED ON RUSSIA.'

In Ardgay, Ian kept close to his desk, his ear to the wind, trying to learn when the posse would be coming and what its size and makeup would be. A constable friend from Culrain told him *he'd* been ordered to stand by for 'rough duty.'

"Soon," he'd told Catherine as they stood in her doorway. He'd ridden hard to Greenyards with the news. "They'll be here within a couple of days. That's all I've been able to find out. They mean business this time," he warned.

She clenched her jaw. "So do we."

"They'll be after the village leaders. Like you and your uncle."

"We'll be ready."

He made one last plea. "Come away with me now. There's still time. You and Finn can stay at my apartment until we find you other lodgings."

She hesitated. There it was again, that siren call of safety and comfort. But it was getting easier to ignore. She knew her duty.

"I canna do it. I've got to see this thing through. If we stop them here, we can strike a blow for crofter's rights that will ring all the way across Scotland. The high and mighty in Edinburgh and London will have to pay attention to us. Don't ye see, if we just stand fast, we could end the clearances once and for all."

"Och, lassie, you're a stubborn one. I'm defeated as much by your logic as your determination." He smiled and put his arm around her, leaning his forehead against hers. "I'll do what I can to help. But promise me this, find a safe place for Finn. Don't bring him along. It'll be no place for children."

She agreed.

"And tell that hot-headed Macdonald lad to leave his old revolver at home. They won't know it's not loaded. It could get him killed."

She kissed him on the cheek. "When this is over, ye said there would be time for us."

"Aye," he answered. "There will be, lass. I promise." He exhaled slowly, praying he could keep that vow.

Doubt wrapped itself around him like a shroud. Time held its breath.

He finally pushed her out to arm's length. Tears etched her cheeks. He caught one on his fingertip.

"We'll find a place to be together. Maybe not in your world. And probably not in mine. But we'll make one of our own."

She sobbed and grabbed at him like a drowning sailor clutching a floating spar.

In Inverness, Superintendent Scott collected an additional fifteen constables. They left the city the next day for the eighteen-mile trip to Dingwall. The force now numbered twenty men. Most of the Inverness lads were on foot, so the next part of the journey was slower. Scott feared he'd be late. But the men were in good spirits and talked excitedly as they marched along. For many, this was high adventure, a chance to get away from the sounds and smells of town living. And they'd heard there would be some real police action at the end of their journey.

They traveled due west at first, skirting the southern end of Beauly Firth, where they were greeted by sea gulls swooping in from the sea. At Beauly Town, they headed due north again. James Gillanders, whose home at Highfield Cottage was close by, met them late in the morning with food and drink.

"Be firm with them, Scott. All the landlords of Easter Ross will be grateful to you," the factor said, slipping him twenty pounds for 'extra expenses.'

After refreshments, the posse took off again, climbing over the Muir of Ord. Although tiring to reach, the view from the top of this steep hill was magnificent in all directions.

Some of the veterans teased the young lads from Inverness, who'd been told the Highland line began in their city.

"No true Highlander is home until he's gone o'er the Ord," they said. "Only then are you truly in the Highlands."

They marched on through scattered sunshine past Strath Conon, emptied of people years earlier by their luncheon host, James Gillanders.

Later that afternoon, tired and hungry, they arrived at Dingwall on the Cromarty Firth. The men were billeted at several inns throughout the town, while Scott dined with Sheriff Mackenzie and Robert Cumming, Superintendent of the Dingwall Constabulary. When they started out again, Cumming and his men would swell the ranks of Scott's posse by an additional fifteen lawmen.

Now numbering thirty-five, the posse left Dingwall the next day shrouded by the early morning darkness. A cold wind swept off the Firth. Gray skies blocked out all moonglow and starlight. At times, lanterns had to be used to guide the way. They took the road past Alness, the menacing silhouette of the Ben Wyvis escarpment arching high on their left. They were now in Easter Ross proper.

The posse climbed up and over the Great Pass, then down to meet the road from Tain. They marched a mile farther on to the Inn at Midfearn, where they stopped to await the arrival of Deputy Sheriff Taylor and the additional men he was bringing. It was just after 6:00 a.m., and the weather had become dismal, the air cold, the sky threatening rain. After a light breakfast, the men drank liberally of whisky, porter, and ale while they waited.

Taylor and the lord's lawyer Donald Stewart arrived about an hour later with ten more men: Dugald MacCaig and his two friends, plus seven other Tain sheriff officers. They helped themselves to the liquor. Since none had eaten anything for breakfast, the alcohol quickly went to their heads.

Taylor greeted Superintendents Cumming and Scott and offered them a ride in his carriage. Next, he lined up the men in rank and file formation, called the roll, and administered the oath making them all Ross Shire sheriff officers. After briefly describing their mission—to put down disobedience and restore order in Greenyards—he made them draw their batons for inspection. All were painted black, menacing in appearance, and inscribed with the initials 'VR.'

Then they set off again, some pulling carts in which they'd stowed additional bottles of whisky and ale. Others carried liquor in baskets slung over their arms or in pouches. They drank liberally as they marched.

In *his* pouch, lawyer Stewart carried forty Writs of Eviction.

Talking loudly, laughing and joking, they passed through Kincardine.

From his bed, Angus Mackay heard them go by and looked out his window. His stomach knotted. He dressed quickly, hitched his old mare to the carriage, and chased after them.

The posse continued noisily onward, passing through Ardgay. Ian waited for it there. Grim-faced, but clear-headed, he took up a position at the back of the two ragged lines of marchers. No one paid him any attention. He was just another lad with a uniform and badge. He didn't know yet what he was going to do. But he quickly identified Dugald MacCaig and his friends from their loud voices. They were all drinking heavily.

On horseback, Alex Munro and Samuel and Roddy Howard joined the lines of marchers just east of Gledfield. They received warm greetings from Deputy Taylor. Munro had no official baton, but had armed himself with a stout oak cane. Howard and his son had homemade clubs. Munro massaged his sore arm. The elder Howard licked his lips, his eyes full of malice.

As they entered Strath Carron proper at Gledfield, the whistles and shouts on Ardgay Hill began. The men halted, milling about in confusion and alarm. Several drew their batons.

Taylor emerged from his carriage. "Easy lads," he said. "They're only children." He pointed to the hilltop. "That's just the way they sound the alarm here."

As they listened, the men heard the whistling march its way up the strath, finally fading away in the distance like a wailing spirit. The posse started out again, but many of the men were unnerved and gripped their batons nervously.

"Children?" some asked. "Are we here to march against children?"

They covered the five miles from Midfearn and arrived at Easter Greenyards at 8:00 a.m. As the road emerged from a small stand of trees, it veered down towards the Carron. There, a large, flat, grassy meadow flanked the road on the side facing the river. Here the men got their first view of the 'rioters' they'd come to put down.

About ninety villagers awaited the posse, mostly women. A few teenagers were scattered among them; a dozen men stood in back. Some had sticks or stones. Catherine viewed everyone from the front of the crowd. Christy and Margaret Ross stood on either side of her. Davey Macdonald was next to his mother in the middle of the pack. The old Waterloo veteran Donald MacNair leaned on his walking stick at the back, shoulder to shoulder with Pete Ross. Catherine's Uncle John stood next to the clan's bard. She faced the men who'd arrived to deliver the writs.

The posse was called to a halt ten yards in front of Catherine. The two sides eyed one another. Dugald MacCaig and his friends elbowed their way to the front. MacCaig raised his baton and glared malevolently at her. She watched Ian work his way slowly forward until he stood immediately behind MacCaig.

"I am Deputy William Taylor," one man yelled as he stepped out of a carriage, accompanied by two other men. The other lawmen clustered around him. He took several steps toward Catherine.

Before he could say anything, she held up her hands. "And I am Catherine Ross and I speak for our town. What is your business here, Deputy Taylor?"

"Stand aside," Taylor ordered gruffly. He spoke in Gaelic so all the clansmen would understand. "We're here on the court's business, to deliver legal papers." He nodded to lawyer Stewart, who pulled a sheaf of writs from his pouch and held them up for the crowd to see.

"Sir," Catherine said evenly, "our tacksman, Mr. Munro, denies ever having applied for those writs. And I have a paper from him stating he has no intention to evict us." She held the statement out at arm's length.

She nodded toward Munro who quickly dismounted and concealed himself in the crowd.

Taylor brushed the paper aside with the back of his hand. It fluttered out of her grasp, was caught by the wind and carried over their heads. It landed in the river. They watched it for a moment, sailing away on its short trip to the sea.

"I'm not interested in any damned piece of paper from you," Taylor snarled. "We have writs to deliver. Now stand aside!"

The men in the posse drew their truncheons. Their muscles bunched. Catherine saw Ian, watching MacCaig's every move, rise on the balls of his feet.

Suddenly, a shout broke the stillness. Angus Mackay had caught up with them. He leapt from his carriage and walked rapidly over to stand next to Catherine.

"Sheriff, there's no reason for this force. I'm sure we can still settle the matter peacefully. Why don't we adjourn to my manse and discuss it civilly."

Taylor put his baton on the minister's chest and gently but firmly pushed him aside. "Reverend, this is no concern of yours. You'd be well advised to keep out of it."

He turned back to Catherine, his face flushed, his look fierce. "For the last time, will you stand aside?"

Catherine shook her head.

"Then be damned!" Taylor waved his baton in her face and yelled to the men, "clear them away, lads. Clear them all away. Knock them all down if you have to!"

Chapter Twenty-eight

For two blinks of an eye, no one on that road by the river moved. The constables had heard Deputy Sheriff Taylor's order, but didn't act on it immediately. A few shifted uneasily from foot to foot. The rest stayed put.

The Greenyards villagers remained motionless as well. Some gripped their primitive weapons tighter. But no one breathed. Not a sound was heard. The two sides eyed one another across an imaginary line.

Then, with a communal yell, the men in blue charged.

Dugald MacCaig, his face contorted with rage, spittle and obscenities flying from his lips, raised his baton high and lunged straight for Catherine. But when he brought his weapon down on what he thought would be her head, he found it blocked. Ian had been quicker off the mark, had gotten to Catherine first, and leapt in front to protect her.

He parried MacCaig's blow with his own truncheon and, for a split-second, relished the look of astonishment in the bully's eyes. He jabbed a short, sharp thrust to the fat man's gut, knocking the wind out of him and doubling him over. He was on the verge of following up with another smash when MacCaig's friends caught up with him. One hit Ian across the back at kidney level. The pain brought him to his knees. The second thug crashed a baton down on his shoulder. Ian heard the snap and felt the sharp pain of his collarbone breaking. By now, MacCaig had recovered and clubbed him in the face, breaking his nose.

With a last glance at Catherine, Ian yelled, "Run, save yourself!" Under a rain of blows and kicks from all three attackers, he fell to the ground unconscious.

Catherine watched him go down defending her. In that instant, he won her heart completely. He'd finally chosen sides, finally made his commitment to her and the village, against the establishment he represented, had sworn allegiance to, and had expected so much from.

"No," she screamed. Horror stricken, her first instinct was to rush to his rescue, and she stepped towards him.

But his insistent order to flee galvanized her into action. Kirtling her skirts for freedom of movement, she accelerated to full speed and headed for the road, hoping to reach the relative safety of the village.

She'd seen Alex Munro glaring at her from the moment Taylor gave the order to attack. Her initial hesitation gave him time to close the distance between them. Still, she almost made it. She heard the overweight tacksman huffing and puffing behind her gaining ground as she gradually slipped farther back as she ran. Her bad foot proved to be her Achilles' heel. After about a hundred yards she began to limp. The more she tried to speed up, the worse she limped. Finally, her foot dragged in the dirt. Since she couldn't outrun him, she decided the alternative was to turn and fight. Teeth bared, she raised her arms, hands balled into fists.

Munro appeared astonished when she stopped, turned, and faced him. He pulled up short, cowed by the resolute defiance. Obviously, he hadn't expected this from a woman.

"Do ye think we would not try to defend our homes? Ye will be judged for this, for the liar and coward ye are!"

He advanced cautiously, still breathing hard, his cane upraised to strike. But Catherine preempted him and launched a first-strike of her own. Balancing on her good foot, she aimed a vicious short kick with the other.

It caught him squarely in the groin. Holding his crotch, he doubled over and puked.

"You feckless, lying bastard!" she cursed.

Then MacCaig and his thugs caught up to and surrounded her. She put her hands up to defend herself, but they came at her from all sides, raining blows down on her head and face. Blood streamed from her nose and scalp. She was finally knocked to the ground. Instinctively, she curled into a fetal position for protection, but the blows and kicks continued. They stopped only when she ceased to move.

Temporarily paralyzed from the beating, she lay in the grass, not believing what had just transpired. She felt them move away and cautiously opened one eye.

They'd stomped away, looking for fresh victims.

The meadow by the river was normally a restful and bucolic place, a place where Catherine, Ian and Finn had frequently picnicked. But on this day, it was a fearsome scene of pandemonium and bloodshed. The men in blue, their blood lust up, vented their drunken rage on anyone they could bring within reach of their truncheons. Since the crowd consisted mainly of women, most of the victims were women. The lawmen chased them across the road and into the meadow, then chased them to the river's edge, in some cases into the water itself, beating and kicking at them, tearing their clothes, pulling their hair.

There remained no further obstacle to the posse's passage. If they had wished, the lawmen could have continued on to Greenyards without interference. But they were frenzied and would not be stopped, even if someone in authority had tried. But neither Taylor nor the two Superintendents made any move to rein them in.

From where she lay, Catherine could see everything that was happening, but wished she couldn't. Looking away would have been easy, but an inner voice insisted she watch the hideous scene unfolding in front of her.

Some of the Greenyards clansmen standing at the

back of the crowd clearly realized they had no chance against the rampaging constables. They grabbed their wives and daughters and fled when the posse charged. A few escaped across the river, others up the braes.

Uncle John, seeing no chance of escape for his wife Christy and his daughter Margaret, rushed to their defense. Although Catherine couldn't distinguish his words, she heard him yelling as he ran towards his wife and child. He hadn't gone more than a few steps before he was surrounded by a pack of constables, roughly handcuffed and led away. They were on him so quickly she was certain someone—probably Alex Munro—had pointed him out as one of the 'trouble makers.' He struggled against the handcuffs and kicked at the men restraining him. But it was useless. As he watched his wife and daughter's ordeal, he bellowed like a caged animal, his cry clearly a combination of impotent rage and searing pain.

Catherine still couldn't move her legs. She looked toward Aunt Christy, who'd not budged since the posse's initial charge. She appeared frozen in time. Oh, auntie dearest, Catherine thought. She could no longer watch this massacre. She buried her head between her arms and unleashed the pent-up tears.

Christy Ross couldn't believe what her eyes were seeing. She finally came to her senses, grabbed Margaret, and made a run for it. But she was too slow and was hit across the back of the head almost immediately. As she went down, one of the men grabbed at her blouse. It tore away in his hand and exposed her from the waist up.

She cried out, "Please, leave us be!" She crossed her arms over her breasts. But this uncovered her head and face, which now became the new target of attack. She tried to stand, but one of the men stood on her chest to keep her down. His hobnail-boots punctured her skin.

When the men started beating her mother, Margaret threw herself onto the back of one of them, clawing and scratching at him like a spitting bobcat.

"Leave her alone, you evil bastard," she yelled. He twisted and turned and bucked to get her off. But she held on. When her mother finally lay unmoving on the ground, another man pulled Margaret off and threw her down. Then he kicked her in the chest and groin and clubbed her in the head. Groaning and holding her chest, she crawled over toward her mother.

Blood seeped from her mother's nostrils and her scalp was torn in several places. She was losing a lot of blood from the chest wounds. Margaret started crying, tending her mother's wounds as best she could. Ripping portions of material from her skirt, she patted them against her mother's chest to staunch the blood flow. She pulled her mother's blouse closed and slipped the few remaining buttons into their holes.

Margaret looked around. Catherine lay nearby, and she saw her shoulders shaking. Seeing her strong cousin beaten and in tears, she slumped her shoulders and collapsed on top of her mother's body.

Donald MacNair, the old Waterloo veteran, stood his ground. He had little choice. Even if he'd wanted to flee, he wouldn't have gotten far on a gimpy leg and a crutch. But it was more than just disability that kept him on the field. It was pride—he'd never run from a fight before and wasn't about to start now. More than that, he was enraged when he saw his friend and neighbor Margaret Macgregor Ross, the widow with seven children, lying on the ground taking kicks and clubbing to her head and face. Her clothes were torn, her red shawl half-ground into the grass beside her. She bled profusely from both ears. Two of her sons, ages twelve and thirteen, had accompanied her. They were getting similar treatment. Two men held them while another beat them with a club.

The old veteran hefted his walking stick like a claymore, and hopped over to the widow's aid as fast as he could. The men attacking her were surprised and hesitated at first. Then they saw who it was. Laughing and joking, they knocked down first the walking stick, then the old veteran himself.

Davey Macdonald and his mother, Naomi, were in the center of the crowd when the mêlée began. His first thought was for her safety. But with action swirling all around them, he saw that getting her off the field would be difficult, if not impossible. He spotted Reverend Mackay up ahead. Despite his mother's protests, he led her to the minister and left her in his protection.

Davey's next concern was to find Margaret Ross. He headed in the direction where he'd last seen her, dodging villagers running and small knots of deputies chasing them. He was suddenly blocked by a man with a gnarled club in his hand and a fiendish grin on his face. None other than Samuel Howard, the sheep farmer. Roddy, his son, stood beside him with a similar weapon.

The elder Howard must have spotted Davey in the crowd from the beginning and followed him and his mother across the field. Now ready to exact vengeance for the destruction of his house and barn, he gripped his club in both hands like a baseball bat and advanced slowly, probably intending to trap Davey against the river. Roddy, his courage clearly emboldened by his father's presence, darted in and out, challenging Davey to fight. But Davey remained level-headed. He backpedaled slowly, never taking his eyes off his enemies.

When he was fifteen yards from the river, Davey saw his chance. He spotted a baton on the ground. Discarded, dropped, or knocked down, it didn't matter why it was there, it was serendipity, and he seized upon it.

Making his move suddenly, he dove for the weapon. The elder Howard swung, sailing his club in a wide arc. It missed its mark and flew harmlessly over Davey's head. In one continuous motion, Davey scooped up the baton, did a shoulder roll away from his attackers, and ended up on his feet just as the sheep farmer cocked his club for another stroke.

But he would get no second chance. Using the baton like a piston, Davey drove it straight into the man's gut. Gasping, the elder Howard dropped first to his knees, then onto all fours. Roddy, his courage rapidly evaporating with his father out of commission, swung his weapon timidly. Davey easily blocked it, then brought his own weapon down on the boy's face. Blood squirted out of the gaping wound. Roddy screamed in pain and ran off.

His adversaries now incapacitated or having fled, Davey returned to his original mission—to find Margaret Ross. He'd gone barely a few yards when he ran into Dugald MacCaig and his two thugs.

"Hello, laddie," MacCaig said malevolently. "Remember me?" He slapped his baton into his hand. His two companions spread out to encircle Davey.

Backpedaling again to protect himself, Davey got closer and closer to the river. The three men kept coming. Davey looked over his shoulder, then back at his attackers. Three against one. Not very good odds. He could take a hard beating, or he could take his chances with the roiling river. He made a snap decision. Hurling his baton at MacCaig, he turned and ran. He didn't stop at the riverbank but plunged headfirst into the foaming water.

Thinking their quarry had escaped, the three tormenters shouted curses at him. These turned to cheers when the boy's head disappeared beneath the surface. They waited for a very long time. It didn't appear again.

Naomi Macdonald, watching from her spot next to the minister, screamed and sank to her knees, sobbing her son's name over and over.

Some villagers stood firm and defied the lawmen when they charged. One such man was David Munro, the thirty-five year old crofter distantly related to Alexander Munro. Pugnacious by nature, he stood his ground like a rock. He was soon surrounded by four deputies. He dared them to come and get him. They approached him warily. He managed to knock one of them down with a hard right to the jaw. His fist coiled to strike again, but the other three overpowered him. They clubbed him until he was barely conscious then jumped on him when he was down. They finally handcuffed him and dragged him away.

Fiona Macleod, a widow from Langwell, was chased zigzag across the field by a young deputy who evidently thought it great sport. She finally tired of the chase and turned to face him. Glaring, she snatched the baton out of his hand and sent it flying. But other deputies came to his rescue and chased her down to the river's edge. Just when they thought they had her cornered, she ripped off her heavy skirt, jumped into the water, and swam to the other side. Climbing out naked from the waist down, she gave them an obscene gesture and stalked off towards her home.

The drizzle had turned to a cold, steady rain. Injured villagers lay shivering on the field, some in shock and hypothermia. Two had wounds which would prove fatal. Some of the deputies had grown weary of the sport and drifted back toward the sheriff's carriage, dragging bleeding prisoners in handcuffs behind them.

For other villagers, it wasn't over yet.

Helen MacIntyre of Western Greenyards was the eighteen-year old daughter of Thomas MacIntyre. She couldn't escape the posse's charge and was trapped between the river and the road by two constables who looked so drunk they teetered on the brink of falling down. She thought she might be able to outrun them if she could get back to the road. Kirtling her skirts high above her knees, she set off with all her strength. But the men had the advantage of interior lines, and they weren't as incapacitated as they'd seemed. They chased her, cut off her escape, and finally caught up with her.

She received several blows about the back and shoulders, then staggered off the road and crawled into a bush, one of the few shelters anywhere close by. But her tormentors pursued her, kicking at her within the bush until she crawled out again. Then they clubbed her a few more times for good measure and led her away in handcuffs.

The rampage by the constables continued.

Anne Mackinnon, wife of Peter Mackinnon the stonemason, was hit across the face and head, knocking her backwards. When she recovered her balance, she was temporarily blinded by the blood in her eyes and dizzy from the concussion. She stumbled toward the road but toppled into a ditch, breaking her leg. She lay shivering in the cold for two hours until someone heard her cries for help.

Elizabeth Gunn, age twenty-six, wife of a Greenyards tenant-at-will, was hit over the head by a deputy. She fell into the river but was pulled out—near-drowned—a half mile downstream.

In Dingwall, Sheriff Mackenzie fired up his favorite briar and paced nervously about his office. What was happening in Greenyards? He'd given Deputy Sheriff Taylor firm orders to avoid bloodshed. But would the orders be obeyed?

At Highfield Cottage, James Gillanders finished a leisurely breakfast. He ordered his horse saddled for the ride to Tain, confident his Greenyards problem would be resolved by the end of the day.

Chapter Twenty-nine

The tumultuous debacle on the meadow by the River Carron was over in about thirty minutes. Weeping, bleeding women, and a few men and boys, lay scattered prostrate across the field. Some unconscious, others moaning in pain. Pieces of torn and crumpled clothing festooned the grass like giant red, blue, and yellow wildflowers. The deputies, their blood sport finally sated, returned to Taylor's carriage. He congratulated them on a job well done. None of the constables was seriously injured, though many had broken and bloody batons. Alex Munro and Samuel Howard had recovered from their encounters with Catherine Ross and Davey Macdonald.

Roddy Howard bled from a laid-open face wound. Someone helped him to Taylor's carriage and the deputy sheriff tended his wounds and bandaged them. Then the boy and his father mounted their horses and headed for Dingwall to get proper treatment.

No one had seen Davey Macdonald emerge from the river. Nor his lifeless body.

When Ian regained consciousness, his nose and mouth were full of liquid. He thought he'd fallen into the river and was drowning. He coughed and choked to catch his breath. Gradually, he realized it wasn't the peaty water of the Carron he tasted, but his own blood. He sat up, spat, and examined himself more carefully. He staggered to his feet and was met by bolts of pain and nausea. He headed for the river to clean his wounds.

Through still-blurry vision, he watched the posse

depart. He spotted Catherine, her Uncle John, Anne Ross of Greenyards—a woman with three children and no husband—and two other villagers being led away in handcuffs. The women were covered in blood. Other villagers had been arrested, but deemed unfit to travel and released.

Ian also saw the lord's lawyer, Donald Stewart, walking among the wounded. Some of the moaning, semiconscious clansmen thought he'd come to help them. When they reached out to him, he gave not aid, but slapped a Writ of Eviction into each hand.

When the posse and its prisoners reached Green-yards, Stewart handed out the rest of the writs to the clansmen cowering in their houses. Even the prisoners didn't escape this final humiliation. He tucked the papers into their coats or blouses.

The posse crossed the river at the bridge south of The Craigs. Alex Munro was in high spirits, leading the way on horseback. He looked back with satisfaction at Catherine Ross' distress. Some women had grown faint and had to be placed into Taylor's carriage. No effort was made to bandage their wounds or treat their discomfort. The lawmen laughed, joked, and recounted 'war' stories of the 'battle' they'd just fought.

The posse stopped at Braelangwell. Alex Munro invited the men into his home and passed out drinks all around, toasting them heartily for a job well done. They made no move to offer anything, not even water, to the prisoners.

The posse arrived in Tain with the setting sun. When they reached the tolbooth, a local doctor was called in and the prisoners' wounds were finally cleaned and dressed. Then they were locked up. Gillanders arrived in time to witness it all. He congratulated Taylor and the two superintendents. Then he took all the men to the inn next door for food and drink.

The lawyer showed Gillanders his empty pouch. "All the writs have been delivered. You can start preparin'

Greenyards for the sheepmen."

In Strath Carron, the clan carried twenty-one wounded women off the field in blankets or litters. But this wasn't the total number of wounded. It didn't include the four injured prisoners, or the many others who, like Donald MacNair, had struggled home under their own power or with assistance.

The twenty-one severely injured villagers were taken to the little schoolhouse. Angus Mackay had set up a first-aid station there. He recruited and organized a small cadre of volunteers and soon had the situation under control. A cheery fire was lit to ward off the cold. The villagers brought in fresh water for drinking and to cleanse the wounds. Bleeding was staunched with compression. Lacerations were bound with strips of cloth held in place by heather ties. Moonshine whisky was administered as an anesthetic and a stimulant.

Mackay sent a messenger galloping to Tain to request immediate medical help. Two doctors arrived by late afternoon. They treated and released those well enough to be cared for at home and made arrangements for transport to the Tain Infirmary of those needing additional care. They extracted numerous black painted splinters of ash wood from the scalp wounds of many of the women. Both doctors, but especially Dr. Gordon, made careful and detailed notes of the nature and types of injuries they discovered. These notes would be important evidence in the subsequent investigation of the mayhem and killings. Some women had hobnail-boot marks on their chests, backs and legs where they'd been stood upon or stomped on by the deputies. Dr. Gordon drew detailed anatomical pictures of these. Many women had missing or torn clothing.

The old widow, Margaret Macgregor Ross, had slipped into a coma. With his finger, Dr. Gordon felt the 'step-off' sign of a depressed skull fracture beneath her deep scalp wound. Too ill to move, she was left in the schoolhouse for her children and friends to comfort and weep over. She died two days later without regaining consciousness.

Another woman, Janet Macpherson of Greenyards, whose husband was in the army, was unable to move her arms or legs. Dr. Gordon diagnosed complete paralysis from a broken neck. Her breathing became labored and raspy. The next day she spiked a high fever, and by the following morning she was dead.

Davey Macdonald was still missing and presumed drowned. But his body hadn't washed up along the river bank or been found drifting in the Kyle of Sutherland.

In Tain, James Gillanders discreetly slipped Deputy Sheriff Taylor a fat payment for his loyalty and zeal in finally getting the writs delivered. It had been a trying month for the factor. But he thought the lord would be pleased with the final results. Greenyards would soon join the rest of Ross Shire as a land completely empty of people.

Chapter Thirty

By the next morning, the rain had ceased, but the ground on the meadow by the river was still soggy. It squished underfoot. Bits of clothing, lengths of broken batons, and pieces of human scalp were scattered across the grass from the road to the riverbank. Wild dogs licked at puddles of congealed blood and fought over bits of flesh.

When Ian awoke, he hurt everywhere. But despite the pain, he felt more alive, more hopeful and filled with a greater sense of relief than he'd known in months. His personal dilemma was finally over, his own crisis resolved. He'd discovered what really mattered to him, what he truly wanted—a life with Catherine and Finn. Now that the fog of indecision had lifted, he could go after it.

He'd spent the night with the other injured villagers in the little schoolhouse. Reverend Mackay and Dr. Gordon had washed and bandaged the large gaping gash over his left eye, repaired the missing piece of scalp, and fashioned a sling for his broken collarbone. Wounded and weary, Ian assisted with those more severely hurt.

After a few hours sleep and a meager, but gratefully-accepted breakfast of scones and milk brought by one of the villagers, he left the schoolhouse to look for Catherine. Stopping at his apartment in Ardgay long enough to change into civilian clothes, he set out for Tain on horseback. It was a bruising and painful ride.

Deputy Sheriff Taylor greeted him with outright hostility at his office in the tolbooth. "Macgregor, you're through. You'll never work as a peace officer around here again. Some of the men even want to see you charged with obstruction of justice. Or maybe dereliction of duty. What do you think of that?"

Ian remained silent.

Taylor kept him standing while he spoke, stabbing the air with his baton for emphasis. "What about that badge of yours? And your oath? Don't they count for anything with you?"

"Lawmakers should not be lawbreakers." Though seething inwardly, Ian spoke calmly, looking Taylor straight in the eyes. "I took an oath to protect and serve the people. Not to assault them. As far as I could tell, I was the only one on that field yesterday who tried to carry out his oath."

Taylor scoffed and dismissed the answer with a wave of his hand. "I've advised Sheriff Mackenzie what to do with you. He said your faithful past service should count for something. So I'm not goin' to charge you. But you've got two days to clear out your desk at Ardgay. And you'll get a week's severance pay. Be thankful you're not behind bars yourself. Now, get out."

Ian didn't move. "One question, sir. Has the Macdonald boy turned up yet?"

"No, not that I've heard. I've got men in row boats dredging the Kyle and others scouring the riverbank. But nothing so far. Most likely he's dead and his body washed out to sea."

Don't count on it, Ian thought. *That boy's a survivor.*

Taylor went on. "I've gathered more evidence about his crimes. I aim to charge him—*in absentia,* if necessary—for assaultin' the Howards yesterday and threatenin' Dugald MacCaig with a gun last week." He looked at Ian and cocked his head to one side. "And then there's the matter of that suspicious fire. Sam Howard's convinced it was the Macdonald boy who started it. I have still got the moonshiner's flask. If I can prove the boy used it, I'll charge him with arson as well."

Ian shook his head. "If he's dead, why not let him rest in peace?"

Taylor slapped the desk. "It's the principle of the thing. I aim to enforce the law. Alive or dead."

Ian placed his folded uniform, baton, and badge on the desk. "May I see the prisoners?" he asked.

"Help yourself," Taylor said brusquely, then turned back to his paperwork.

Catherine's first night in jail had been a hard one, her sleep cold and fretful. She awoke aching all over, depressed about what she'd seen yesterday, and worried about Ian and Finn. Relief surged through her when Angus Mackay had arrived with hairbrushes, soap, hand mirrors, and fresh clothes for everyone. He'd also brought news.

"Have no worry about Finn," Mackay had assured her. "He's staying with one of your neighbors. I looked in on him, told him you were all right, and promised he'd be seeing you soon."

She'd stuck her hands through the bars and squeezed his. "And Ian Macgregor?" she asked hopefully. "What have you heard about him?"

Mackay had smiled. "Banged up, but recovering. I suspect he'll find some way to get to you today. But from the talk I've heard, he's none too popular with the other deputies right now."

Everyone had been greatly saddened to hear about the serious injuries to Margaret Macgregor Ross and Helen MacIntyre. And shocked Davey Macdonald was missing and presumed drowned.

"I'm working to get you released on bail," Mackay told them. "I'll be heading to Inverness tonight to plead your case before the Lord Justice-Clerk himself."

Before he left, the minister promised to have some personal messages the prisoners had written delivered to their families. "I'll try to return tomorrow. Hopefully with good news for you."

After Angus had gone, Catherine gathered her courage for a look in the mirror. She gasped! What a mess! Her hair was disheveled and matted with blood, dirt, and bits of grass. Her scalp was swathed in a bandage which crossed above her eyes, wrapped around her head, and tied at the back. Both eyes were swollen and black. *I look like a raccoon,* she thought. Her face was scratched, her lips puffy and cut.

She reached into her pocket. It was still there, her mother's comb. She pulled it out and stared at it.

At that moment, Ian arrived.

When she first spied him, she recoiled and turned away, hiding her face in her hands, moving into the shadows at the back of the cell. Her four cellmates came forward, patted Ian on the back, and thanked him for his actions yesterday. Then they moved away and stared at Catherine.

"Cath," Ian said softly, "come on, lass. It's all right. Come over here."

"Oh, Ian," she said from the shadows, "I can't bear for you to see me like this."

"Don't worry," he coaxed. "I'm not such a pretty sight myself!"

She looked up slowly. He *was* a mess too! His head was covered with bandages, his eyes swollen and black like hers, and he had one arm in a sling. He looked so pathetic it was almost funny. She took her hands off her face and ran to him.

They embraced as well as they could through the cell door, occasionally grimacing in pain when one of them bumped an injury.

"Och, my love," Ian sighed, caressing her face. "I thought for a minute they'd killed you. But when I saw you being led away, I knew you'd be all right."

"I will."

They held each other in silence for a long time. "I've been let go," he said. "Fired. I've turned in my uniform and badge. It's all over for me here." He shrugged. "Not that it matters much anymore. I could never work with these men again after what they did yesterday."

He lifted her chin and looked deeply into her eyes. "I

don't know how I'll support you and Finn now, but if you'll have me, I want you for my wife. We'll face the future—whatever it holds—together."

She put her arms through the bars and wrapped them around his neck. "Aye. The three of us—you, me and Finn—partners against the world."

Her cellmates clapped at the marriage proposal and its acceptance. Anne Ross lifted her skirt and did a little jig. She looked a sight in her bandages and torn clothing, but her joy was real. The others cheered and applauded her efforts.

Catherine held Ian's arm. "Why don't you move into my house until I find out what's going to happen to me?"

"I will. And look after Finn."

She forced a smile. "Thank you."

"I'll be back tomorrow," he promised, "with more clothes and whatever personal items I can find for you in Ardgay."

He reached to kiss her, but banged his head on the bars. They both laughed then looked at each other, their eyes moist.

Late the next day, Ian and Finn, along with Christy Ross, Dr. Gordon, and Angus Mackay, arrived at the tolbooth. They were accompanied by the bailiff. The minister who had ridden all night from Inverness looked weary, but was smiling.

Mackay held up an official-looking piece of paper. "You've been released, all of you. As soon as the doctor cleans and re-bandages your wounds, you can go. I've posted a bond for your bail."

Within the hour, they were all released and headed back to Greenyards.

On the way home, they passed Jenny Munro, a young woman they all knew and whose husband had gone off to war a year earlier. She had three little children and was leading a horse pulling a cart piled high with her possessions. She stopped briefly to speak with them.

"I've had enough of the Highlands," she said. "I'm going to Glasgow. Maybe I can find work and shelter there, at least 'til my husband returns." She looked back down the road and nodded in the direction of the village. "They've already started tearing down my house." She wept. "God, how we loved that house." She wiped her eyes, blew her nose, and waved goodbye.

As they neared Greenyards, they met more departing villagers, displaced persons evicted from where they'd been born and thought they would be buried. Displaced by a man they'd never met—the lord—and against whom they'd never given offense.

Catherine hugged or stroked or patted the back of each of the refugees, her former neighbors, spoke brief words in hushed Gaelic to them, then sent them on their way. Sad figures coming from somewhere, on their way to anywhere.

That evening, while Ian amused Finn with a wooden toy he'd fashioned, Catherine strolled down to the river, tucked her skirt under her hips, and sat on a rocky outcrop. The waxing, gibbous moon glistened off the Carron, the melodious sound of its rushing water a balm to her troubled heart.

An owl passed above her, its call breaking her reverie.

She stared into the foamy water. An image of David's face appeared. "Och, my love," she whispered, "I must let ye go. For I have met another—Ian, he is called—and he has won my heart."

Water puddled in the corners of her eyes.

"He is a good man, David. I am certain if ye knew him, ye'd find him a fast friend. And he is good to me and to Finn."

She sighed, turned her head, and looked at white water swirling around a tree branch wedged between two rocks. The river pushed insistently at the limb, and for a time the woody obstruction held firm, defying the water's will. But the Carron would not be denied, and with a groan the branch finally released its grip on the rocks and was swept away.

Catherine uttered a soft cry, then spoke again to David. "But Ian canna replace ye. No one can. Ye were my first and love, and will always have a place in my heart. And I will see that Finn never forgets ye."

She captured on her fingertips some of the tears tracing unckecked down her cheeks, dipped her hand into the river, and allowed the cool water to carry off the tears, finally releasing her love for David.

She stood, wiped her face with the hem of her skirt, and headed back to the house. The owl returned over her head. This time she answered its hoot with a joyous laugh.

A week later, on a bright, blue sunshiny day, Catherine and Ian were wed. A gentle zephyr wafted in from the Kyle. Angus Mackay performed the ceremony in a meadow next to the little schoolhouse on the banks of the Carron. Catherine collected a handful of wildflowers blooming on the hillsides of Bodach Mor for her bridal bouquet.

The whole village turned out, except those in hospital, those still missing—like Davey Macdonald—and those already cleared out. Many arrived in bandages and splints or on crutches. But they hobbled along anyway, glad for a day of joy to make up for so many days of sadness. Old Pete sang the wedding songs in Gaelic.

After the ceremony, the bride threw her bouquet into the river. The crowd watched in silence. The current swept it away, just like their own lives were being swept away by a current of change they didn't understand and were powerless to resist. A fiddler and a piper broke into a reel. Those who could, danced and sang the old songs together one last time.

When the party was over and all the guests departed, Ian, Finn and Catherine sat on chairs by the front door of their house and watched the last of the sun's glow disappear below the western horizon. When the first star appeared in the sky, Ian told Finn a bedtime story, tucked him in, and went back to his bride, still sitting outside.

"Well, what now, wife?" he asked, smiling.

"Hello, husband." Her face radiated affection in the twilight.

"How are ye feelin'?" He worried she might not be physically up to their wedding night.

She stared distantly at the horizon and answered, "Equal parts sadness and joy."

He nodded. "I understand. Me too."

They held hands in the silence as the evening slowly laid itself out above them.

Finally standing, she whispered, "Give me a moment."

When she called to him, he went to her bedroom. She awaited him there in a thin, lacey gown, a gift from Aunt Christy. A shaft of moonlight from the window bathed her in an ethereal, luminous glow. The gown, tented by her breasts, flowed over perfectly curved hips, clinging like a vine to her legs all the way to the floor.

Ian stood transfixed.

When he finally lifted his gaze, he saw she'd arranged her hair to partially cover the right side of her face. A sudden puff of wind from the open window billowed the rich dark tresses over one eye before they nestled back against her cheek again. Her dark green eyes were luminous, her full lips, accentuated by moonglow, glistened with anticipation.

She held his gaze for a long moment, then opened her mouth, "Husband?"

"I canna lie," he said, moving to her. "I've been waitin' for this a long while."

"And wonderin'?"

He looked at her with those handsome eyes, darkened in a way she'd never seen before. "Yes. And wonderin'. But I don't want to rush it."

"It's been a long time for me," she murmured.

"For both of us." His mouth sought out the birth-mark on her neck. When he bit it gently, she moaned and grabbed two handfuls of his hair and pulled hard.

He yelped, lifted her off her feet, and carried her to the bed, kissing her, searching hidden places as she offered them.

Later, she felt the musk of him, the sweat and passion fading. They could hear Finn's regular breathing in the next room.

"Your first husband," he said, "do you still think of him?" The question came out as something pent up for a long time and begging to be answered.

"He was a good man." Her fingertips traced a line down his chest. "Losing him was not like a divorce...or from some sickness. Our marriage was still growing, still developing. Two people getting closer."

She exhaled slowly. "But time does heal, Ian. It really does. The bed stays empty, but you smell his clothing, tryin' to smell him before dropping off to sleep. But even that fades, replaced with nothing. Just emptiness."

She stroked his cheek. "Until you came along"

"Was it all right? I mean what we did. Was I—"

She put a finger to his lips. Images of those erotic drawings in Dingwall ignited her. She pulled his head down to her breasts and reached for his manhood.

"Ye make me lose all sense of shame, husband," she whispered.

The next morning, Finn noticed Ian was still there for breakfast. He didn't ask what it meant. It seemed completely natural to him, the way things ought to be. He was glad for it.

On Friday, May 15, messengers-in-arms accompanied by two sheriff officers were dispatched from Tain to Greenyards with warrants of arrest for three villagers—John Ross, Catherine Ross and Anne Ross.

They were taken before a Tain magistrate and charged with obstruction of justice. For Catherine, charges of rioting and inciting to riot were added as well. They entered their pleas—not guilty on all counts—and were released on bail pending trial.

Davey Macdonald, his body still not recovered, was charged with armed rioting and arson *in absentia*. His mother, dressed in black, stood weeping before the bar of justice while the charges against him were read.

Deputy Sheriff Taylor stood next to her, smiling smugly.

Chapter Thirty-one

While awaiting trial, Catherine and Ian lived as normally as possible given the circumstances. They planned for the future they thought would be coming. She tried to sell her furnishings and dragged them onto the grass by the front door. But most of her neighbors, soon to be cleared themselves, had no need for—nor the funds to buy—any of them. They'd only have to pay to ship the items later themselves. Ian finally loaded a horse cart with the chairs, dressers, beds and tables and hauled them to Ardgay, where he sold them at nearly give-away prices. The house was left with only heather pallets to sleep on and wooden boxes to sit upon and eat from.

Finn thought it a grand adventure, like camping out.

The oats stored in the shed from last year's harvest Catherine turned into as many bannocks as she could. None of them went for whisky. The two chickens she had left became stews, carefully portioned out at their evening meals. Along with a few root vegetables Ian had picked up in Ardgay, their repasts were frugal.

As she prepared supper one evening, she glanced out her window as she worked. The sun had just set, and the sky was a pallet of dark colors ranging from baby blue near the horizon, through the twilight colors of azure and ultramarine at higher elevations, with inky navy blue dominating the view overhead.

She shifted her gaze to the vegetable garden and spied the green tops of carrots, turnips, onions and kale pushing up through the ground, omens of a good crop to come. But not for her. Families headed out of the strath, their possessions stacked in carts or carried on their backs, some prodding reluctant cattle ahead of them.

Gillanders' workmen noisily pulled down the houses as soon as they were emptied, leaving only piles of rock and rubble where families had once lived.

Her concentration was abruptly broken by an insisttent call from Ian. "Cath! Come out here. Hurry!"

Alarmed, she stopped what she was doing and rushed out the door. She found him waiting near the shed, his arm on Finn's shoulder.

The boy was transfixed, staring open-mouthed. "Wow!" he whispered over and over.

"What is it?" she asked. "What's the matter?"

"Look." Ian pointed to the northern horizon.

She followed his gaze and saw a shimmering curtain of light, a dancing apparition of pale yellows, magentas, pinks and blues spread out across the evening sky.

"The northern lights!" she cried.

He grinned. "Aye, the *aurora borealis.*"

Finn looked up at him, puzzled.

He patted the boy's shoulder. "Never mind, lad. Northern lights will do just fine."

They stood there, side by side, the three of them, her arm around Ian's waist, her head on his shoulder.

"Never seen 'em so...so..." She groped for the right word.

"Dazzling?"

"Aye. Never seen 'em so dazzling."

They lingered an hour more, watching the celestial light show.

Catherine looked at her new husband. "Ian, have you given any thought to what we might do when all this is over?"

"Aye, I have. There'll be no land for us anywhere in the Highlands, that's for certain. We could move to the coast and try our hand as fishermen—

"I don't like fish," Finn interjected.

Ian grinned at the boy. "A bit of herring now and then is fine. But I'm with you lad, a steady diet of it would not be to my liking. Besides..."

Catherine waited. "Besides what?"

"I canna swim."

She laughed. "Nor can I. I guess that settles that. We'll never be fishermen."

"I have another idea." He hesitated. "I could join the army." When she started to protest, he continued quickly, "Hear me out. They're recruiting for the 78th Regiment right now. And paying good bonuses for joining up. I could set you and Finn up in an apartment in Tain before I go. I've saved some money, and we'll get something from Gillanders for leaving and from the sale of the animals. I'll send you my army pay every month. You and Finn should get along fine."

Her stomach knotted, and a cold hand of fear settled upon her back. She grabbed his hand. "I'll not risk losing another husband"—she glanced at Finn—"or Finn another father. Promise me you'll not go asoldiering?"

He backed off. "Easy, lass, I hear ye. I'll nae do it. It was only a suggestion. I didn't realize you'd be so dead set against it."

She relaxed. "We could try our luck in Edinburgh or Glasgow. I'm handy with a needle and thread. Maybe I can get work in one of the new clothes factories."

"Aye, and maybe I could find a constable's job there." He lightly tapped Finn's shoulder for emphasis. "That's it then, we'll head for Glasgow."

The next morning, in the thin sunshine of an early dawn, Catherine, Ian and Finn met Angus Mackay in his carriage by the roadside. He'd agreed to drive them to the Dingwall courthouse, where Catherine would learn her fate. They were joined by John, Christy, and Margaret Ross in their own cart. They all headed out at a brisk trot for the long ride ahead.

Catherine looked back at the village. Only a few houses still stood. Gillanders' agent had agreed to let her and her uncle remain until their court cases were decided.

Unlike the make-shift courtroom in Tain, the one in Dingwall was a right proper one, with a high-beamed ceiling, paneled walls, and a raised judge's bench which towered over the spectators. The Greenyards' villagers filed in, cowed by the awesome majesty of the room.

Sheriff Mackenzie, Deputy Sheriff Taylor, and James Gillanders were seated in the front row with other landowners. Taylor shot Ian a hostile look, but said nothing.

With three tremendous thumps of his staff echoing off the walls, the bailiff called the room to order. Lord Justice-Clerk Michael Hope entered, dressed in a magnificent white wig, which reached to his shoulders, and drapes of black robes that touched the floor. He climbed the stairs to his bench, banged the gavel firmly, and motioned for all to be seated.

Justice Hope glanced over half-spectacles and shuffled papers in front of him. "Let's begin," he announced.

The trial itself was a sham, lasting barely half a day. The Queen's Prosecutor paraded Deputy Sheriff Taylor, the two superintendents, and half a dozen constables as witnesses for the government's case.

The villagers had no money for a competent lawyer to defend them, and the court-appointed barrister could find no way to refute the charges. When it was over, the defendants were found guilty as charged on all counts.

Clearing his throat, Justice Hope commanded, "John Ross of Greenyards and Anne Ross, also of Greenyards, step forward."

The two walked resolutely down the aisle and stopped before the bench. They craned their necks up to look at him.

"You have both been found guilty of the crime of disturbing the peace. This is a serious crime and must be punished accordingly. Both of you are sentenced, therefore, to the maximum—a fine of 50 pounds or six months in jail." He slammed down the gavel.

The two defendants looked dazed. Neither offered resistance nor word of protest when the bailiff led them out. Their friends and families in the back, however, howled in anger. Anne's children called for their mother. Christy Ross, still bandaged, stood up and shouted something in Gaelic.

Lord Justice Hope gaveled for quiet.

"Catherine Ross," he called out next. "Come before the bar."

Catherine adjusted her clothing, brushed a hand through her hair, and, in as dignified a manner as she could muster, walked to the bench and stared up at the judge.

"You, Catherine Ross, have been found guilty of the additional crime of obstruction of justice. You are the leader of the rioters in Strath Carron. On your shoulders, therefore, must fall the greater punishment. You are sentenced to eighteen months at hard labor in the Tain Tolbooth or a fine of 100 pounds."

Ian gasped and jumped to his feet. "No, no! There's no way we can come up with that kind of money."

"Quiet." Hope ordered. "Take your seat or I'll have you arrested as well."

Angus Mackay pulled him back down.

The bailiff headed for Catherine, handcuffs at the ready. Hope started to bang down his gavel again. But Angus Mackay stood and loudly demanded to be recognized. The gavel stopped in mid-arc.

"Yes, yes, what is it now? Who are you?" he asked gruffly.

"I am Angus Mackay, minister for the Parish of Kincardine. These villagers are part of my flock. I beg the court at least to give them time to settle their affairs. Time to gather the money for the fines. I'll pledge my own bond for them."

Hope glanced at Gillanders. He received a barely perceptible nod in return.

"Very well. They have five days. I expect them to

have their fines paid by then, or"—he aimed his gavel specifically at Catherine—"present themselves at the tolbooth." He slammed the gavel down one last time. "This court stands adjourned!"

Chapter Thirty-two

Two days later, the three convicted and sentenced Greenyards' villagers, along with their families, crowded into Angus Mackay's study in Kincardine. The mood was glum. The injustice of the sentences imposed by His Lordship Michael Hope pressed on their minds and hearts like unbearable weights. It seemed none of them would avoid jail time.

Catherine scanned the room. "Where's Margaret?" she asked Aunt Christy. They were sitting next to each other near a sideboard table. "I haven't seen her in days."

"She'll be along. Don't worry about her." Christy winked at her husband.

Catherine didn't have time to ask more questions. The minister was beginning to speak.

"Friends, I have good news. With the help of some generous kirk members in Edinburgh, we have found the money for John and Anne's fines. Neither will have to spend even a day in the tolbooth."

Everyone clapped. Christy hugged her husband.

Anne Ross grabbed the minister's hand and pumped it, then impulsively pecked him on the cheek. "God bless ye, sir," she said.

"What will you do now?" the minister asked.

She sighed. "I have an aunt in Dingwall. She's invited me and the children to come stay with her. As soon as I settle accounts with the factor, we'll be on our way there."

"And you, Mr. Ross, what are your plans?"

"I want no part of city livin'," John answered. "I couldn't stand it. Besides, I have no skills this so-called Industrial Revolution has any use for. No, Christy and I will head for the Lowlands. I'm still a good farmer. Maybe I can find work on one of the large estates there."

Then Mackay looked at Catherine. "I'm sorry. But we could not find the amount for your fine. It was just too..." He couldn't finish. He blew his nose into a handkerchief.

Catherine had been staring into her hands. She finally looked up, her eyes flashing fire. "I'll not be persecuted just for standing up to them. For daring to fight an unjust policy. I'll not go to jail for that."

"If you flee, you'll be branded an outlaw," Mackay warned. "You'll be hunted down like a common criminal."

She took Ian's hands. "Do ye understand, husband? I'm not frightened of going to jail. But to give in to them now would make everything I've worked for meaningless." She squeezed his hands tighter. "It wasn't meaningless, was it? We tried to do something here, something important. I'll not degrade the sacrifices we made by agreeing to a further injustice." She searched his eyes. "Are ye with me, husband?"

He pulled her close, put an arm around her shoulders. "Aye. I am with you lass, for better or for worse. If this is what you want, then so do I." He ran a hand through Finn's hair and got a gap-toothed grin in response. "And so does the lad."

"Where will you go?" John asked.

Catherine answered slowly. "We've talked about it. We've decided to head for Canada. My mother and father have begged me to join them there for years. It's time I did. I want them to meet my new husband."

She held out a heavy purse toward the minister. "Mr. Mackay, Ian and I have collected every penny we have. We've sold the animals and some extra barley, and gotten Ian's savings together. It's all here. I know ye've posted a bond for me. This won't nearly cover it, but it's a start. We'll pay ye back every bit of it when we get to Canada."

Mackay hesitated.

"Take it, sir," Ian urged. "It's little enough for all you've done for us. And you'll get the rest, you have our word on it."

Angus' eyes filled with tears. "No, you keep it. You'll need it. You'll have many expenses ahead of you." He blew his nose again. "Besides, it is I who owe you—all of you here. You've opened my eyes. I was lost before, confused. But now I've found my way." He wiped his eyes. "And don't worry about me. This collar I wear and the faith I bear are all I truly need."

John Ross faced his niece and her new husband. "Ye'll have to hurry, and be ever watchful. There'll be a reward on your heads. Anyone could turn ye in."

"We're Highlanders," Catherine boasted. "We'll take to the heather and head through the hills." She squeezed Ian's hand reassuringly. "I know the way, husband. We'll make our way to Fort William and book passage on a ship bound for Nova Scotia."

"Nova Scotia," Ian said ruefully. "'New Scotland. A place settled by displaced Scots."

She squeezed his hand again. "We'll be fine."

Mackay held up his hands for attention. "Now that it's settled, I have another surprise for you." He walked into the bedroom and emerged a few minutes later with Davey Macdonald. The boy looked gaunt and haggard, but otherwise alive and well. Margaret Ross held one of his arms, his mother the other. They led him into the room.

Everyone gasped, then cheered and rushed to envelop the three of them in tearful embraces.

Catherine could only ask, "How in the world...?"

Davey grinned sheepishly. "When I dove into the river, I hit my head on a rock. I must have blacked out for a moment. When I came to, I was near-drowned. But the river had carried me downstream around a bend and out of sight of the men who'd been chasing me."

"That bastard MacCaig." Ian swore.

"Aye. I thought I was done for. But I managed to

grab a tree branch wedged between some rocks. I stayed hidden there until everyone had gone. Then I headed for Angus Macleod's cave. I've been there ever since."

"It's a miracle, for sure," the minister said. His eyes glowed. "The bootlegger told me the next day the boy was safe. I informed his mother immediately. We agreed to keep up the pretense of his death to save him from the authorities. They're still looking for him."

Naomi Macdonald squeezed her son's arm. "It was all I could do to keep my wits about me when he was charged. I wanted to scream out that he was alive and would be here soon to defend himself. But I held my tongue."

"What about the charges against ye?" Catherine asked.

"I considered facing them. To clear my good name. Right up to yesterday I planned to turn myself in. But when I heard what happened to the three of you at Dingwall Courthouse, I knew I'd never get a fair trial." He looked at Catherine. "I have decided to come with you to Canada, if you'll take me. Angus Macleod has given me some money and a horse for the journey to the coast. It'll carry our supplies."

Margaret gripped Davey's arm tighter. "I am coming too." she said defiantly. "We've pledged ourselves to each other. We'll be married as soon as we get to Canada."

Catherine arched an eyebrow and looked at John and Christy Ross.

"She's a grown woman, now," Christy said. "She must follow her own heart. She has our blessings."

Catherine looked at Ian.

He nodded.

"Very well." She turned to the two young lovers. "Ye are both welcome to join us. Be ready to leave the day after tomorrow."

Two days later, right before daybreak so as not to be noticed, a little band of travelers along with a fully-laden garron beside them headed into the west. From a rise in the road, Catherine turned back for one last look at Strath Carron. One last look at her home. She could just make out a flock of Cheviot sheep grazing next to her house, soon to be a pile of charred rubble like most of the others.

When they reached the western end of Strath Carron, it divided into three finger-like ravines, each carrying its own rivulet. Catherine selected Strath Glencalvie, and within a half hour they'd reached the rubble of what had been her father's village. They surveyed the ruined settlement.

Ian started back down toward the main trail.

Catherine stopped him. "This way, husband."

He arched an eyebrow.

"A slight delay. I want ye to see somethin'."

A mile farther up the strath, they came to a clearing in the wind-swept trees. A church nestled within it. A simple grey stone cabin, like so many others built in the Highlands during the past few decades, the kirkyard and cemetery were enclosed by a low stone wall. Two dozen grave markers dotted the yard in random arrangement.

Ian looked at his wife. "What's this about...?"

Without a word, she led the way through a gate in the wall. Margaret hooked her arm through Catherine's.

"This is where it happened," Catherine said. "This place is called Croick. It is where the survivors of the Glencalvie Clearances took shelter...includin' yer new bride and her family."

Ian removed his cap and bowed his head. "I know the story, but never been here...no reason to."

She walked up to one of the windows and pointed. "Come, Ian. See for yerself."

He approached and began to make out scratchings on the panes, writings etched into the glass itself...all in English. He read aloud,

"Glencalvie peoples here, May 24, 1845
John Ross shepherd

The Glencalvie Rosses
Glencalvie people...the wicked generation."
There were many more, but he stopped.

She ran her finger over the writings, feeling for the spirits of those who'd left them. "We used a bit of diamond from someone's ring...held the wee ones up just so they could make a mark." She smiled. "I wrote many of these myself, translatin' from the Gaelic. They wanted a testimonial to their sufferin'...to *our* sufferin'... wanted to leave somethin' to be remembered by..."

She stopped suddenly, catching her breath, unable to go on.

Ian's arms wrapped around her.

With tears in their eyes and hearts in their throats, the travelers turned their backs on the Kirk at Croick and its memories and climbed over the hills into Strath Alladale. They followed the river due west, toward its headland. It gradually diminished to first a brook, then a creek, then a mere trickle, finally disappearing altogether among the rocks and heather. Catherine trudged in silence at the front. Ian, with Finn in hand, followed. Margaret, arm in arm with Davey—who led the garron—brought up the rear.

To conserve their meager funds and escape detection, the little group of displaced citizens avoided the main roads and kept to narrow paths and tracks. At night, their beds consisted of pallets of leaves, with only plaids for covers. They ate scones, berries and an occasional trout Ian managed to pull from a nearby stream. Despite the hardship, they looked forward to the dawn of each new day because it would bring them closer to journey's end.

The lands they passed through were mostly empty of people. They saw only sheep, thousands of Cheviot sheep, a ragged quilt of dirty white rolling across the grassy lands of the eastern and southern Highlands.

From Strath Alladale, the group headed almost due south to Strathglass, former home to generations of

Clan Chisholm but now devoid of most two-legged creatures. They made camp in a shallow cave on a hillside overlooking the river, ate their supper and slept under the stars.

By evening of the next day—their third on the road—they reached Lochaber, where the Glen Garry Highlanders had lived until they were cleared over the thirty-year period from 1785-1817. They camped under a bridge east of the town of Invergarry and awakened to a crimson sunrise.

And to their only real scare.

As they broke camp, a horseman suddenly appeared out of the west. A burly, rough-looking man with a stubbly beard, threatening eyes and a scowling countenance approached them.

Ian stepped out to meet him.

"What are ye doin' here," the man demanded. "I'm factor for the estate of Lord Ranaldson. This is his property." He stabbed his riding crop at their still-smoking campfire. "And so are those trout you've eaten freely of."

Ian answered calmly. "We did not know we were on the lord's property." He took a few coins from his purse and offered them up. "And we'll gladly pay for our breakfast."

The rider ignored the money. "What's your business here?"

"Traveling south," Catherine answered. "Headin' for Fort William. And we meant no harm campin' here."

The horseman studied her for a moment, then barked, "Just be on yer way. If I return and ye're still here..."

"Yes, sir," Ian answered, pocketing his purse. "We'll be gone within the half hour."

The factor nodded, smacked his horse across the rump, and galloped off.

The travelers let out a collective breath, hastened their packing and were soon on their way again.

It took them another day-and-a-half to cover the

fifteen miles to Loch Linne, the finger-like strait of water connecting Fort William to the sea. They followed the loch to the port, where Ian booked passage on the *Hector,* a brig sailing for Nova Scotia in two days.

They sold the garron and treated themselves to a night's rest at a local inn. With bellies full of cooked food for the first time in days, they slept soundly on real mattresses.

They boarded ship the next morning.

When Catherine hadn't reported to the Tain tolbooth by sunset of the last day of Justice Hope's stay of sentence, Deputy Sheriff Taylor immediately executed a warrant for her arrest. Notices were hurriedly printed and nailed to bulletin boards in public houses, inns, courthouses, and other governmental buildings, and sent by messenger to law enforcement offices throughout the Highlands.

Now a wanted criminal, Catherine could never return to Scotland without fear of arrest.

As the *Hector* sailed on the morning's ebb tide, Catherine and her family stood on deck until the ship's bow met the foaming sea and the last glimpse of Scotland disappeared over the horizon. She clutched a sprig of heather to her breast while a piper played a mournful dirge.

Softly, barely audible, she sang the words of an old Gaelic lament:

"Cha till, Cha till, Cha till—mi tuille!"
We return, we return, we return—never more!

Liquid pooled along her eyelids and lined down her cheeks. She captured the tears on the backs of her fingers and cast them, and the heather, into the water. Turning her back on the Old World, she faced her family and gazed hopefully toward the New.

Epilogue

The crackle of a sycamore log in the fireplace startled Catherine out of her reverie, from her mental journey back to the Highlands and how that cruel day by the River Carron had come to be. She jumped when one of the logs hissed, spit and snapped. A smile curved her lips. She was still not used to the way real wood burned, so unlike the soundless peat fires back in Scotland.

The voyage on the *Hector* had been long and fraught with sea sickness, brackish water, weevily bread and stringy meat. They disembarked wearily at Pictou on the north shore of Nova Scotia—New Scotland—and barely had time to regain their land legs before they were off again, this time aboard a coastal schooner heading north along the maritimes into Hudson's Bay. When the ship stopped at York Factory long enough to discharge its cargo and passengers, Catherine and her family left the sea for good.

"Are we there now?" Finn asked.

"No, son," Catherine answered patiently. "We still have a ways to go, and ye must be strong."

The travelers indeed had another three full weeks ahead of them: first, down the mighty Nelson River by canoe into Lake Winnipeg; then south across the lake by flatboat into the Red River; finally down the Red in canoes again. Along the way, they'd seen the topography of their new country change dramatically—from rugged hills and forests of fir, pine and spruce; through valleys as green and lush as any Highland strath; to rolling prairies which seemed to go on forever.

Exhausted but full of faith in their future, the little band from Greenyards finally reached Fort Garry near the junction of the Red and Assiniboine Rivers. There Catherine reunited in a teary but joyful celebration with her mother, father and two brothers. And there she introduced them to her new husband.

They'd reached the end of their journey. They'd come to their new home.

Their first year in Canada had been hard. Winter was upon them before they knew it. Everyone in the community—neighbors as well as family—had pitched in to build the new arrivals a sod house for temporary shelter. The following spring, Ian picked out some farmland on the edge of the settlement, cleared it, and planted their first crop. Then he built Catherine a proper house of wood, with a porch, and with oil lamps instead of candles for light.

They grew potatoes, turnips, carrots, and corn in a garden by the side of the house. But their principal cash crop was wheat. Catherine turned some of it into bread. But it wasn't like making scones and bannocks out of oats; it took some getting used to.

Ian snored softly in the bedroom. He'd turned into quite a good farmer, despite his earlier misgivings. Finn, now eleven and a strapping lad, was a great helpmate to his da and playmate for James, his four-year old brother. The wounds of the past had healed. Catherine was happy and fulfilled, and indulged herself in a contentment she'd long denied.

Davey Macdonald and Margaret Ross lived with them that first year, even after their wedding. Both only seventeen, Catherine had doubts about marriage at such a tender age. But in the end, considering what they'd already been through, she felt she couldn't refuse them. Ian gave the bride away in a simple ceremony on the banks of the Red River. Catherine's tears had been as much for Margaret's happiness as a remembrance of her own ceremony along a different river thousands of miles and another life away.

The young couple set out to make a home of their

own. With Ian's help, Davey put up a small house and cleared forty acres of farmland. But he didn't plant wheat. He grew corn. Putting to good use the experience he'd gleaned from watching and working with Angus Macleod, he fashioned a crude still and soon produced the best corn whisky in the territory. Guides hauled it to the forts and trading posts up and down the Red and Nelson rivers.

Catherine stirred the fire and returned to the letter she was reading, a letter from Minister Angus Mackay. The two of them communicated once or twice a year:

"Dear Catherine,

"Much has happened here in the Highlands since I last wrote. The trickle of anti-landlord sentiment which was just getting started before you left has become a torrent. Hardly a week goes by that some letter or sermon doesn't appear in one of the newspapers, or some new pamphlet is published railing against the clearances.

"I firmly believe that the awful incident along the Carron five years ago—and your determined resistance which brought the matter to a head—was the impetus for much-needed changes here. You should be very proud of what you accomplished. There have been no further large-scale clearances since then. I am only sorry you aren't here to witness the results in person.

"As for myself, I have left the manse at Kincardine and accepted a position with a parish near Inverness. I am very pleased with it and get to play golf much more often now (you can imagine how I like that!). I have also been very active in the Society for the Protection of the Poor. We find shelter, food, and clothing for displaced Highlanders and other unfortunates."

Catherine made herself another cup of tea, then returned to Mackay's letter.

"Here's news of some of your old friends and neighbors (and a few adversaries) from Greenyards.

"John and Christy Ross live in Edinburgh. But you probably know that, since they're kin to you. John gave up farmwork a couple of years ago and now works in a factory. Whenever I visit them, we reminisce about our days in the Highlands.

"Old Pete Ross died last month. I guess Clan Ross has little need for a bard any longer.

"James Gillanders has been the subject of much revilement in the newspapers and sermons. He mostly keeps to his home at Highfield Cottage.

"Alexander Munro is hardly ever seen away from Braelangwell. He's recently remarried, to a younger woman, I hear.

"Donald MacNair, the Waterloo veteran, is in the Old Soldier's Home here in Inverness. I stop by to see him whenever I can.

"Sheriff Mackenzie retired from active law enforcement and is living out his years near Dingwall. I have seen him once or twice. He told me he regrets he didn't do more to prevent the brutality of that posse. He said he should have led it himself.

"William Taylor is the new Ross Shire sheriff. But his overly-aggressive enforcement of the law has been tempered. Revelations about his cozy relationship with Gillanders and the landlords have kept him in the glare of public scrutiny.

"I visited Strath Carron last week, just for old time's sake. There's nothing there but sheep now, sheep everywhere. I stopped at the field by the river where that terrible onslaught took place. The grass is grown high, and the meadow itself is fenced off from the road. It looks so peaceful you would never imagine the awful things that took place there five years ago.

"I have one other incident to tell you about. Some government agents were in my kirk in Inverness last week. They'd spent all summer in the Highlands trying to recruit lads for the army and stopped by to see me after Sunday services.

"'Where are the Highlanders?' they moaned. 'We've

been up and down the glens and straths and there are no clansmen left. No stout lads for our armies in Europe, no pipers to lead them into battle with tunes of glory, no Highland Regiments to defend us.'

"I sat them down and lectured them on how the Highlands, with the Queen's blessing or tacit approval, had been depopulated by greedy landowners eager to make money from sheep.

"As you can imagine, they were none too happy with my cheekiness. They said they'd pass the message on to their higher ups. It would have been rather amusing, were it not so poignant.

"That's all for now. I have enclosed a recent copy of the *Inverness Courier*. You might turn to the obituaries. There's an interesting item there.

"My best to Ian, the boys, and the rest of the family.

"Affectionately, Angus."

Catherine leafed through the newspaper, then turned to the obituaries. There were six items. One was about an excise officer named Dugald MacCaig who'd been murdered in a brawl at an Inverness tavern.

"The killer or killers are still at large," it noted.

She put down the newspaper and went to bed, snuggling up against Ian. At peace finally, with the world and with herself, she drifted off into a contented sleep and dreamt about her home in the Highlands.

A Historical Note

The above story—based on actual events and real characters—is typical of the little known chapter in British history called the Highland Clearances. Beginning in the late 18th century and peaking in the mid-19th, these mass evictions emptied the Highlands of people and replaced them with sheep. The 'white plague,' the fleeced creatures were called, or the 'four-footed' clansmen.

Scattered like barleycorn on the winds of change, many Highlanders made the sad journey to Edinburgh and Glasgow. There they sought unfamiliar work in the textile mills of the Industrial Revolution, living desperate lives in the crowded housing of the cities' growing slums. Others were put aboard ships, sometimes at the point of bayonet, bound for Canada, New Zealand or the Carolina coast of America, where today Scottish surnames are mute testimony to their history.

Sir Walter Scott, in his book, *Manners, Customs and History of the Highlanders of Scotland*, wrote of the Highland Clearances as follows:

"...the glens of the Highlands have been drained, not of the superfluity of population, but of the whole mass of inhabitants, dispossessed by an un-relenting avarice, which will one day be found to have been as shortsighted as it was unjust and selfish."

Scott was right, of course, but only to a point. Not all the population loss from the Highlands can be blamed on the clearances. Many clansmen left simply because their increasing numbers had outgrown the capability of the land to sustain them, even at the subsistence level they'd always known. There were also many who doubtless thought they would find greener pastures in the cities of the Lowlands or the colonies of North America.

By 1854, the clearances were over for the most part. Although individual evictions continued here and there, the wholesale emptying of the glens had come to a halt. This was partly because the Highlands had been substantially emptied already. During the hundred years from 1786-1886, over 100,000 clansmen were forced from their straths and glens. Many emigrated to the new world. But there's no way of knowing how many left the Highlands yet remained in Scotland, although the populations of Glasgow and Edinburgh were doubtless swelled by their numbers.

A second reason the clearances abated was the same one that started them: the laws of economics. The import into Britain of cheap foreign wool caused prices to plummet. This made Highland sheep farming after 1870 much less profitable. Evictions after this date were mostly by landlords wishing to turn their estates into sporting lodges for the well-to-do. But even this was resisted by a growing tide of anti-eviction sentiment and actions. The goal of these reformers was not only to prevent further clearances, but to protect the crofters who remained from other injustices, such as exorbitant rents.

By the 1880s, the crofters themselves had become emboldened to action. Taking their cue from working-class trade unions in the Lowland cities and England, they banded together to form Land Leagues, which organized strikes to protest unfair rents and evictions. In some cases, the Leaguers even raided the sporting estates and seized land back from the owners. Some of the confrontations were violent, and this period is known as the 'crofters' war.' In 1883, on the Isle of Skye, the violence reached the level of a pitched brawl—called the 'Battle of the Braes' by historians—between crofters and gunboats full of soldiers.

That same year, 1883, the Government finally acted. A Royal Commission headed by Lord Napier was appointed to investigate the crofters' plight. The Commissioners came to the Highlands, conducted interviews, and saw for themselves the disastrous results of a century of 'improvements.' They submitted their final report in 1884, which recommended a series of land reforms. But Parliament dragged its feet; not a single recommendation was enacted into law that year.

However, the tide against the landlords was now at full flood. The crofters were finally gaining some political power. In 1884, the Third Reform Act gave crofters the vote, along with three seats in Parliament. Two years later came the Crofters' Holding Act. This finally gave them tenure on the land, fixed their rents at reasonable levels, and created a Crofters Commission to oversee its provisions.

Some of the social and economic forces which brought on, and finally ended, the Highland Clearances operated entirely at the local level. The collapse of the clan system and its lord/tacksman/tenant farmer relationships was merely the bitter end of the Highlands' unique version of feudalism. Into that vacuum poured the power of the Industrial Revolution. But the collapse was not only an economic one. The disruption of clan traditions and customs, which had held the Highlands together for centuries, now worked to transform it socially and politically as well. The loss of clan integrity, plus the pro-landlord position of the High Kirk of Scotland, also explains why there was such little organized resistance to the clearances until much later.

Other changes in the Highlands were symptoms of more globally occurring events. The American and French Revolutions at the end of the eighteenth century, and the rise of liberalism in Britain in the early nineteenth, defined the rights of the individual *vis-a-vis* the state. These upheavals left the Highlands initially untouched. But when the crofters were finally enfranchised, there was a receptive political soil in which reform could take root, although the reactionary power of the landlords, the state, and the church—individually or combined symbiotically—did much to delay the growth of these nascent reforms. It wasn't until the three institutions had been separated and separately reformed that full political change finally came to the Highlands.

Other forces for change were the urban reform movements of the mid- and late nineteenth century. They were guided by the spirit and ideology of Romanticism. All sought to correct the excesses of the Industrial Revolution. In literature, Romanticism was typified by the works of Dickens and Hugo, with their descriptions of the plight of the downtrodden heroes Oliver Twist and Jean Valjean. In social reform, Romanticism was evident in laws which restricted child labor, improved working conditions in mills and factories—including health care for those injured on the job—and put into place public health measures for clean drinking water, sewage disposal, and the control of epidemics.

Scotland's loss was the world's gain. The clansmen who left the Highlands brought their values of hard work, thriftiness, and steadfast loyalty to their homes in North America, New Zealand and Australia, to name but a few places where Highland names are common today. Often rising to positions of respect and influence, they contributed vitality, wit and wisdom to their new countries, though in Canada not all their influence was favorable.

The North West Company, rivals to Hudson's Bay Company, was led by Highlanders. Their alliance with the Métis Indians at the massacre of Red River settlers at Seven Oaks remains a stain on Highland honor.

Furthermore, aggressive Highland whisky makers contributed to alcohol abuse by Indians and others on the plains. Some trading posts in the bush country—along Lake Winnipeg and the Nelson River, for example—sold so much liquor they became known as 'whisky forts.'

All in all, however, the Highland contribution was a positive one. In 1867 Canada became a Dominion. Three years later Manitoba became a province and Catherine Ross' settlement on the Red River was incorporated into the city of Winnipeg; it was, in many ways, more Scottish than Scotland itself. This was the sweetest revenge of all for the Highlanders. Whatever Canada had become, they had made it themselves. And that was worth more to them than all the haggis and black pudding in the Highlands.

About the Author

Chris Holmes is an epidemiologist whose medical career spans pediatric practice, academic preventive medicine, and U.S. Navy Medical Service. He holds a B.A. in History from the University of California, Riverside; an M.D. from the University of Cincinnati; and an M.Sc. in Public Health from the University of Utah. He has authored fifteen professional articles in peer-reviewed journals on topics as diverse as pediatrics, occupational medicine, biomedical ethics, and the history of medicine. He was a consultant for the 19th Edition of *Taber's Cyclopedic Medical Dictionary*, and has served as a reviewer for several professional journals.

Chris' four published books are: *The Medusa Strain*, a *Foreword Magazine* finalist for best mystery of 2002 and a gripping novel of bioterrorism; *Spores, Plagues and History: The Story of Anthrax*, a non-fiction work which traces anthrax epidemics and bioterrorism from the time of Moses to Saddam Hussein. It has been favorably reviewed in the *Lancet, The British Medical Journal, The Journal of Emergency Medicine, The Bulletin of the History of Medicine* and the *FBI Law Enforcement Bulletin; The Garden of Evil*, a novel highlighting the threat of food-borne terrorism; and *Blood on the Tartan*, his first historical romance.

Chris lives in Escondido, California with his wife and two dogs. He is an avid gardener and enjoys playing contract bridge, working jigsaw puzzles, long-distance running, and spoiling his four granddaughters.

His website can be accessed at:
www.chrisholmesmd.com

Also Available from Highland Press

Leanne Burroughs
Highland Wishes
Leanne Burroughs
Her Highland Rogue
Jannine Corti Petska
Rebel Heart
Cynthia Owens
In Sunshine or In Shadow
Isabel Mere
Almost Taken
Ashley Kath-Bilsky
The Sense of Honor
R.R. Smythe
Into the Woods
(A Young Adult Fantasy)
Phyllis Campbell
Pretend I'm Yours
Jacquie Rogers
Faery Special Romances
(A Young Adult Romance)
Katherine Deauxville
The Crystal Heart
Rebecca Andrews
The Millennium Phrase Book
Jean Harrington
The Barefoot Queen
Holiday Romance Anthology
Christmas Wishes
Holiday Romance Anthology

Holiday in the Heart
Romance Anthology
No Law Against Love
Romance Anthology
Blue Moon Magic
Romance Anthology
Blue Moon Enchantment
Romance Anthology
Recipe for Love

Upcoming

Holiday Romance Anthology
Romance Upon A Midnight Clear
Holiday Romance Anthology
Love Under the Mistletoe
Anne Kimberly
Dark Well of Decision
John Nieman & Karen Laurence
The Amazing Rabbitini
(Children's Illustrated)
Isabel Mere
Almost Guilty
Chai/Ivey/Porter/Young
Mail Order Brides
Candace Gold
A Heated Romance
Romance Anthology
No Law Against Love 2
Eric Fullilove
The Zero Day Event
Jannine Corti Petska

The Lily and the Falcon
Romance Anthology
The Way to a Man's Heart
Romance Anthology
Love on a Harley
MacGillivray/Burroughs/Bowen/
Ahlers/Houseman
Dance en L'Aire
Lance Martin
The Little Hermit
(Children's Illustrated)
Brynn Chapman
Bride of Blackbeard
Sorter/MacGillivray/Burroughs
Faith, Hope and Redemption
Anne Holman
The Master of Strathgian
Romance Anthology
Second Time Around
Jannine Corti-Petska
Surrender to Honor
Romance Anthology
Love and Glory
Sandra Cox
Sundial
Ginger Simpson
Sparta Rose
Freddie Currie
Changing Wind
Molly Zenk
Chasing Byron
Cleora Comer
Just DeEtta

Printed in the United States
104034LV00003B/1-39/A